ITALIAN IMMIGRANTS IN PHILADELPHIA

1926

HOLE IN THE CEILING

Robert DiSpaldo

authorHOUSE®

AuthorHouse™
1663 Liberty Drive
Bloomington, IN 47403
www.authorhouse.com
Phone: 1 (800) 839-8640

Published by AuthorHouse 07/14/2017

ISBN: 978-1-5246-9066-3 (sc)
ISBN: 978-1-5246-9065-6 (e)

Library of Congress Control Number: 2017907231

Print information available on the last page.

Contents

CHAPTER 1

The morning was already hot, much as it had been since school had let out for the summer vacation. If the weather pattern continued like it had been in the past week, the afternoon would become unbearable from the humidity, and by three in the afternoon, a thunder-shower would cool things off somewhat.

Joey Nocelli, already browned by the sun, sat in his back yard and splashed his feet in a bucket of spigot water. He hugged the back of the two-story row house where two or three feet of morning shade remained. Anticipating the heat, he wore only his 'knickers with drawers underneath. His dark hair was sopping wet and lay flat against his head. At nine years of age, he showed signs of becoming a muscular young man. He would probably grow to just about medium height, however, as was his father.

At the moment, he wondered when Sammy Cohen, his best friend, would come ambling down the alley with that funny gait of his. Sammy lived in the store at the end of the block, and usually came down the alley that separated Joey's house from the houses on the next street. The gate in the wooden fence was already unlocked for him.

"Joey," a tiny voice called.

Instinctively, Joey looked up at the wooden fence that separated his house from next door. The wooden slat fence was approximately five feet high, and a grown-up could easily look over it. The carrot-topped face that peeped over the top, however, was that of seven-year-old Carmela Richetti. "Come here, Joey," she said. "I got something to tell you."

Joey was reluctant to leave the coolness of the water, but he liked Carmela. She always had some little secret to tell him. There were some things that only he and she shared. They were their secrets and not even Sammy knew of them. He stepped out of the bucket and went to the fence.

"Come up the ladder," the girl whispered. Another, of her secrets.

Joey moved a short ladder so that it was opposite her. He climbed up the ladder so that they faced one another, their faces almost six inches apart. A speck of dried jelly was still on the corner of her mouth. "I saw my brother naked, and he's different from me," she said, seriously.

"What do you mean?"

"He's got a little thing like a finger that he pees out of."

"I have too. Don't you?"

"No, silly," the girl giggled.

"Let me see." Joey honestly believed that everyone was made like him. His little brother had the little finger. And so did Sammy Cohen, Sammy's looked funny because some of the skin was missing. It looked like a ball-headed man with one eye. "Let me see," he repeated.

The little girl looked back at her kitchen door. Her mother had left for the store, and her brother Nunzio was still in bed. "I'll show you if you show me yours," she said.

Somehow, Joey knew that this thing they were about to do was forbidden. Hadn't his mother warned him about coming into the bathroom when she was in there, or when she and his father were in the bedroom alone and the door was closed? He knew that they should not go any further, but the curiosity was so overwhelming at the moment, that he had absolutely no fear of the consequences. "You first," he said.

The girl's dark eyes were bright with excitement. "I have to get up higher," she whispered. She climbed higher up on the ladder until the hem of her cotton dress showed above the fence.

"Be careful," was all that Joey could say.

"You ready?"

"Yeah."

Instantly, the hem of the dressed was raised, and Joey was staring in astonishment at the smooth, pale legs, at the tiny slit. No "tiny finger" like his. Just as quickly, the hem of the dress dropped. "Now, you gotta show me yours, Joey," the girl said triumphantly.

"Aw, you saw your brother's. Mine's like his."

"You promised, Joey." The girl took several steps down the ladder and held on to the top of the fence. "Go ahead, Joey. I can see from here."

Joey hesitated. It wasn't that easy for him. He had to unbutton his fly, then find his penis inside his drawers.

"I'll never tell you another secret," the girl insisted.

Joey looked through his kitchen window. There was no sign of his mother. He unbuttoned the three buttons of his fly, then struggled with the slit of his underwear while balancing precariously on the ladder. Finally, he pulled out his penis. It felt cold and clammy in spite of the heat. "There," he exploded. "I hope you're satisfied."

"I can't see it. Your hand is hiding it."

"If I let go, it'll go back into my pants."

"Well pull them down."

"Are you crazy?"

"Then come up higher and I'll hold it out."

At that moment, there was a loud screech from a house on the other side of the alley. A woman's head popped out of an upstairs window, and she began screaming. "I see you. I see you, you little dago pigs. You got no shame. You ought to go back where you came from."

Joey's mother came storming out of the kitchen door. Luckily, Joey was already down from the ladder and little Carmela had disappeared. Without a word, Mrs. Nocelli scooped Joey up and carried him into the kitchen and sat him on one of the chairs. "You stay there," she ordered him grimly in Italian. She went to the kitchen window and peeped out. The woman had never stopped with her tirade, her voice penetrating the calm morning with its ugliness. Other heads had popped out of some of the other windows,

"Them two dago kids wuz gonna do it on top of the fence like two alley-cats. Can you beat that? It's a shame what's happening to this neighborhood. Dago pigs"

"Aw, lay off, Peg," called a woman, her head poking out of the next door window. "It ain't nothing your kids ain't done."

"Oh yeah. I'd whip hell out of them, they done something like that,"

"Oh, go back to bed, you lush," came from another window.

Suddenly, the woman. Peg, disappeared amid sounds of laughter from the other houses.

"Puta!" Joey's mother turned away from the window, her beautiful face still livid. She turned on Joey. "What have you done?" she asked in a strange mixture and English and Italian.

Joey knew it would not do to lie. It would be better to get it over with before his father got word of it. He found it difficult to explain, however, considering the nature of the subject. The words came out in a jumble of English and Italian, much like the words of his mother. He explained that Carmela had accidently seen her brother naked, and she was curious to know if Joey was made like him . . . down there. He did not mention the fact that she had exposed herself first.

"And did you show her that you are the same?"

"Yes." He lowered his head in obvious shame.

"And you know that this is wrong?" Her voice had softened, and her broken English was readily understood by the boy. "A boy and a girl should not look at one another until they are married. Your father and I, we are married, so it is right. It will be right when you are married. Do you understand?"

Joey nodded, keeping his head down. He knew it was over. His mother's voice was soothing, caressing, as she took his head and held it to her bosom. "You should not be so anxious to grow up. There will be much time to be a big man and to be married. Do you understand, Joey?"

"Yes, Momma."

"Now, go outside and wait for your friend. And if you see that terrible woman, come in quickly and do not speak to her. Understand?"

It was over.

That night, while in bed in the back bedroom, he could hear his mother speaking softly to his father in Italian. All the windows and doors were open upstairs because of the heat, so he could hear quite clearly at times. He listened fearfully because his mother was telling his father about the morning's event, but he somehow felt that all would be forgotten. His mother's voice was soft, tranquil, and not at all anxious. She even laughed gaily at times. But when she was through, making it all sound like a humorous incident, he heard his father murmur, "I will speak to him tomorrow."

"No, Giovanni. There is no need. He has learned his lesson." His mother's voice had become lower, seductive. She knew enough to keep her husband from getting involved with the problems she might have with the neighbors. She also knew how to do so.

"Then, there is no problem," murmured his father. "Shall we go to sleep."

"If you wish."

There was a long silence, then Joey heard his mother begin to moan and his father giggle. His father never giggled except when he was in bed with his mother. Finally, she whispered, "Close the door, Giovanni."—Her voice was hardly audible.

"It is too hot."

"Please."

There was the sound of his father getting out of bed, a loud, squeaking sound of bed-springs, then the sound of the door closing. There was silence for a time, then his father's loud grunting, the rhythmic creaking of the bed and his mother's tiny shrieks of pleasure. It ended with his mother moaning his father's name over and over again. "Giovanni caro . . . ti amo . . . ti amo tanto," (dear I love you, I love you so much) she whispered finally.

Joey remained awake long after she had gone to the toilet, and everything in the house was still except for his father's snoring. His mother must be made like Carmela, he reasoned. And he was made like his father. Why the difference? What was it that, his mother and father had just done? His mother had seemed *to* enjoy it, but his father sounded as though he had been doing some real hard work.

He finally fell asleep, knowing full well what he must do. He would ask Carmela. If she didn't know, she would find out. She would tell him because she would be grateful that he hadn't snitched on her.

CHAPTER 2

In spite of the unfortunate incident, and a few others which were minor in comparison, the summer of 1926 was one that would not soon be forgotten by Joey Nocelli, for it was the year of the Sesquicentennial Exposition in Philadelphia. On May, 31, in spite of various incomplete buildings and inadequate paving, it was opened to the public, and for a glorious summer, it was the premier place to visit. The people of South Philadelphia, especially, could take afternoon strolls there, and even picnic on the vast grounds. There was something for everybody, and people from far and near came to celebrate the one hundred and fiftieth anniversary of our nation's birth.

During the early spring, Before the exposition opened to the public, Uncle Guido had driven Joey and his family up Broad Street many times in order to show them the progress of the work that was going on. They all marveled at the huge replica of the Liberty Bell that marked the entrance to the exposition. It straddled Broad Street just south of Oregon Avenue, which was then the southern-most street in Philadelphia, and was supported by huge, concrete columns and an overhead beam shaped like the support of the real bell.

The cars had to drive underneath it, and every time they did, Joey would wonder if they would all be killed if it fell on them.

Once in the grounds, they drove around, staring in wonder at the strange, exotic buildings from the different nations that were represented. The work on these buildings was going on everywhere, so there was not much they could stop to look at. Of course, Joey's father was the most interested in all of this since he worked for a construction company. He would have much to tell his friends on the job the day after such a trip.

On one of these trips, Uncle Guido had driven them to the end of Broad Street to the Philadelphia Navy Yard. They had even gone inside one day when it was open to the public. Joey remembered how amazed his father had been to see the row upon row of huge, gray battle-ships, at the size of the guns. Uncle Guido pointed with pride at one of them as he told them that he had served on it during the great World War. Giovanni Nocelli said nothing, for he had spent most of the war in an army hospital, a victim of the flu epidemic that had gripped much of the world and had almost caused his death.

On the way, it was impossible to miss the new Municipal Stadium, now almost complete. They drove around it one time, and it seemed to take forever. They passed one archway gate after another as they drove around the horseshoe shaped, high brick structure. It would seat over a hundred thousand people, Uncle Guido explained, and it would hold the coming Dempsey-Tunney heavy-weight championship fight. He promised to take Joey's father to the event.

Uncle Guido had also driven the family over the brand new Delaware River Bridge the very first day it was opened for traffic, and Joey's father had commented that the blue-gray suspended bridge would outlast everyone who crossed over it that day. He marveled at the mass of cables that supported the structure. Even as they crossed into New Jersey, he was designing, in his mind, a miniature replica to be built in his house, perhaps separating his living room from his dining room. Naturally, it would be built of wood. Joey's father was very handy with wood.

The return trip across the Delaware River was made by ferry, and they had all gotten out of the car and stared at the Philadelphia skyline, the pleasant breeze blowing through their hair and cooling them off. Uncle Guido promised to drive them to Atlantic City someday. He tousled Joey's hair and told him that he could brag to all of his friends that he was one of the first to cross over the new bridge.

Uncle Guido was not really Joey's uncle. Guido Manzoni, a boyhood friend of Joey's father, had left Italy as a boy with his family. He had been reunited with Giovanni Nocelli c when Joey's father and his bride came over, many years later. He had become a very close friend of the family and had christened Joey when he was born, making him his godfather . . . Compare Guido, in Italian. And from the moment that Joey had learned to speak, Guido Manzoni had taught him to call him Uncle Guido. "That's what they do here in America," he explained. "Compare Guido don't sound so good . . . it don't sound American."

Uncle Guido was the only person that Joey knew who had an automobile, and when he came to visit, the shiny, black touring car was the only one parked on the street. Joey would watch it proudly so that the kids would not scratch it or dirty it. Uncle Guido would come for Sunday dinner, then off they would go. Uncle Guido and Joey's father would sit in the front, and his mother, little Jimmy, his three-year-old brother and he would sit in the back. Joey would wave as the neighbors enviously watched them drive off.

On Sundays, Uncle Guido would drive the whole family to the various places, but during the week, he would come after supper, and Joey and Sammy Cohen would ride off with him. At these times, Uncle Guido would drive to a certain corner on Broad Street and pick up a tall, blonde girl with laughing, blue eyes, Joey liked her because she was always hugging him and always laughed. Her name was Fanny Coyle. He knew she was not Italian, but he liked her anyway.

Uncle Guido was generous. When he got to the fair grounds of the exposition, he would give each boy fifty cents to do with as he pleased. In the meanwhile, he and the girl would leave. After an hour or two, they would return to pick up the boys and drive the girl back to the corner on Broad Street. She would lean over and kiss Joey good night, then wave at them until the car was out of sight. Although he never saw her kiss Uncle Guido, Joey knew that she did when they were alone, because his face was usually covered with lipstick. And Uncle Guido wasn't even jealous when she kissed Joey. Instead, he laughed at the boy's discomfort, Sammy Cohen would tease him all the rest of the evening.

On one of the family trips to the Sesquicentennial, they found the grounds still damp and muddy from a heavy rain almost a week before. By the time they reached the gaming area where it was comparatively dry, Mrs. Nocelli was almost in tears as she looked at the mud on her shoes and hem of her dress that came to her ankles. Uncle Guido was begging forgiveness for bringing them there. And Joey was looking at the bright red, toy automobile. It was just right for Jimmy, but he was sure he could squeeze into it. It was the raffle prize for the week.

All about them were tents with games of skill, games of chance, games of luck. The crowd, however, was sparse. Joey's father put little Jimmy down and flexed his muscles. He wasn't very tall, looked short compared to the "American men" that milled about. But he was muscular, and Joey knew that he was stronger than they were. And he knew that his mother was the prettiest lady there, with her long brown hair that was trying to escape from under her wide-brimmed hat. Uncle Guido was taller than his father and thinner. He looked more like the "American men" with his pale blue eyes and straight hair. The most notable sign was his speech, there was absolutely no sign of a foreign accent, unlike his mother and father.

Uncle Guido saw Joey admiring the red car. "You want that little bugger?" he asked. "It's too small for you."

Joey nodded his without looking up. "It's just right for Jimmy," he said.

A young lady sat at a table next to the car. She had a roll of tickets before her. "Only ten cents a ticket," she said, smiling and flashing large, white teeth. Her eyes beckoned Uncle Guido.

Without a word, he pulled out a roll of bills, found a five-dollar bill and handed it to the girl. "When is the drawing?" he asked.

"About an hour from now," she answered. "How many?"

"All of it. The boy needs a car real bad."

The girl's eyes widened, impressed. Mr. Nocelli protested. "Per molto (to much)?" he muttered in Italian. "That is a day's pay."

"No, Guido," Mrs. Nocelli said, lamely.

"Lucia, the boy wants the automobile bad." Uncle Guido could still speak in Italian, in spite of the many years in America. "He really wants it for Jimmy." He smiled at her. Joey knew Uncle Guido liked his mother.

The girl smiled broadly as she counted the tickets. She was highly impressed by Uncle Guido's generosity. And my, what a roll of bills. After counting fifty, she tore off five more. "They're eleven for a dollar," she explained, she handed the tickets to Uncle Guido. "Lots of luck," she said.

They roamed about, the men trying the various games. Everybody laughed when Mr. Nocelli tried to knock down three wooden bottles stacked like a pyramid. Never in his life had he handled a baseball, and it was reflected in his throwing. "Pop, you pitch like a girl," laughed Joey.

Needless to say, none of the balls even touched the bottles. Uncle Guide, on the other hand, wound up, imitating a pitcher on the mound, and proceeded to knock down the bottles. He won a large teddy bear and handed it to Mrs. Nocelli. "For Jimmy," he said. All the while, Joey kept a wary eye on the little red automobile.

Finally came the drawing. A man with a megaphone announced the event, explaining that two lesser prizes would be won first. One was a beautiful doll with all her finery. The second was a wooden rocking horse. The tickets for the raffle were in a large, wire cage, in plain sight of everyone.

The man shook the cage vigorously, causing the tickets to tumble every which way. Then, a little girl from the crowd was called upon to pick the tickets. She stuck her arm through a small opening in the cage and gave one to the man. "Number one, zero, eight, nine, three," he announced.

A squeal of delight was heard, and a woman led a small girl to receive her doll. The rocking horse was won by a family with several children who all seemed the right age for it.

"And now for the big prize," shouted the man. He gave the cage one last shake. "The person with the winning ticket must be present in order to pick up the prize. If the prize is not collected, we will draw again until there is a winner."

Joey felt his mother's hand squeeze his as she held on to both children. Uncle Guido groaned as the number was called. He turned and shook his head. He knew exactly what range of numbers he had, the first two digits excluded. They were the same on all the tickets.

The man repeated the number, waited a moment. A miracle! No one responded. "Please, Madonna," Mrs. Nocelli prayed, "let them pick another number."

The man repeated the number again. The crowd tensed. No winners. "Okay, here we go again," he shouted.

Uncle Guido shouted exultantly as soon as the new number was called. Then, he searched through the tickets and raised his arm with the winner. He turned to get Joey. His eyes met Mrs. Nocelli's. There were tears of happiness there . . . and laughter. God had answered her prayers for the happiness of her children.

For days afterwards, Joey played outside with the car, the envy of all the kids in the street. Beside little Jimmy and Carmela, next door, He allowed only Sammy Cohen to ride in it, while the other kids begged for a ride. Sammy would ride to the corner, to his parent's store, and when he returned, he would have several lemon-drops that he would share with Joey.

After those first days of excitement, however, Joey suddenly lost interest in the little car. More and more, he let little Jimmy ride it, until the little boy became quite good at pumping his legs and driving it. "Can I have it when I get big like you?" the boy asked one day.

"It's yours, Jimmy," Joey said.

"Now?"

"Yep. From now on it's yours."

"Gee, thanks, Joey. I'll take good care of it," said the little boy somberly.

From that moment on, Joey never sat in the car again.

CHAPTER

3

One day, after a heavy downpour that left huge puddles of water in the street, the area in front of Joey's house became like a playground, with almost every child in the street splashing about barefooted. The street echoed with their laughter and screams. The mothers sat on the white-stone steps, gossiping, smiling contentedly with the knowledge that their children were enjoying themselves and their men were at work. Things were good. America had been good to them. Even Donna Catarina, who lived to the right of Joey's house, was smiling. From inside her window, she stared wildly at the children, her senile grin showing many missing teeth, her disheveled hair looking as though it had never been combed. She never sat on her steps, and hardly any of the women sitting about had ever seen her outside her house in the past several years. "Povera donna (Poor woman)," Joey's father often said. "E pazzo (And crazy)," he added, making circling motions about his ear with his finger. Mrs. Nocelli would shake her head sorrowfully.

Joey's mother sat on her steps with Angelina, little Carmela's mother. She was Lucia Nocelli's best friend and lived to the left of Joey's house. The two women spoke in low tones, every once in a while bursting into laughter.

Joey watched them warily, wondering if they were discussing him and Carmela. He had spoken to the girl shortly after the incident in the yard, and she had made no mention about being punished. His mother had probably not told her . . . yet. "You were swell for not snitching on me. She would have killed me if she knew," she had whispered, standing close to him.

Now, as he sat on the curb, his feet in a shallow puddle, he saw Carmela coming toward him, an impish grin lighting up her torn-boy face. Her hair was matted down on her head, her flimsy cotton dress clinging to her body. Somehow, she had managed to get soaked to the skin, and now intended to do the same to Joey, a pail full of water poised.

"Carmela!" screamed her mother. But it was too late. The water splashed against the back of Joey's head as he tried to duck away. In a flash, he was up and wrestling with the girl, both falling to the wet street.

"Joey!" Now it was his mother who was screaming as he straddled the girl's squirming body. He scooped up some water in the pail she had used and poured it on her face.

He refilled it and once more splashed her before his mother dragged him off amid the squealing and laughter of the other children. Little Carmela was crying as her mother helped her up, lowering the hem of her dress. It had risen, exposing her chubby, brown legs and panteloons. Without a word, each woman took her offspring by the arm, and into their houses they went. Good friends, they knew better than to argue over the children. They had both witnessed what had happened.

From inside each house, however, came screams and sounds of crying. Both children had been punished.

A half hour later, Joey sat alone in his back-yard. The brick pavement of the yard had dried out, and he could no longer hear the sounds of the children in front of his house. There had been no signs of little Carmela either. She had probably been forbidden to go out back to speak with Joey. Across the yards, in the upstairs window of the house of the woman who had screamed at him and Carmela, he thought he saw shadowy movements. He was ready to bolt inside if she so much as showed herself.

He heard Sammy Cohen walking down the alley before he appeared. Sammy was the only kid in the block who was not allowed to go barefooted, and his sneakers made a dragging sound with one foot. Sammy, who was several months older than Joey, was slightly pigeon-toed and tended to swing his right foot around in a slight circle with each step, dragging it at the last instant. As usual, the wooden gate was unlocked and Sammy came into the yard. He had not been playing out front with Joey because his parents forbade him to play in the water puddles. "Look what I've got, Joey," he said. He showed Joey a brand new Ken Maynard card.

"Boy, that's neat," Joey said, admiring the glossy four by six card with his favorite cowboy's picture on it.

"Keep it. Here's some gum."

Joey took the stick of gum, part of which had come with the card. Sammy Cohen was chewing busily on the rest of it. "Gee, thanks," he said. He proceeded to stuff the gum into his mouth. "It's a shame your mom won't let you play out front with us. We had a lot of fun."

"Yeah, I saw you jump on Carmela, though." The grin caused Sammy's mouth to become a half-moon, with his upper lip practically hidden by his longish nose.

"Yeah, I got a good licking from my mom, too."

"It was her fault. I saw her throw water on you."

"It don't matter. We both got a licking. I could hear her screaming through the wall."

"Yeah, I guess."

"You sure I can have this, Sammy?"

"Yeah, I can get more."

"Thanks. Wanna play dolly-buck? I'll go get my other cards and we can play for fun,"

"Nan." After a moment, Sammy spoke up again. "Can you get out?" he asked.

"I don't know. I gotta ask my mom. I'm supposed to stay in and mind Jimmy," answered Joey. "Why?"

"I gotta show you something."

"What?"

"A neat hiding place. I found this in it." Sammy took a folded piece of paper out of his pocket and unfolded it. He handed it to Joey. It was soiled and had probably been torn out of a copy book. In each corner, written diagonally, were the names Bart, Shawn, Brett and Jamie. And in the center of the page was a skull and cross-bones. Under each name was a thumb-print, apparently in blood. Each boy had probably pricked his thumb and pressed it under his name.

"Wowi, you found this in the hiding place?" Joey's curiosity was instantly aroused. He stared at his friend wide-eyed as Sammy nodded.

"You think they were thieves?" When Sammy shrugged, he looked at the sheet of paper again. "Maybe Mr. Glatfelter knew them. He's been living around here a long time."

"Let's go see."

"Okay, let me see if I can get out." In a moment, he was inside. Little Jimmy was asleep on the sofa, exhausted after the excitement of the past hour. Joey's mother was snapping the end off of fresh string-beans, then snapping them in half. "Can I go out, Mom?" he asked in Italian.

"Non andare fuori(no go out)," she said, shaking her head vehemently.

"Please, Mom. I'll be good."

"No.. no..no!" This son of hers needed to be taught a lesson.

"Please. I'll come right back. Sammy wants to show me something at his house," Joey lied. "See, he gave me this, and he wants to show me some more." Joey showed his mother the cowboy card.

Mrs. Nocelli looked at the card, at the handsome "American" face on it. And she suddenly realized why she liked Sammy Cohen with his prominent Jewish features. The Cohens were just like her and her family: foreigners in an Anglo-American land, despised and ridiculed by those who had also come to these shores, but at an earlier time. "Is he a good man?" she asked, handing back the card.

"Yeah, Mom. He's a good guy."

Mrs. Nocelli nodded thoughtfully. She was sure there were some good people. She remembered how the neighbors of the woman across the way had ridiculed her. They were the woman's own kind, yet they had picked up for her Joey. Then she smiled. Perhaps her children would look like "Americans" when they were grown. Guido could certainly pass for one. And her Joey spoke with no accent. And perhaps if he went to college . . .

"Momma, can I go?"

Mrs. Nocelli was awakened from her thoughts. "Vade," she said simply. "Go, but come back right away,"

Joey followed Sammy down the alley. But instead of going toward Sammy's house, they went the other way. In the middle of the block, they came to an alley at right angle to the main alley. It split the block and led into their street. It was narrower than the main alley and had a ceiling over it. For some reason, the builder had seen fit to cover the alley at the second floor level of the house on either side, making it like a tunnel. It was also off limits to the kids of the street. Joey hesitated when Sammy turned into it. When Sammy motioned for him to follow, Joey shook his head.

"What's the matter?" Sammy had come back to him and was whispering.

"Suppose Mrs. Furguson sees us?"

"We're not doing anything . . . just walking through."

Joey peeked through a knot-hole in the fence. Satisfied that no one was in the Furguson back yard, he pushed Sammy, "hurry up," he said.

Walking softly, they entered the narrow alley. Halfway through, Sammy motioned up at a hole in the ceiling. The wooden lathe had been broken and the plaster had fallen, leaving a ragged hole about sixteen inches in diameter, large enough for a boy to climb through. The two by four rafters could be seen on either edge of the hole where they were exposed. Inside the hole could be seen only darkness.

The two stopped for only an instant, then they continued through. But as soon as they emerged into the street, they were confronted by the loud, course voice of Mrs. Furguson from her doorway. The caramel-hued face was the only part of her that was visible. The rest of her body was hidden by her door. "What you boys been doin' in my Alley?" she roared. Her voice sounded strange coming from the dark, pretty face.

"We're just walking through, Mrs. Furguson." Sammy answered because Joey was unable to. He was trembling and had to keep his teeth clenched to keep them from chattering. There were rumors that the woman could cast a spell on anyone who angered her. And she probably already knew what he and Sammy were contemplating.

"You sure?" The woman's voice pierced the stillness of the street as children stopped playing and women sitting on their steps stopped gossiping.

"Yes, Ma'am." Sammy seemed to be enjoying the confrontation.

"What you doin' down here anyway? Why don't you go back up the corner where you belong?"

"Yes, Ma'am, we're going." Sammy caught Joey by the arm and had to tug at him before he moved. They walked slowly back toward Joey's house.

"I'll be watching for you'll," boomed the voice. Then, the door banged shut.

16

Some of the neighbors laughed good-naturedly. They had watched in amusement. Others shook their heads in consternation. "Better watch out for her," called out Mrs. Albano, a short, roly-poly woman ^with a jolly, laughing face. "She likes little boys like you. She'll cook you in the oven and eat you."

Joey did not stop trembling until he was safely back in his back yard with Sammy. He had even refused to go see Mr. Glatfelter, the blacksmith, to find out more about the names on the sheet of paper. Mrs. Nocelli was so relieved to see him back so quickly that she gave them cookies. They had hardly been gone fifteen minutes.

"Well, what do you think?" asked Sammy when they were alone.

Joey had seen the hole before, but had never paid any attention to it, had never thought of it as a hiding place. Perhaps because it had been too small to crawl through. "Did you make the hole bigger?" he asked.

"A little," grinned Sammy.

"Well, if you think I'm ever going up in that hole, you're crazy. Forget it."

They did not mention the hole in the ceiling anymore, and a few minutes later Sammy left. Joey shivered at the thought of going up into that dark hole . . . and being discovered by Mrs. Furgson.

CHAPTER 4

St. Martha's boy's center was only a block and a half away, so Joey was allowed to go play there at night. And with him, even though he was Jewish, went Sammy. They went once or twice a week to play basketball in the large gym. At times, when there were enough boys to make up two teams, they played baseball with a pimpled, rubber ball that they hit with their fists. At other times, usually in the winter, Father Brandon laid down the mats and the boys boxed or wrestled. The priest, lean and muscular, and with a smashed nose, had boxed at the seminary school he had gone to, and boxing was his first love.

The first night that Sammy had come in with Joey, some of the boys had begun to pick on him, subtly bumping him and tripping him. There was no name calling, for they knew that Father Brandon would never tolerate it. Finally, one boy tripped Sammy from behind and caused him to fall. The priest promptly blew his whistle. Sammy slowly got up, eyed the boy who was several inches taller and some ten pounds heavier. "You do that again and I'm gonna kick you right in the balls," he said, not mincing any words. Then, he began to walk off the court.

"Where are you going, son?" called Father Brandon.

"Aw, these guys don't want me to play with them. I guess I'll just watch," Sammy replied.

"Do you want to play?"

"Sure."

"Well, you come back here and play," said the priest. Then, in no uncertain terms, he made it absolutely clear that no sort of prejudice would be tolerated in his gym. "I don't care what nationality you are or what your faith is, if you would rather come here to play instead of hanging out on some street corner, then you're welcome to come. Anybody who has trouble with that can leave now. And anybody picking on this boy, or anyone else, will be told to leave. Is that clear?" Then, looking directly at Sammy, he said, "And no more vulgar language." When no one said anything, he took his position between the two centers and tossed up the ball. There was no more harassment and Sammy Cohen actually became well liked in the center.

They were coming home from the center one night and they passed The First in Christ Church. It had once been a store, but now the large show-window was curtained off.

The large door, however, was open because of the heat, and the glistening black faces could be seen singing a gospel. They hurried by, for both of the boys had been warned not to linger near the place. In passing, Joey had glimpsed at Mrs. Furguson, her face shades lighter than the others, her mouth open in song. She did not look at all frightening or intimidating.

"Did you see Mrs. Furguson?" asked Sammy, grinning.

"Yeah."

"We could go up and take a look at the hide-out while she's at the prayer meeting."

"I'm not going up in that hole."

"Maybe you'll like it."

"Why? Have you been up there?"

"It's neat."

They walked silently, Joey admiring Sammy's courage. They usually did everything together, usually after the Jewish boy dared and double-dared him. But Joey wanted no part of this. It was too close to Mrs. Furguson. What if she came back unexpected? What if she trapped them up there? He shivered.

"Come on, Joey. Just shimmy up and stick your head through. It's really neat. Those kids had a neat hang-out. And it wasn't too long ago."

"How do you know?" Joey had almost forgotten the names on the sheet of paper.

"I asked Mr. Glatfelter about them. He didn't remember them at first. But after a while, he did. He remembered that they were a bunch of tough kids and they used to have gang fights with kids in different neighborhoods. Then, the war came, and they all signed up. Only one came back, and he moved away." Only the sound of the gospel singing could be heard faintly from a half block back as Joey rapidly calculated how long ago it might have been.

"Sammy," he exploded. "I thought you said it wasn't too long ago. It was before either of us was born. It was before the war. I'll bet nobody's been up there in fifteen or twenty years,"

"No wonder it was so dusty and dirty." Sammy was getting a kick out of Joey's reaction. "Mr. Glatfelter couldn't remember how long ago it was, and I never gave it any thought. Anyway, they fixed it up real neat. It's got pieces of rugs and all. They even had a bucket to piss in, I guess."

"Aghl", Joey grimaced in revulsion. All the more reason not to go up into the hole. How much dirt could accumulate in fifteen or twenty years?

"C'mon, Joey." Sammy was insistent. Pretty soon he would be daring him. "The house next door is empty and Mrs.

Furguson is at the prayer meeting. There's nobody to worry about."

"Oh yeah . . . what about Sarah and her brother?"

"They're not allowed to come out while Mrs. Furguson is out. You know that."

They had reached the alley and they stood behind Sammy's store. Sammy drew Joey into the alley so that there was no chance that his parents would see them. "C'mon," he said. "We'll walk down the alley and come out into the street." He took several steps then turned. "C'mon," he repeated. Reluctantly, Joey followed.

The alley was lit by gas-light. A lamp-lighter had already lit up the heavy, cast-iron lamp-posts even though it was still not completely dark. The alley, itself, was relatively clean, kept so by the residents of the block. Only that morning, Joey had swept the section behind his house. He had also done Donna Catarina's, for the old woman could not be depended on to do her share. Part way down, someone yelled, "Who's back there?"

Joey recognized the voice of Mr. Alberto who liked to sit in his back yard and smoke his stogie.

"It's me, Mr. Alberto Joey Nocelli."

"Don't do nothing dirty back there."

"I won't, Mr. Alberto."

They continued without incident in spite of the fact that voices could be heard in several of the back yards. They passed Joey's back yard, and soon they were under the hole in the ceiling. Sammy made a motion for Joey to wait. Silently, on tip-toes, he ran to the street entrance, looked up and down the street to see if anyone was coming. He came back. As Joey watched, Sammy shimmied up between the walls of the two houses by spreading both arms and legs and working himself up by using both hands and feet. In an instant, he was gripping the ceiling rafters on each side of the hole. Then, his head disappeared into the hole. With another shove of his legs, he could have disappeared completely. Instead, he came down.

Joey sighed with relief. He thought for sure that Sammy was going all the way in. It seemed easy and he knew he could do it because he was stronger than Sammy. Sammy was grinning at him. That was all it took, he was saying by his attitude. But Joey had made up his mind. He didn't want his friend to dare him. It was too easy. Besides, he was dying with curiosity. "Go look," he said, motioning toward the entrance. Sammy went, looked up and down, then nodded his head.

Joey got into position, spreading his arms and legs and pressing against the two walls. He locked his arms and drew a deep breath. He looked at Sammy, then pressed against the brick walls, lifting his body. About a foot up from the ground, his sneakers pressed against the walls and his legs locked. He repeated the procedure several times, and soon he was gripping the rafters and his head went inside.

He came down quickly, disappointed. He had not been able to see anything. There was only darkness. Even the gas-lamp, some thirty feet away, could not shed enough light to see up in the hole. "C'mon," whispered Sammy. He was already walking toward the street entrance. Joey followed and they walked nonchalantly out into Fremont Street.

Mrs. Nocelli was sitting on her steps with Angelina from next door. All along the street, people were sitting quietly or conversing on their own door steps. Even the children were subdued. A slight breeze showed promise that the evening would cool of a bit, and they were taking advantage of it. Some men were relaxing with only an undershirt covering their chests.

In her curious mixture of English and Italian, Joey's mother asked him why he had not come home from Snyder Avenue, since that was where the center was.

"We went through the alley, Mom. I wanted to make sure the alley gate was locked," Joey explained.

"You sure?" asked his mother.

"Ha fatto una pisciatta (did a pee)," laughed Angelina.

Mrs. Nocelli joined in the laughter.

"No we didn't, Mom," Joey protested. On several occasions, when the need to urinate had come upon him,

Joey had peed in the alley. All the kids did it. But now, he denied it vehemently, since he had not done so this time.

"Go see if Jimmy is sleeping. There are some cookies in the cabinet." Mrs. Nocelli smiled proudly as the boys squeezed through, between the two women and into the house.

Her Joey was such a good boy.

CHAPTER 5

Saturday morning was a busy one for Joey. First stop was the grocery store on the corner. Sammy Cohen's parents owned it. For reasons that Joey could not understand, except that it was a religious one, the members of the Cohen family could not light the gas burners on Saturday. It was like Joey's family couldn't eat meat on Friday, explained Sammy, and it was this service that Joey performed for them each Saturday.

When he knocked on the side entrance of Sammy's house, the boy let him in. A tiny black yarmulke was perched snugly on his head. They went directly into the kitchen where Mr. Cohen greeted Joey. He was a tall, spare man, and a shaggy mustache and beard hid almost all of his face, making him appear many years older than his thirty-five years. He looked much too old to be Sammy's father. He also wore a yarmulke. "Ah, good morning, Joey," he said. "You came early. That's good." He spoke in concise, clear English, much like Joey's teacher. But somehow, he sounded different. He sounded like Mr. Fishbaum, who he would visit later. Mr. Fishbaum also spoke good English. Mr. Cohen handed Joey a box of wooden matches.

Joey took one of the matches, went to the gas range and lit the two front burners. Solemnly, as Sammy watched from behind his father, a devilish grin on his face, Joey returned the matches.

"Thank you, Joey," said Mr. Cohen. He reached into his pocket and gave him a nickel. "You're going to Mrs. Levine and Mrs. Fishbaum?"

"Yes, Mr. Cohen."

"Good boy."

Sammy winked at him as he left. He had not said a word in all the time that Joey was there. He knew he would not see him for the rest of the day.

Mrs. Levine lived in one of the big brown-stone houses across Snyder Avenue from the Cohen's store. Mrs. Fishbaum lived next door. Snyder Avenue was extremely wide and trolley cars ran in both directions. It was the southern edge of the burgeoning Italian neighborhood that tended to envelope almost all of the section of Philadelphia. Seventh Street was the eastern edge. Beyond that, from there to Fourth Street, in a long swathe that took in some twenty blocks, the Jewish residents had resisted the invasion of new immigrants. The row of brown-stone houses had also resisted the influx of Italians. But only because they were too expensive for the new arrivals. And they were still owned mostly by old Jewish families such as the Levines and the Fishbaums.

"They're the rich Jews," Sammy had once said, inferring that his family was a poor Jewish family, "Maybe someday you'll move into one of those houses."

"What about you?" Joey answered. "Maybe you will."

"Nah. If we ever move, it'll be far away . . . in another part of the city." Sammy was wise beyond his ten years.

Mrs. Levine usually let Joey in because Mr. Levine was already at the synagogue where he would stay all day. He was different from Sammy's father. Joey wasn't sure when he went to the synagogue. It seemed like he was always in his store.

"Ah, Joey," the matronly woman gushed when she opened the door. "Come in . . . come in." Joey liked Mrs. Levine. She always smelled so nice and always had store cookies for him besides the usual ten cents she gave him. One time, she gave him a bag full of clothing for his mother. Upon seeing the expensive dresses and blouses, Mrs. Nocelli told Joey to be sure to thank her. She had hastily altered a gown that Mrs., Levine had grown out of and wore it at a wedding that they were invited to. The other women, mostly from her home-town in Italy, were impressed by the black, beaded, silk gown. Their envy was obvious, so Mrs. Nocelli boasted a little, saying that her Giovanni had insisted that she buy something nice for the occasion.

The only thing that Joey hated about going to Mrs. Levine's house, was that she used every ploy she could think of in order to get him to stay after he had lit the gas jets. "Here, Joey, I have for you a blintz. I make for you some cocoa," she would say. Or she would simply pour her heart out to him. "Stay and talk a while with me, Joey. Mr. Levine is gone to the synagogue already, and I'm so lonely. I like you a lot, Joey." She would take the boy's face in between the palms of her two hands, and a look of sadness would be reflected in her eyes. "I wish I had a little boy like you, Joey," she would say. Mrs. Levine, already in her fifties, had never had children of her own.

Joey always used the excuse that the Fishbaums were waiting for him. And Mrs. Levine would sigh and lead him to the door. "Such a gorgeous boy," she would say.

Mrs. Fishbaum was no problem. She would lead him to the gas jets that she wanted lit, then she would give him the dime she always had waiting on one of the fancy tables in the living room. The Fishbaums already had electricity in the house, and large, ornate Tiffany lamps were usually lit on them, making the living room alive with the rich tapestries and furniture. A colorful oriental rug reached to the edges of all the furniture. Sometimes, Mr. Fishbaum would be sitting in one of the chairs. He would either be reading or listening to their radio. He would nod to Joey then go back to whatever he was doing.

Joey would go straight home with enough money for the Saturday matinee at the movie. He usually had some of Mrs. Levine's store cookies that he would share with little Jimmy.

The Grande Theatre was in the same block as St. Martha's center. Still, he was only allowed to go there in the afternoon. He had attended a movie only once at night. The whole family had gone to see Rudolf Valentino in the Sheik. He had not thought too much of the movie, but it had had a strange effect on his mother. When they had gone to bed that night, Momma had cautiously closed her bedroom door. But Joey had heard the strange sounds far into the night: sounds that little Carmela had explained as love-making. And the next morning at breakfast, his father had playfully asked when they could go see a Valentino movie again. Momma had laughed shyly and her lovely face had turned crimson. She had hummed all day long.

Joey wasn't interested in the main feature playing that Saturday. But he scanned the large placards in the glass enclosed show-cases in front of the theater as he waited in line for it to open up. "William Desmond" in large, bold letters was on the top of one of the placards. Beneath it was the figure of a cowboy on a horse. He was dressed all in black, including a black mask and a flowing, black cape trailing behind him. The horse, a white stallion, was up on its two hind legs. On the bottom of the placard was the title, "The Phantom." And just below it, a narrow strip had been stuck on. On it was printed, "Chapter six."

Last week's chapter had ended when the masked Phantom had been lured into an old, abandoned mine by the villain. He had the heroine tied up in one of the mine shafts. A stick of dynamite was ready to explode, its fuse already lit. The explosion would surely cause the mine to cave in and kill her. The Phantom had come to the girl's rescue, when he stepped into a pit that had been cleverly covered over. The chapter ended when the hero hurtled down into the pit with several steel spikes sticking up out of the bottom of it.

Even as the line of eager children waited for the theater manager to open up the cashier's cubicle, Joey pondered the question uppermost in the mind of practically every child in the line. How was the Phantom going to get out of this one? He could not figure it out. But he knew that the hero would not be killed. There were still nine more chapters to go. He reached into the brown, paper bag he carried and ate one of the sandwiches his mother had packed for him.

It was after five when he left the movie. The main attraction had been better than he had anticipated, and he had seen the good part over again. He had eaten his other sandwich and a banana, and now he was hungry. He walked swiftly because he knew it was close to supper time. The thought that they might have begun eating without him caused him to break into a run. Being late for supper was not tolerated by his father, and Joey had been sent to bed more than once without it for breaking this cardinal rule. Of course, his mother always brought him something to eat later on. So it was with great relief that Joey found his mother still setting the table when he arrived. From a large, cast-iron frying pan on the stove came the fragrant smell of pieces of chicken being fried with sweet peppers, onions and potatoes. Several loaves of bread were baking in the oven.

At the table, Joey's father asked him how the "Good guy" had saved himself and the heroine this week. He already knew his predicament. Joey had told him all about it last week. He seemed just as interested as Joey.

Joey cleared his throat, beaming at his mother. She smiled, showing the same interest that his father did. It made him feel quite important. He tried to make it as interesting as he could. "Well, you know that the good guy always carries this whip with him," he began.

His father nodded. Of course he had heard of the whip. Had this Phantom not used it before to save himself?

Joey continued, bringing his audience up to date. "Remember last week . . . the Phantom was about to fall into this hole with the spikes sticking up. Well, when he started to fall, he flicked the whip and it wrapped around a big, wooden beam that was holding up the ceiling. He swung over the hole then picked up the dynamite and threw it into it. The explosion was muffled and didn't do any damage. Then, he released the girl."

His father was nodding approvingly. This Phantom is a brilliant man," he said in his broken English. "Is he not, Lucia?"

"Yes. In America there are many such people," she agreed.

"Someday, I would like to see this Phantom," said his father, in earnest.

"Can I come with you next week?" asked little Jimmy. He had never been to a matinee with his brother.

Giovanni Nocelli said nothing. This was a decision for his wife to make. Even Joey looked to his mother, hoping that she would say no. The boy was much too small to sit through an afternoon of movies. "When you are big like Joey, you can go, my baby," Lucia Nocelli said softly. Little Jimmy continued eating without another word.

"And what kind of trouble is our hero in this week?" Joey's father knew that each week the movie ended with a new cliff-hanger.

Joey was already picturing the scene in his mind. "Well, the Phantom is chasing one of the bad guys on his horse, and he is almost catching up to him. But the bad guys set this trap. Another guy is hiding behind a rock and he shoots him as they ride by. The chapter ends with the Phantom and his horse rolling over and over,"

"Mm..these bad guys are smart fellows too. They are always setting traps for this Phantom." Mr. Nocelli looked forward to these conversations

27

with his son. He was learning more English from these talks than he did from speaking with any of the men at work, since most of them were newly arrivals the same as he. But he knew that in order to keep Joey's interest, he had to find a common ground. And he had found it in the weekly discussion about the Saturday afternoon serial. He had even insisted that Joey speak only in English. As a result, he found himself speaking almost at his son's level. He nodded agreement when Joey assured him that the Phantom would escape this latest trap.

They ate quietly until dinner was done. Mr. Nocelli was paring a peach then slicing it and dipping it into a glass of wine. He held a sliver in front of little Jimmy who promptly took a bite. The boy's face twisted wryly at the wine taste, but ate the morsel. Joey's mother chided her husband. He laughed and offered the boy another piece. The boy ate it, after making the same face. "See, Cara, he likes it." Mrs. Nocelli shook her head as she began clearing the table.

Joey was about to get up from the table, when his father asked, "Did you go to light the gas for the lady with the electric?"

"Yeah, Pop . . . why?"

"Paolo, the man who does the electric work for the company, has promised to show me how to put it into our house. He said he will help me."

Mrs. Nocelli's ears perked up. She had seen the wonders of this strange phenomenon: lights that went on and off simply by pushing a button, large, beautiful boxes where people kept their food fresh instead of in messy ice-boxes. She had even heard of a machine that washed clothing. How wonderful it must be to have this electric. "Can you do this, Giovanni?" she asked, eyes bright.

Her husband looked offended. "Did I not put in a toilet, a bathtub and a sink for you, Cara?"

"Sure, he can do it, Mom," Joey said excitedly. He remembered when he and some of the kids in the street used to go down in Petey De Fabio's cellar and Petey's father would show them movies. He remembered that the movie projector had to be plugged into what Petey called a receptacle. Petey had bragged that they had sold his house for a lot of money because of the electricity. "Petey said his father got a lot of money for their house because they had electricity," he added.

Mr. and Mrs. Nocelli exchanged glances. This was indeed something to consider, for they had discussed the possibility of moving more than once. And if simply putting this electric into the house could get them more money, then perhaps they could see their dream come true. Perhaps they could move into a nicer house.

Mr. Nocelli knew that his wife had only one true friend in the street . . . Angelina from next door. Most of the friends that they had grown up with in the old country, now lived about eight blocks away and closer to the Italian market on Nine Street. And except for special occasions, they rarely saw each other. It would be good for her if they lived closer. He had seen a row of houses with porches and tiny gardens in front of them. Some even had a fig tree. It was into one of these houses that he would like to move his family.

Then, there was the matter of going to church. The Italians were still a minority group in the neighborhood when they had first moved into it, and it was obvious from the beginning that there was animosity in the stares of the parishioners when they went to church. As a result, they had begun to attend the St. Nicholas of Tolentino Church, some seven blocks away and close to where their friends lived. After mass, they would visit them and have coffee and cake before they went home for Sunday dinner. It was ideal in the summer time, but it was a chilling ordeal for the children in the winter, for it was a long walk home.

Although Joey never entered into the discussion, they were certain that he would like the idea. He was quite close with Nicolina Flaviano, the daughter of Mrs. Nocelli's closest friend from their village in Italy. It was to their house that they usually went to after mass, and it was noted, with quiet satisfaction, that the two youngsters spent hours laughing and giggling over the Sunday comics. There were high hopes that the two would someday marry. If they moved, they would be living a block apart.

So it was that Mr. and Mrs. Nocelli smiled at each other. "I will tell my friend that I am ready to put in the electric," said Giovanni Nocelli.

CHAPTER 6

The morning had started out hot and muggy, and by early afternoon, it was obvious that there would be a summer storm. In the distance, loud cracks of lightning could be heard as the dark sky lit up. And the bolts were coming closer. Large drops of rain were splattering against the back yard paving at a leisurely pace.

Next door, Donna Catarina could be heard screaming with each crack of thunder. It happened with every thunder storm. One time, after such a storm, as was her habit, Mrs. Nocelli went next door to check on the old lady. For a time, she could not find her. Finally, upon hearing the faint wails of the old lady coming from the cellar, she went down to look. She found Donna Catarina in the coal-bin, her body and clothing as black as the coal pile she had tried to burrow under.

So it was with great concern that Lucia Nocelli listened to the cries of the old woman. The bolts of lightning were now almost overhead, and each flash was accompanied by a resounding crack that seemed to shake the house. And from next door came the blood-curdling screams, one after the other. Little Jimmy cringed and clung to his mother's dress, more because of the screaming than because of the lightning and thunder.

Finally, Mrs. Nocelli could stand it no longer. Telling Joey to mind little Jimmy, she went next door. The door was unlocked, which was not unusual. Donna Catarina usually forgot to lock her door even at night when she went to bed. Mrs. Nocelli found the woman easily, her screams coming from inside the doorway to the cellar. Her face was pressed tightly against the wall at the top of the stairs. Each crack of lightning made her jerk as though charges of electricity were coursing through her body.

"Donna Catarina," Mrs. Nocelli called softly. She touched the woman on the shoulder.

The old lady turned and a look of recognition replaced the wild look in her eyes. It relieved Mrs. Nocelli, for the wild, disheveled hair and fierce eyes was the look of insanity. "Ah, Lucia . . . grazia Dio (grace god)!" the woman moaned. She seemed not to hear the thunder any longer. She took Mrs. Nocelli's outstretched hand and followed her out of the doorway and into the kitchen. She sat in one of the chairs at her benefactor's bidding.

Mrs. Nocelli proceeded to shut the door to the back yard and the kitchen window, muffling the sound of the thunder somewhat. Then, she lowered the shades so that the lightning flashes did not light up the kitchen. The dimness also made the room look more presentable. Not so obvious was the pile of dirty dishes and pans in the sink, the scurrying of cockroaches across the dirty, cracked linoleum that covered the floor. She sat at the table with the old woman. She made idle gossip with her as though the summer storm raging outside simply did not exist. She thought of suggesting a cup of coffee, but the coal stove was completely out, and it would take a good while before a fire could be made hot enough to boil water. Instead, she promised the woman a plate of pasta later on.

Donna Catarina smiled happily, her toothless gums gleaming grotesquely in the dimness of the room. She was totally oblivious of the storm, which seemed to be moving quickly by. She listened mainly, but at one point asked how little Jimmy was. They spoke entirely in Italian.

"He is feeling fine, now that you have cured him of the mal-ochi (sickness)," replied Mrs. Nocelli.

Bene . . . bene(Well . . . well). He is such a beautiful baby. You must be careful with people. When they say how beautiful he is, you must be sure to say, 'Grazia Dio (Grace God),' afterwards."

"Oh, yes, Donna Catarina. I always do that . . . ever since you told me."

"Such a beautiful boy. God bless him. Does he walk yet?" The old woman spoke of the boy as though she had cured him only recently, when in fact, it had happened several years ago when little Jimmy was still an infant.

31

It was well known in the street that Donna Catarina performed such cures. Among the newly arrived Italians, she was known as la strega . . . the witch. And it had been on a cold, windy March day that the baby, barely six months old, had begun to cry for no apparent reason. Not even his mother's breast seemed to appease him. At her wit's end, Mrs. Nocelli had called Angelina, her friend from next door. The woman took one look at the baby and suggested calling Donna Catarina. She, herself went for her. They came back, the old woman with an old shawl over her head and her toothless smile, looking every bit a witch.

She waddled into the house and stood over the baby for an instant, then told Mrs. Nocelli to lay him on the kitchen table. Mrs. Nocelli did as she was told, and soon the old woman had the baby's belly exposed. She felt about the tiny groin with fingers that were gentle despite their twisted, knotty appearance. All the while, she mumbled words that neither Mrs. Nocelli or Angelina recognizes. She felt the tiny belly and chest. Finally, she covered the screaming baby with its blanket and asked for a cup. She filled it half full of water, then dipping her finger into a cup of oil, she allowed a drop to fall into the oil. The three women watched as the oil spread. Only Donna Catarina knew what it meant. "Mal-ochi," she said simply.

Without hesitation, she began making the Sign of the Cross on the baby's forehead with her thumb, all the while mumbling what sounded like the Lord's Prayers. Then, there were times that the two women did not recognize any of the words. And all the time the old woman's thumb moved on the tiny forehead.

Slowly, miraculously, the crying subsided. And suddenly the baby was asleep. It woke up several hours later, gurgling and hungry for its mother's milk. Mrs. Nocelli happily sent Donna Catarina a bowl of soup beside a bottle of her husband's best home-made wine that the woman had asked for in payment for her cure.

Now, with the storm all but over, the old woman spoke of the incident as though it had happened only recently. Mrs. Nocelli did not want to confuse the woman. "Yes, Donna Catarina, he has learned to walk. He has also learned to speak," she said. "Perhaps I can teach him to say Donna Catarina."

"Ah, God bless you, Lucia." The woman grinned happily.

Soon the thunder could be heard only in the distance. The storm had passed. Mrs. Nocelli got up to leave. "Will you be all right, Donna Catarina?" she asked.

"Yes, I will be fine. You know, I have finished the bottle of wine."

Mrs. Nocelli knew that the woman referred to the bottle of wine she had received for curing little Jimmy. From time to time she would mention it, and Mrs. Nocelli would refill her empty bottle. It was that time again. "Give me the bottle and I will fill it," she said.

The old woman waddled to a kitchen cabinet, all the while mumbling, "Grazie . . . grazie (thanks . . . thanks)." Mrs. Nocelli took the empty bottle and left.

As soon as she returned home, Joey asked if he could go out. Only a steady drizzle remained of the storm, causing the streets to be empty. Joey ran to the Cohen store and asked for Sammy.

"He's not with you?" asked Mrs. Cohen. The smile she always had for Joey disappeared. They were always together, these two. And her son had left before the storm.

"No, Mrs. Cohen. Maybe he's over at the blacksmith. I'll go see." He ran out before the woman could give him a half a dozen places to go look for her Sammy.

Mr. Glatfelter, the blacksmith, was the biggest man that Joey had ever known. His bulging biceps seemed as big as Joey's waist. Joey knew that it was bigger than Sammy's, because the big, friendly man had gotten a piece of string one day and had made Joey measure Sammy's waist, then his right bicep. Mr. Glatfelter's bicep was approximately one half inch bigger.

Mr. Glatfelter spoke with a deep, guttural accent, seeming to roll his "Rs" in the back of his throat. He liked the two boys and seemed to welcome their friendship. Both wore rings that the big man had made out of horse-shoe nails. They had spent many hours watching the sparks fly as Mr. Glatfelter shaped and fitted the horse-shoes for horses that munched quietly on some hay in the rear of the shop. Mostly, they visited the shop in the winter months when the fire that heated the horse-shoes until they were malleable made the shop warm and *cozy*. They seldom went in the summer months.

"So, Joey . . . vere haf you been? I thought maybe you moved far away." The big man, his huge, hairy chest covered only by a leather apron that reached down to his knees, gripped a horse-shoe with a pair of tongs. He wriggled it in the hot fire while he pumped air with his right foot. His toothy grin and walrus moustache made him look somewhat like Teddy Roosevelt. He had been pleased when the two boys had pointed it out to him, and he had promptly proceeded to make the rings that the boys proudly wore.

"No, Mr. Glatfelter, I didn't move.

"I haf not seen you since Christmas, yah?"

"Oh, no, Mr. Glatfelter. Remember, I came and it started to snow, and you told me to go home because my mother would worry about me. It was just before Easter."

"Yah, yah, I remember. You don't come now because it is hot. And I don't blame you. If I don't haf to vork here, I don't come either." He chuckled. "So vere's Sammy?" he asked.

"I thought he was here. I'm looking for him."

"He's not home?"

"No, I just came from the store."

"Vel, I haf not seen him since he came to ask me about those boys' names that he found."

"Sammy said you knew them."

"Oh, yes. I knew them from when they were little boys like you . . . maybe smaller. They also used to come here to keep me company," Mr. Glatfelter paused in his work and stared into the fire. The memories were good ones, for he smiled. "They were good boys," he said sadly. "Ven the war came, they all signed up at the same time."

"Did you go to war, Mr. Glatfelter?"

"No, I vas too old, Joey." Now, the memories had become painful. Mr. Glatfelter frowned. "Vel, if you vant to look for Sammy . . . okay," he said gruffly. "If you vant to watch, you sit over there." The roughly shaped horse-shoe was cherry red from the heat. It was ready to be shaped, and the giant could not waste any more time in idle talk. He had to fit it while it was soft and pliable.

"I think I know where to find him, Mr. Glatfelter," Joey said. "I'll see you later."

The big man nodded his head as Joey left the shop. Large drops of sweat from his face caused the fire to flare up and sputter.

Joey looked out of the entrance to the alley. Satisfied that no one was about, he went directly under the hole in the ceiling. "Hey, Sammy," he hissed.

Instantly, Sammy's grinning face looked down at him from the hole. "Come up," he whispered. When Joey hesitated, he said, "Hurry up, before somebody sees you."

Without a second thought, Joey shimmied up the wall, and with Sammy's help was through the hole and sitting on a solid floor made up of boards nailed to the ceiling joist. There was even a piece of rug to make it quite comfortable.

When his eyes became accustomed to the dimness, he saw that there was plenty of head-room . . . all the way up to the roof of the two houses.

"Come on," whispered Sammy. "Don't worry, you can't fall through. There's boards all along. And I cleaned the dust."

In spite of Sammy's assurance, Joey crawled gingerly as he followed his friend toward the back of the houses. It grew darker as they moved away from the hole, and Sammy's body was just a shadow in front of him. But now, he heard voices through the brick wall of the Ferguson's house. Joey estimated that they were coming from the rear bedroom of the house and that Mrs. Furguson was shouting at someone. He heard the black woman quite clearly.

"I told you can't wear your good clothes around the house," she yelled. "I can't be buying you clothes just to be wearing around here. Ain't nobody gonna see you no how."

There was only the muffled sound of crying for answer. n

"And stop that silly crying. You hear me, girl. And go on and clean up these bedrooms." The voice seemed to trail off as Mrs. Furguson apparently went down the stairs. Only the pitiful sound of crying could be heard for a time, then subsided.

"Sarah," whispered Sammy. They sat facing one another, their backs against the walls of the houses. Joey knew; the girl, a pleasant twelve-year-old, several shade lighter than her mother. Although she was twelve years old, she was one grade lower than Joey, therefore, he hardly ever saw her. As soon as school let out, she would hurry home and disappear as though she never existed. He had not seen her since school let out for the summer. Once in a while, Joey thought he saw her peeping from behind lowered shades at the girls her age skipping rope or playing jacks on the step across the street. He had never seen her at play with them. Somewhere in the house was also a little boy of five. Joey had never seen him playing outside either.

By now, Joey's eyes had become accustomed to the dimness, and he could see Sammy's face clearly. He was grinning, as usual. "How do you like it?" he whispered.

"It's neat." Joey had to agree that it was indeed a marvelous hide-out. Directly over the hole, he could see the brick walls of the two houses all the way up to the underside of the roof, and the boards and the pieces of rugs continued beyond the hole and to the front of the houses. The four boys had gone through great pains to fix the place up. What fun they must have had. What strategies they must have planned for their fights with the other neighborhoods.

"Look here," Sammy whispered. He had moved several feet toward the rear of the house, putting him approximately outside the rear bedroom of the empty house. In the dimness, Joey could see that several bricks were loose, with no signs of mortar to hold them together. Carefully, Sammy took out four bricks. The hole was not clean through, however. The plaster inside the room had not been broken through, and only a mere half inch of plaster was the only thing that prevented anyone from getting into the empty house.

"We could take out a couple more bricks and get in," whispered Sammy.

"You crazy?" Joey caught himself as he realized that he had blurted the words out too loudly.

"It's empty."

"I said no." The thought of Mrs. Furguson, just on the other side of the opposite wall, made him shiver. If she ever trapped them up there . . . he began to crawl toward the light. "I'm getting out of here," he hissed.

"Okay. Look, I'm closing it up." Sammy began to put the bricks back in place. Joey stopped moving. He sat, once more facing Sammy. He relaxed, knowing that Sammy had been teasing him. But he knew that sooner or later, Sammy would try to get into the house. He also knew that he might go along. The adventure was too tempting.

Except for the steady drum of the rain on the roof above them, all was still. Sammy broke the silence. "You think that the hole was a way out in case they got trapped by somebody in the alley?"

"Maybe one of the guys lived in there, and he could come in and out anytime he wanted . . . maybe meet the other guys after he was supposed to go to bed," Joey thought out loud.

"Yeah," agreed Sammy. "Would you break through if you lived there?"

"Are you crazy? My father would kill me."

They were silent for a time, each with his own contented thoughts. There were no sounds from the Furguson house. Don't tell anybody," Sammy whispered.

"I won't. Joey hardly needed the warning. This was their secret.

CHAPTER

7

There had been an air of excitement and expectation from the moment they had picked up Fanny Coyle at the agreed upon corner. She had gotten into the front seat with Uncle Guido and had given him a long kiss right in front of the boys. This had never happened before. Although there had always been signs of lipstick smudges and disheveled hair and clothing afterwards, the girl had never kissed Uncle Guido in front of them. Sammy had nudged Joey and Joey knew that he was grinning. They had gotten out of the car at the entrance to the exposition, as they had done on numerous other times, and Uncle Guido had given them some money and told them to have a good time. Then, he and the girl had driven off.

The automobile was waiting for the boys when they finally came out. Uncle Guido and the girl were sitting in the front seat, the girl leaning heavily against him. She nuzzled her face against his neck, leaving a trail of kisses from his ear to the hollow of his throat. They seemed oblivious of the boys. But finally, Uncle Guido started the car and drove around awhile before he left the girl off. They seemed reluctant to part. Finally, the girl gave Uncle Guido one last kiss and left them after kissing Joey on the cheek. Her lips were warm and moist, unlike any time before.

When Uncle Guido finally spoke, he sounded happier than he had ever sounded before. Something special had happened tonight, surmised Joey. He sounded like Poppa did the morning after he closed the bedroom door and all the strange noises could be heard. As a matter of fact, Joey had seen his mother behave much like the girl had, before and after they closed the bedroom door. Sometimes they went to bed extra early when it happened.

"Guess who's coming to town?" Uncle Guido asked.

"Babe Ruth!" Both boys shouted it out simultaneously.

"You better be extra good if you wanna come with me, Joey."

"You bet. When are we going, Uncle Guido?" Joey was leaning over the back of the front seat in his excitement.

"Saturday, I guess. They'll be here for three games."

"I hope Babe Ruth gets a homer," said Joey.

Sammy sat quietly. He knew he had not been included. He had been invited to go with them to a Saturday game last season, but his father had sternly advised him that a Jewish man should be in a synagogue on Saturdays and not at a ball game. Sammy did not argue that he had not yet been bar-mitzvah, so technically he was not yet a man. What did his father know about baseball anyway? He thought Shibe Park was a place where people went for picnics and Connie Mack was a lady who owned the park. Anyway, he had not been asked since. Now, he waited, heart pounding, hoping that he would be asked. He would do anything to go. He might even defy his father.

"How about you, Sammy?" Uncle Guido was in a grateful mood, and could think of no other way to express it, other than by giving.

"I can't go on Saturday. Me and my father go to the synagogue on Saturdays."

"How about Friday?"

"Yeah, I can go on Friday," Sammy said happily. "We'll be home by sundown, won't we?" he continued lamely. He knew his father expected him to be home at sundown on Friday in order to begin the observance of their holy day.

"Your friend is pretty hard to please, Joey," Uncle Guido said. It looked like it would have to be Thursday. You never knew about a ballgame. A tie game going into extra innings could last forever. And he would not want to leave if that happened. And why not Thursday. Uncle Guido was feeling absolutely magnanimous. For over a week now, everything had gone his way. The poker game of last week-end had netted him close to a thousand dollars. Then he had picked up over five hundred dollars at the race-track. And to top it off, Fanny had been so exciting and tender in the back seat of his car. He had never seen her like this. She had been insatiable in her love-making. And the best part was that her husband would be out of town for several days, and she had promised to go to Atlantic City with him. "Would Thursday suit you fine, sir?" he asked, kiddingly.

"Yeah!" Sammy shouted. "Thanks, Mr. Guido. Thank you." Sammy didn't know what more to say. At the moment, he wished he had an Uncle Guido.

"Make sure you tell your father. He's teaching you good, and I want you to respect him, you hear?"

"Yes, I will, Mr. Guido."

The automobile pulled up in front of Joey's house. Joey's mother was sitting on the front steps with Angelina. Joey and Sammy jumped out of the car, and Uncle Guido looked on with envy as he saw Lucia Nocelli's beautiful dark eyes light up when Joey told her of the promised trip. For an instant, her eyes met his, and he would have joyously given everything he owned, even Fanny Coyle, if he could have her as his own. Of course, it could never be. He had too much respect for Giovanni, his boyhood friend, and even more for Lucia. He kept his love a secret, but at times he felt that she knew it and respected him for not making it too obvious. The look she had given him, he knew, was not one of adoration, but one of thanks for making her son happy.

"Thank you, Guido," Lucia Nocelli said. She felt that she needed to do something more to thank him, but she didn't know what. "Giovanni is inside," she said. "He has new wine."

"No, thanks," Uncle Guido said. He was still in his automobile, motor still running. "I have business," he laughed.

"Yes, I know that business," Mrs. Nocelli scolded. She knew that he was undoubtedly on his way to a card game, and that he would gamble all night. As far as she knew, it was his only source of income. That he was so lucky was a wonder. He always had so much money in his pocket. Sometimes she worried about his safety. Terrible things happened to people with all that money, and she had told him so many a time.

"Say good-bye to Giovanni," he said. He pulled away as the two boys waved vigorously.

Soon Joey and Sammy wandered off. Angelina, who had once admitted to being forty years old, sighed. Pretty in a plain sort of way, and overweight, giving her face a jolly appearance, she none-the-less was a romantic and dreamed of Rudolf Valentino. "Eh, Lucia," she said, "do you think that if I got rid of my Tony, your friend would go out with me?" She laughed, and it was when she laughed that she looked her prettiest. She had come to America as a child and did not speak broken English.

Lucia Nocelli looked her up and down. She knew that her friend was having fun with her. "I do not think so," she said, joining in the laughter. "Perhaps if you lost some weight."

"I think he would go out with you." Angelina had stopped laughing and spoke softly. "I think he is crazy for you." She had spoken in the Italian that she remembered as a child so that her friend would understand her.

"It is you who is crazy," laughed Lucia. But she knew that what Angelina said was true. She had known it for a long time. Not that Guide had ever made any advances. He went out of his way to appear aloof when in her company. But at times he forgot himself, and his eyes on her made her nervous. She loved her Giovanni, but she loved this man who had known her husband longer than she. She loved Guido like the brother she had left back in Italy, and she wanted desperately for their friendship to last forever.

"No, Lucia. I think you know that I'm right." The two friends confided in each other like sisters.

Lucia listened with ears close to the screen door. Somewhere in the house, she could hear the pounding of a hammer. It was safe to talk. "You are right as usual, my friend," she said in a low voice. "Sometimes I worry about it. I do not think that Giovanni senses it. I would not want their friendship to come to an end. They were friends as young boys in Italy. I swear that I do nothing to . . ."

"Of course. I know that, Lucia. Perhaps if he should find a nice girl and get married . . ."

"How I pray that this would happen. But he only goes with women who are married. He says that as long as they are already married, he will not have to marry them."

"Smart fellow." admitted Angelina.

"Yes, perhaps he is too smart," lamented Lucia. "One of these days, a husband will catch up to him. And that is another thing that I worry about."

From inside, Giovanni could be heard calling his wife. The two friends looked at each other. "I hope he has not heard any of this," laughed Angelina.

"I think not. I think my dear husband has other matters on his mind." And indeed, Lucia recognized the strange tone in his voice, a sound that only she knew. He was tired of what he was doing and wished only to hold his wife and feel her breasts and thighs against him.

And Lucia felt her body respond to the sound of his voice. She was as ready as he. It would be quick, she knew. They would be done before Joey came home. "Wait for me," she told her friend. "I will be down soon."

Angelina saw the strange smile in Lucia's eyes. "You are going to him?" she asked, mildly surprised.

"He is my husband."

"What if Joey comes home?"

"Greet him loudly. I will hear you."

"Go, then," laughed Angelina. "Go, puta."

"I will pray that your Tony will be good to you tonight," laughed Lucia. She entered the dark living room, saw that little Jimmy was still asleep on the sofa. Upstairs, Giovanni waited for her, his trousers already off. "Is it done with, Cara?" he asked.

"yes . . . yes," she gasped as he took her in his arms. God, how she hated this woman's sickness. It had been so long . . . such a long week.

CHAPTER
8

In spite of the fact that it was a week-day, the stands in Shibe Park were almost filled to capacity. It was a beautiful day, with not a cloud in the sky. It was a day befitting the arrival of Babe Ruth and the New York Yankees. Everywhere there was laughter and signs of anticipation. Whole families, even tiny infants in their mother's arms, were there with bags stuffed with food and pops. It was like one huge picnic.

From behind third base, Uncle Guido, Joey and Sammy sat facing the short fence in right field. Enterprising home-owners across the street from the park had set up benches and chairs on their roofs and spectators were already making themselves comfortable while waiting for the players to take the field. Home plate and the infield were clearly visible to them. As one, they hoped that the legendary Babe Ruth would rocket one out to them. What a souvenir it would be, and what a story they would have to tell their children and grand-children.

Many of the fans had come to see the legend, but more had come to see their beloved "A's". With such greats as Mickey Cochrane, Jimmy Foxx, Al Simmons and Lefty Grove, it was just a matter of time before the team would recapture the greatness of the club that had become the scourge of the league only ten years before. It was inevitable. The crowd that filled the park sensed it, and they had come to cheer their team on. Today, however, in spite of the fact that he was a "Yankee", it was Babe Ruth who captured the imagination of every fan there.

The crowd came to its feet when the New York team came on to the field, shouting, "Bambino . . . Bambino." Babe Ruth, his huge upper body looking top-heavy and awkward on spindly legs, waved his cap to the crowd. He then took his turn at batting practice and proceeded to swat homers over the short right-field fence. Some sky-rocketed out to the fans on the roofs across the street. Each homer brought forth thunderous shouts of approval. Joey and Sammy applauded every time he hit one.

The New York Yankees, with power at just about every position, scored two runs in the first inning. Babe Ruth hit a long fly which would have been a homer had it not gone foul by several feet. Then, he flied out deep into center field. Even without his power, they scored easily. It looked like it was going to be a long afternoon for the "A's" pitcher, Lefty Grove, even though he struck out the last two batters.

"I'll bet a hot-dog that the Yankees score ten runs before this is over," laughed Uncle Guido as the Athletics came to bat.

"You got a bet," Sammy shouted above the sound of the crowd. "Lefty's settled down now. The Yankees will be lucky if they score again. You saw what he did to those last two guys."

Betting was a malady that Uncle Guido had succumbed to many years ago. Even as a boy, he would bet a penny that the telephone in the candy store where they hung out would ring for somebody in the neighborhood within two minutes of the time he arrived. Betting was a challenge he could not resist. Now, he took the challenge with as much intensity as though he were betting a hundred dollars. "Okay, smart guy, I'll tell you what I'm gonna do." He winked at Joey. "I'll bet you a dollar to a quarter that the Yankees win by five runs." How could he lose? The Yankees already had two runs. Babe Ruth was sure to hit a homer with somebody on. Then there was Lou Gehrig. He was on a hitting streak. And the others? He was betting on a team with the most batting power ever assembled, the team that was sure to go on to win the World Series again. There was no way he could lose.

"You're not serious, are you, Mr. Guido?" Sammy had suddenly turned red.

"Yeah, I'm serious. A dollar to a quarter that the Yankees win by five." Uncle Guido was having fun. "As a matter of fact, I'll tell you what. Make it a dollar to a dime." Uncle Guido was grinning . . . a teasing, cocky grin.

"Okay, you've got a bet." Sammy's face had now turned pale.
"Where's your dime?"

The boy dug into his pocket and brought out a dime. Uncle Guido took out a roll of bills and peeled off a dollar bill. He held out his hand. "We'll let Joey hold the bet," he said, trying hard to keep from bursting out laughing.

Sammy dropped his dime into Uncle Guide's well-manicured hand. The "A's" had a man on base and the crowd was screaming for a hit, but he heard none of it. His eyes were on the money until it disappeared into Joey's pocket. He finally came back to earth when he shook hands with Uncle Guido. The bet had been completed. Suddenly, he could hear the crowd cheering. Jimmy Foxx had driven in a run with a double, and the Athletics were beginning to close the gap and to go on to win the game.

The game ended with the score four to two. Connie Mack, the Athletics' owner and manager, looking as though he was dressed for a dinner party, his tie neatly knotted and snug against his stiff collar, stared impassively at the imposing figure of Babe Ruth as he sauntered to the plate. He motioned with his score card. The outfielders who had already been playing deep, moved back another fifteen feet. With two out and men on first and third, the legendary manager did not want an extra base hit by Ruth. A homer would put the Yankees ahead, and an extra base hit would possibly score two runs to tie. A single, on the other hand, would keep the man on first from scoring.

Lefty Grove, pitching like a magician since the first inning, tried hitting the corners. With one ball and one strike on the batter, his curve ball came in a little too close on the outside corner, and Babe Ruth got his bat on it. There was not a sound in the park except the crack of the bat as the ball rose in a high arc out toward deep center. The crowd held its breath. They were not looking for the game to end with a loss for "Lefty" after such a superbly pitched game. Even if it was Babe Ruth who would end it.

The crowd erupted with a great roar as the ball dropped safely into the center-fielder's glove. He had caught it without moving a step. Had the ball been pulled to right field, it would have been a homer. Connie Mack calmly got up and headed for the locker room as soon as the umpire signaled the last out.

Uncle Guido rose to his feet, secretly glad that-the "A's" had won. It would have been a shame for Lefty Grove to lose this one. He had given up only three hits after the first inning, and was never in trouble except in that last inning. That Sammy was certainly a shrewd one, he mused. Knows his baseball. Maybe I ought to talk to him more. I could have made me some money today, if I had listened to him. He turned to look for the boy. Sammy was no longer with them. "Where's Sammy?" he asked Joey.

"I don't know," said Joey, looking around.

"Oh, no," groaned Uncle Guido, looking at the crowd. Everyone in the park had stayed until that last out, and now they were streaming out. "We better wait here. Maybe he'll have sense enough to come back here." He sounded angry.

Soon the throng had disappeared. It was obvious that Sammy wasn't coming back. "Let's go," muttered Uncle Guido. They waited at the main entrance for ten minutes. Now, Uncle Guido was no longer angry. He was worried. "Never again," he kept muttering over and over again.

"Maybe he's waiting at the car," Joey said, hopefully.

Uncle Guido doubted it. It would be a miracle if he himself found it. And he had made it a point to memorize the street and spot where he had left it. He would be willing to bet the boy would not find the car. But, when Sammy did not show up, he led Joey to the car. A small boy met them. "I thought you forgot the place," he said. "I was getting ready to leave."

"Thanks," said Uncle Guido. "Did the other boy show up?"

"Nope."

"Damn! What do we do now?" exploded Uncle Guido.

Joey had not been too concerned until now. He had never seen Uncle Guido this worried before. He was always so sure of himself. "You think we ought to call a policeman?" he asked timidly.

"Where do you find a cop around here anyway?" Uncle Guido asked, mostly to himself.

"Wait here." said the boy, who appeared to be Joey's age, but had the street-wise look of an adult.

They waited, both helplessly looking about for Sammy. A friendly man came over to them. He told them not to worry. "Kids from the ball-park get lost every day," he said. "He's probably over at the police station right now. I can take you there if you want."

Several minutes later, the boy came back leading a policeman. "This here's Officer Mulhane," he said. He waited while Uncle Guido found a quarter and gave it to him, then he ran off.

"He'll make a million dollars, that one," Officer Mulhane said, chuckling. He seemed unperturbed. "I understand you lost one of them," he said to Uncle Guido.

"Yeah, Officer. A little kid about his age." Uncle Guido pointed to Joey.

"A little Jewish kid by the name of Sammy?"

"Yeah, that's him." Uncle Guido already sounded relieved.

"Well, you don't have to worry about that one." The policeman winked at them. "He's a smart kid, he is."

"He's okay, then?" Uncle Guido insisted.

"Yes, sir, he's just fine. He came up to me and told me he went down to the A's locker room to get some autographs. Got himself some, too. Foxx and Cochrane and Grove . . . some others. Couldn't get near the Yankees."

"Where's he now?" Uncle Guide's anxiety was quickly replaced by impatience.

"Over at the precinct, about a block and a half down the street. Be a lot easier for us to help these lost kids if they'd come straight to us," the policeman said.

Uncle Guido was already getting into the car, "C'mon Joey. We better go get that kid before he gets lost again," he said. "Thanks, Officer." He waved.

The officer waved his stick, and by the time the car had pulled away, Officer Mulhane was deep in conversation with the friendly man who had spoken to them.

On the long ride down Broad Street, from North Philly into South Philly, Uncle Guido drove silently. He had not said much at the police-station except to answer some questions. In the back seat, the two boys exchanged glances, Joey shrugging his shoulders. He knew Uncle Guido was angry. Sammy was just beginning to realize the gravity of his act. Up until now, he could not comprehend why Mr. Guido should be so angry with him. But he was. He hadn't spoken one word to him since leaving the police-station. He hadn't even answered him when he said he was sorry that he had caused all the trouble. That should have straightened things out between them. It usually did with his father. Maybe Mr. Guido hadn't heard him. "I'm sorry I caused you all that trouble, Mr. Guido," he said again.

Uncle Guido drove without a word. He had heard the boy apologize before, but he had not sounded sincere. He sounded as though the apology should make everything right.

Well, he would teach him a lesson. He was no longer angry, but he played his little game of silence. Let the boy worry a little . . . keep him off balance. It felt like when he had the winning hand in a game of poker, but he wanted the other players to think that they had a chance of winning the pot. It was like playing cat and mouse.

Through the mirror, he saw the boy nudge Joey, then shrug hopelessly. He was beginning to worry. He could see it in his eyes. He could see it by the missing cocky grin. It was enough. "I hope you learned your lesson," he said finally.

"Yeah, I did." There was a note of relief in Sammy's voice.

"I don't think you did, Sammy. Don't you think that Joey would have liked to get some autographs too?"

"I didn't think that Joey was that much interested. I'll give him two of them. One of the policemen wanted to give me a quarter for one of them. They'll be worth a lot of money some day when the A's win the pennant."

Uncle Guido couldn't help but chuckle. Officer Mulhane was right. The kid was shrewd alright. He had a regular Jew business head on him. How many did you get?" he asked, forgetting the sermon. Somehow, he had the feeling that everything he said was going in one ear and out the other.

"Seven."

"You got Foxx and Cochrane?"

"Yeah . . . and Simmons and Lefty Grove," Sammy said, proudly. The others did not matter.

"Which ones you want?" Uncle Guido asked Joey.

"You can have anyone except Lefty Grove."

"Aw, that's alright, Uncle Guido. I can get some, some other time." Joey wasn't that crazy about sport figures. He preferred the cowboy cards. "Sammy always gives me his cowboy cards," he added.

48

"Mm . . . Tom Mix and Buck Jones?"

"Yeah, he gives me lots of them."

"Well, you take two autographs anyway. Maybe, someday they'll be worth a million dollars, like Sammy says. And by the way, give him the bet money."

"That's okay, Mr. Guido. Forget about the bet," Sammy said quickly.

Uncle Guido smiled at himself. He had the pot won, and the boy was putting more into it than he had figured on, in the hopes of getting back into his good graces. The gambler in him told him to take the offer. He had won.

Joey had the money in his hands. Through the mirror, Guido could see the funny look on the boy's face. Joey was waiting to see if he would accept the offer. And in that instant, Uncle Guido knew that he had lost. He had been bluffed by the Jewish kid. If he took the dollar back, Joey was sure to think less of him. "Give him the money, Joey," he said. "He won it fair and square." He saw the relief that flooded Joey's face. He smiled. Actually, he had won also. "Don't ever forget, you two . . . you win a bet, make sure you collect. And if you lose, don't be a welcher . . . pay up."

They rode home, detouring around the section of Broad Street where they were building the new subway line that would take a passenger deep into North Philadelphia and south to South Street. Someday, prophesized Uncle Guido, a person would be able to ride the whole length of Philadelphia, from North to South, underground.

CHAPTER 9

The pimpled ball was a boy's most precious possession. Slightly smaller than a regulation baseball, it was made of rubber and filled with air. It could be bought for a dime at any candy store or toy shop. With it, two boys could play catch, they could bounce it off a wall and play a sort of hand-ball, or they could draw a chalk-line in the street and play a game of tennis, slapping the ball with the palms of their hands. They could place a coin on the ground, and with each boy staying approximately six feet on either side of it, they would aim at it with the ball. Every time the coin was hit, it counted a point. It was two points if the coin turned over.

If enough boys could get together, they could play baseball. And the only place where enough boys of Joey's age could get together in the daytime was at the Snyder School playground. In the summer, the vast school-yard became the neighborhood playground, and a corner of it became a baseball field. No gloves or bats were needed. Only a pimple ball.

One morning, Sammy showed up in Joey's back yard with one. "Let's go to the school-yard and see if we can get into a game," he said. He tossed the ball underhanded to Joey who caught it easily. Joey bounced it on the brick pavement. It was brand new and full of bounce. They were sure to get into a game with it.

"Okay, let me tell my mother," Joey said. He went inside and was back almost immediately. "I have to be back for lunch," he said.

"Me too."

"You have to take a leak?" Joey was already unbuttoning his fly as he headed for the out-house in the corner of the yard. Most families still had the toilet facilities in their back yards, even though some now had indoor plumbing. Many were still in use. Sturdily built of brick, some were used as storage space. Joey's father had lined one whole wall with shelves, but the toilet still worked. Joey used it at times such as this, when he did not feel like running upstairs in the house.

The school-yard was crowded with children of all ages. One corner, next to the school building, was used for girl's activities, organized and supervised by some of the very teachers who taught during the regular school term. They were loved and respected by most of the children, some of whom had been in their classes. Here, mostly 'small girls played "pick up jacks" or skipped rope. The smaller children slid down a shiny slide or were swung on strap-in swings. These were supervised and helped by the bigger girls. There was something for every little boy and girl.

Out in the far corner of the yard was the baseball field. A game was already in progress when Joey and Sammy arrived. It was only a pick-up game and anyone could play. The league games were played in the afternoon, and a boy could play only if he was on the team designated to play that day.

Joey and Sammy sauntered over to the third base side of the field. They waved to some of the boys they knew. Sammy kept bouncing his ball, making sure it got a good bounce. For a short while he and Joey played catch. They waited patiently. Sooner or later the ball being used in the game would be batted over the fence of the neighboring back yards, and usually was not returned. In that event, Joey and Sammy would be invited to play, since Sammy had a ball. Of course, two of the boys already playing would have to be sacrificed. Certain boys were expendable.

It wasn't long before one of the boys misjudged the ball as it was pitched in on one bounce. His clenched fist failed to hit the ball squarely, and it veered foul along the first base line. The batter held his breath as it flew toward the back yards. It did no good. The ball dropped into one of the yards, bounced against the back window of the house which fortunately did not break. A moment later, the ball came flying out in two parts. The two halves were retrieved. They would be used to play half-ball at another time.

In a few minutes, the game was continued with Sammy's ball. Both Joey and Sammy were now playing right field, one for each team. The two boys they had replaced, the smallest on each team, retired to a wooden bench along the first base line. They sat quietly. Sooner or later, one of the boys playing would quit or be called home, and one would get back into the game. Someday, in a couple of years, there would be boys smaller than they were, and they would be big enough to remain in a game that was ruled by the biggest and best players.

In the three innings that they played, Joey hit a ball between left and center and brought home a run. He reached second. He was driven home by a sharply hit ground ball through the infield. He also made an easy catch of a high fly that he had momentarily lost in the sun. He was making a good impression on the boys who had never seen him play.

Sammy chased a ball that had been slapped over first base and caught it on the run for a third out and prevented runners on second and third from scoring. At bat, he slapped the ball with a limp hand and placed it over second base for a hit. In the ninth, with two out and a boy on third, he played deep for the best hitter on the other team. He saw the boy eyeing the vast, open space between the second baseman and himself. Anyone could place the ball into the space for a hit. The boy was sure to try for it, scoring the boy from third.

Just as the boy began his swing, Sammy began running in, and was parked under the ball almost twenty feet behind the second baseman when the ball reached him. It was an easy out and the game was over. Sammy's team won. The boys from both teams were impressed. They urged both to join their teams.

"Nah," said Sammy. "1 can't. My family's going down to the shore." He winked at Joey.

"What about you, Joey, you want to play for us?" The boy believed Sammy. All Jew kids went away for the summer.

"I can't either, Tony," Joey said, taking the hint from Sammy. "My family is going to New Jersey to pick tomatoes as soon as they get ripe. Maybe we'll go sooner if some of the other stuff is ready."

"Well, if either of you guys want to play, just come around. I"11 put you in left or center." It was quite an incentive. Nobody liked to play right field.

"I'll see when I get back. We're only going for three or four weeks," Sammy said. He walked away, bouncing his ball. Joey waved to the boys and joined him.

Up in their hide-out, Joey giggled, but not too loud, for they could hear voices in the Furguson house. "That was pretty clever," he said. "Sorry, I can't play because we're going down the shore." He mimicked his friend.

Sammy laughed. "It's a shame we can't get a team together and get into the league. We could whip them good."

"Yeah," agreed Joey. "We could win the championship easy. Too bad all the guys from around here have to go to the farms. I wish I could go with them one summer," he added whimsically.

"Well, I don't wish you could,"

"Why?"

"I'd go crazy without you around, Joey. You're the best friend I ever had."

Joey was surprised at the sincerity in his friend's voice. He felt the same way about Sammy, but they had never talked about it. "Don't worry, Sammy, I wouldn't go" he said. "It wouldn't be any fun if you weren't there."

The voices in the Furguson house had become quite clear and seemed to come from the rear bedroom. Joey recognized the girl, Sarah's voice. She was screaming at her small brother. "You tell Momma about me wearing my new dress, and I'll lick your ass. You hear me, Hebert?"

"I will . . . I will," the five-year-old screamed back. "How come you can get dressed real nice and not me?"

"Cause you dirty yours, and Momma'll kill us both."

"I won't. Honest I won't, Sarah."

"Hush, Hebert. Look, I'm gonna take it off." After a moment of silence, the girl's voice was heard again. "Okay, Hebert . . . you satisfied?"

"Okay, Sarah."

"You won't tell Momma?"

"No."

"Okay. Now, get out of my room. You ain't supposed to look at me when I'm naked."

The two boys stared at each other in shock, their eyes barely visible to each other in the dimness. In Joey mind came a vision of little Carmela from next door. Obviously, she had seen her brother naked. But then, so had he seen his little brother Jimmy naked. It must be different if one was a boy and one was a girl.

From beyond the brick wall, the boy said, "Aw, let me stay, Sarah. I like to see you naked. You look nice . . . nicer than Momma. She be all big and fat."

Obviously pleased, the girl could be heard laughing. "Okay, Hebert, you can watch. Pretty soon I'll be big like Momma. When my titties get bigger and I get a lot of hair down here, I'll look a lot prettier. You won't be able to look at me then."

"You pretty right now, Sarah. Betch that white boy, Joey, think you pretty, he sees you like that."

"Hebert!" the girl screamed. "Don't you ever say that in front of Momma. She'd kill me."

"I see you lookin' at him behind the shades."

"Oh Hebert I", The girl sounded frightened. "Don't ever say nothing like that to Momma. You don't want to see your pretty sister dead, do you?"

"No."

"Then, promise me you won't. And I won't tell her you looked at me while I was naked."

"Okay. You promise to let me look at you once in a while?"

"I promise," said the girl. "Come on, let's go down. I got to start supper. You know what Momma'll do if supper ain't ready."

Joey made his way to the entrance hole, listened carefully for sounds of footsteps, then let himself down. He was followed by Sammy. They walked silently out of the neighborhood before either spoke. Finally, Sammy could not contain himself any longer. "She likes you, Joey. Maybe she'll let you look at her." He was grinning from ear to ear.

"Aw, Sammy, you think I'm crazy? Mrs. Furguson would beat her up if she even talked to me or anybody else. Maybe that's why she never comes out of the house."

"Would you want to see her naked?"

"Nah."

"Why not? You looked at Carmela."

Joey was sorry he had finally told Sammy about the episode in the back yard. "Well, there's nothing to see," Joey blurted out. "So why would I want to look at Sarah?"

"Cause she's different. She's colored and she's older. Her titties are bigger. They looked almost as big as my mother's, the first time I saw her without her coat on in school. I'll bet she's got some hair on her pussy, too."

"Hair?"

"Sure, stupid. All ladies have hair down there when they get big. Didn't you ever see your mom naked?"

"You think I'm a peeping Tom?" Joey said angrily.

"Don't get mad, Joey. I only seen mine by accident. She doesn't know I seen her, either. If she did, she would tell my father, and I don't know what he would do."

"Would he whip you?"

"I don't know. He's never hit me."

They had never discussed sex at any length before. The only time, and they had not gone into any great detail, was when Joey had told Sammy about the incident with Carmela. They had not delved into the sexual aspects of it. It was something he had done and had been punished for. Neither had ever mentioned it again until now.

They walked on in silence, Joey wondering what his father would do if he saw his mother naked. He had been warned numerous times to knock on their bedroom door before going in. The same for the bathroom. His parents seemed rather strict about their privacy. And his father had punished him twice with his strap. Not hard, but punished nevertheless. So his guess was that he would be punished severely, as befitted the crime. "I think my pop would whip me good if I did something like that." he said without thinking. "Well, maybe not, if it happened accidently," he added.

They caught the local ice-wagon back. Standing on a wooden running board on the rear of the wagon, they found small pieces of ice and sucked on them to cool off. Even the air as it passed over the huge blocks of ice, was chilled enough to cool them off. This would be a nice job in the summer, thought Joey. It was a good way to keep cool.

CHAPTER 10

For days, Mrs. Nocelli baked and prepared food for the party. The ice-box was stuffed with home-made pasta, sausage and meatballs that would be cooked at the last moment. Mr. Nocelli was sure that the wine he had made last autumn was ready. He sipped from the bottles he had filled and saved for this occasion. And he found that the wine had turned out perfectly, each sip exciting his taste-buds as no other wine had before.

It was early August and Joey would be ten years old. But since his birthday came on a Thursday, the celebration was postponed until the Saturday afterwards. No party such as this was celebrated on a weekday, when the men had to go to work the next day. None would be able to, for no self-respecting paesano (countyman) should remain sober. They could not, and still show respect for their host.

During the week, Joey had gone to the Italian market with Uncle Guido. There, he had picked out his very first pair of long pants, a shirt and a pair of shoes. Next, they stopped at a wondrous store whose inside was fragrant with the pungent smell of cheeses and cold-cuts. There were huge rounds of cheeses on the counters with large wedges cut out, large balls of provolone, whole pieces of prosciutto and salami hanging from the ceiling. Dry sticks of pepperoni and liver sausage made the mouth water.

Inside one glass counter were large bowls of olives, some black and smooth, some green, and some were black and shriveled and soaked in oil with garlic and red flakes of hot pepper mixed in. Uncle Guido knew the owner, a large, fat man who picked on the olives even as he tended the store. "Hello, Mike," said Uncle Guido upon entering.

"Eh, Guido . . . che cosa dire(what do you say)?" greeted the man. "Your kid?" he asked, pointing at Joey with a greasy, black olive in his hand.

"Nan. My God-child. Gonna be ten years old and we're gonna give him a big party."

"Good looking kid," said the man, nodding approval. "So what can I do for you, Guido?"

Uncle Guido proceeded to buy several pounds of the various types of olives, a ball of provolone that weighed almost seven pounds and five sticks of pepperoni. Then, he bought five pounds of salami and five pounds of prosciutto, both sliced for sandwiches. Joey munched on a chunk of the cheese that crumbled in his hand. "Good, eh?" the storekeeper asked. "You eat plenty of that stuff and you grow big like me and your Uncle Guido."

As they made their way back to Uncle Guide's car, the aroma from the food seemed to surround them like an invisible veil, and heads turned and smiled. And by the time they reached Joey's house, the inside of the car was permeated with the wonderful, stomach warming smell.

Saturday night, Sammy came early and brought a gift, a small package wrapped in colorful wrapping paper. Joey did not open it, but he knew that it would be a number of cowboy picture cards with the chewing gum still attached. The two sat in the back yard, picking on some of the food that was set out on a make-shift table. Sammy drank a glass of lemonade. He couldn't stay long, he explained. His father had allowed him out only because he was going to wish Joey a happy birthday. And as soon as the first guests came, he got up. "Happy Birthday, pal," he said. Then, impulsively, he hugged Joey and left.

The first to arrive was Nicolina Flaviano with her parents and brother. The boy, slightly older than little Jimmy, was soon riding about in the boy's red car. When the two began fighting over it, it mysteriously disappeared.

Nicolina looked pretty in a virgin-white dress that came well below her knees. A ribbon in her long, brown hair framed her dark eyes and pouting mouth. Joey looked at the girl in a new light, glancing at her breasts to see if they were as large as Sarah Ferguson's. But her body was as flat as his. She was only slightly taller than he, in spite of the fact that she was over a year older. She seemed a bit nervous, not laughing whole-heartedly as she did when they would lay down on her living room floor and read the comics on a Sunday morning, after church. She waited until they were alone in the back yard before she wished him a happy birthday. Then, she kissed him on the cheek, something she had never done before. Joey was embarrassed. "You didn't have to do that," he said.

"I wanted to," she said.

Soon, more guests arrived, and before long, the house of Giovanni Nocelli was bursting with music and laughter. They ate great platters of baked pasta and meatballs and sausage in delicious gravy. They made sandwiches with crusty roles overflowing with cheese and meat cold-cuts. They drank Giovanni's wine and picked on chunks of pepperoni and olives and provolone.

The women gathered together for a time and gossiped and chattered away. These were women who had come from the village of Monteparesa, for the most part. And now they gathered about the newest arrivals, Amelia Cortolani and her daughter, Clara, and asked questions about parents or old friends they had left behind.

Clara Cortolani was a striking beauty with dark hair and hazel eyes who smiled whimsically when asked if she had broken any young man's heart when she left Italy. In a sweet, lyrical Italian, not yet blemished by harsh English words and sounds, and which brought back memories of home, she told them that there were hardly any young men left in the village. They had all gone to make a living elsewhere: in the large cities, other countries . . . America. There was one young man who would miss her, however, her mother added knowingly.

At age twenty-seven, the girl was an oddity, because women from the village were usually married by the time they had grown out of their teens. Amid much laughter, she was assured that here in America there were many men, and she need not fear that she would become a spinster. Names were mentioned. "There is the son of a neighbor who has just become a doctor," said one of the women. "I think he would make a fine husband."

"Do you mean Lorenzo Magliori?" interrupted another. "He is too short and already balding."

"There is a man who owns a fine furniture store near me . . ." And so it went, the women trying to sell their particular applicant for Clara

58

Cortolani's hand. While she busied herself with her guests, Lucia Nocelli thought of one, her own favorite young man who was sure to sweep the young woman off her feet . . . Guido. He had promised to come.

Rocco Petrucci had brought his guitar and Fernando Columbo his mandolin. Joey's father brought out a small, ancient accordion that he had brought with him from Italy. It was not known how many generations had danced to its music. Together, the three played the music of the mountain village they had left: la Saltarella, la Mazurka and others, while Francisco Pascucci, a short, robust man sang risqué ditties that brought forth hoots of laughter from the men and happy squeals from the women. They danced in the tiny living room, making the floor vibrate to the stomping of feet.

With the men playing the music, only two or three remained to dance with the women. As they tired or began feeling tipsy from the wine, the women were left to dance with each other. Angelina, from next door, looked on with amusement. How had she missed all this happiness and cheer? She could not recall ever having a celebration such as this. She could not even remember her parents having friends from the old country. Surely, she had missed something.

In the back yard, Carmela and Nunzio, her children, along with several others, children of some of the guests, played games that had suddenly become childish. In the dimness of the yard, lit up only by the light bulb from the kitchen, the game of pinning the tail on the donkey had suddenly gotten tiresome. "Let's play spin the bottle," whispered Carmela, giggling. There was a slight hesitation, then it was the girls, some even younger than Carmela, who squealed approval. Joey was still apprehensive when he was called upon to spin the bottle first, since it was his birthday.

Joey became completely unnerved when the bottle pointed to Nicolina Flaviano, and allowed himself to be led into the out-house. "Don't stay too long," whispered one of the boys." Joey could see the girl's face from the light that shone through the quarter-moon shaped vent hole at the top of the door. There was a tiny smile on her pretty face.

"Well," she said.

"I never kissed a girl before," Joey confessed,

"Honest?" said the girl, showing surprise.

"Honest."

"I'll show you," she said. She held his face, tilting it slightly. Her mouth covered his, warm and moist. He felt the tip of her tongue against his lips. She pulled away for an instant. "You're supposed to put your arms around me," she said.

He held her waist. She felt soft, softer than anyone else he had ever held . . . except his mother. He would always remember her softness when she held him to soothe his hurts and fears. But this was different. Her arms were about his neck, and they were smooth and warm. Her lips were trying to force his open.

"Hey, come on out," came the cries from the others.

They came out, but not before the girl had whispered, "That was nice, Joey."

Joey sat in a daze while Nicolina spun the bottle. She went into the out-house with one of the other boys, and they came out almost immediately. She looked squarely at Joey. See, I only like to kiss you, her look told him.

Almost everybody had gone into the "kissing room," as they now called the out-house, when Carmela was picked to go in by a boy of eight. They came out quickly, the boy wiping his mouth with the back of his hand. It was her turn to spin the bottle. She squealed with delight when it pointed to Joey, and as soon as the door closed behind them, she began kissing him with great, splashy kisses that tasted of the soda-pop she had been drinking. They were childish kisses compared to Nicolina's. They came out quickly.

The bottle seemed to be controlled by his brain when it stopped. Nicki, please," he had been praying. Now, he needed no coaching as he took her in his arms. They kissed as naturally as though they had kissed a hundred times Her tiny tongue went deeper into his mouth, and he let his own tongue savor it. He tightened his arms about her waist, squeezing her slim, girlish body to his. And when they came out, Joey felt as though his life had been changed forever. Never had he felt his legs so weak. When he sat down, he noticed how tight his trousers felt around his crotch. He felt as though he had to urinate. He dared not look as the girl spun the bottle then disappeared with her new partner. He felt miserable when they didn't come out immediately.

Before he had another chance to be with Nicolina, Angelina, from next door, came out to announce that it was time for Joey to come in and blow out the candles. "And don't forget to pick up the bottle before somebody trips over it," she said, laughing.

Inside, the music had stopped and everyone gathered about the kitchen table. Mrs. Nocelli was lighting the ten candles and one for good luck that were stuck in the rich, Italian cream cake that had been baked that very day by the Scotti Brothers bakery. When Joey blew out all the candles, everyone shouted and applauded.

It was during the lull in the music and dancing, while everyone sat about eating cake and drinking coffee or soda-pop, that Uncle Guido arrived. Without knocking, he appeared in the doorway, dapper in a white suit, black and white shoes and a straw hat. The carnation in his lapel matched the color of his tie. He looked every bit the dandy, quite out of place among the men in their rolled-up shirt sleeves.

"Guido!" gushed Mrs. Nocelli, rushing to him as though to a lover, turning her cheek for his kiss. Some of the women looked at each other. Was there something here to gossip about the next day? And when she took his arm and introduced him around as Joey's godfather, they kidded Giovanni Nocelli with good-natured remarks.

But Lucia Nocelli, giddy with wine, laughed and led Guido from person to person, finally leading him to Clara Cortolani, who sat demurely next to her mother and father. After introducing him to the girl's parents, she motioned to the girl. "And this is Clara Cortolani. She has just come from Italy with her parents and is not married. And she is looking for a rich, handsome American," she said. "Is she not beautiful, Guido?" she added, as the girl lowered her eyes in embarrassment.

Guido, somewhat embarrassed himself, could only mutter, in his best Italian. "So beautiful, and he meant every word of it. For never had he seen such natural beauty . . . perhaps except Lucia, who still held his arm so tightly that he could feel her soft breast, warm against it. "Clara, I wish you to meet Guido Manzoni, who also has never been married," she continued her introduction. "And he even has an automobile," she added, winking at Mrs. Cortolani, who beamed.

Uncle Guido had to turn from the girl for fear of appearing rude before all these people. He simply could not keep his eyes from the beauty of her eyes, her mouth, her breasts. "And where is my God son?" he asked, trying to regain his composure.

"Uncle Guido!" Joey yelled as he and some of the kids came in from the yard. He ran to Uncle Guido and was given a big hug. It was embarrassing in front of everybody, but he didn't mind.

"Here's something for you," Uncle Guido said, handing him a small, nicely wrapped gift.

"Open the presents," someone yelled.

"Yeah, open the presents," all the kids joined in, and soon Joey found himself sitting in a chair in the middle of the living room. One by one he opened the gifts, smiling happily, even when he was not too excited with it. Finally, he came to Uncle Guide's gift, and when he disclosed a gleaming, gold wrist-watch, every one applauded. Even Clara Cortolani was impressed. She smiled when Uncle Guido caught her eyes.

A little later, when the women once more gathered in the kitchen to gossip and the men resumed their drinking and sang the songs they had sung back in their village, Uncle Guido asked the girl if she would like to go for a ride in his automobile. She shrugged and indicated that she would need her parent's permission. With the best Italian he could muster, he asked first Mrs. Cortolani, who readily gave her consent. Then, he asked the girl's father.

When Mr. Cortolani, a short, bald, pompous man began to hem and haw, Uncle Guido said he would take some of the children along. Still the man looked undecided, looking at his wife who kept nodding. Finally, it was the prodding of the paesanos (countrymen), with their jibes and laughter that convinced him that his daughter would be safe with Guido—"Come, Enzio, you are not in the old country," someone said. "She is not with a stranger." Mrs. Cortolani finally came over to him. "Farli andare(Let them go)," she said. She towered over him.

"But we have never let her out by herself," he said, lamely.

The woman held her ground, and when it was finally settled, Uncle Guido and the girl, her face crimson by now, and Joey, Nicolina and an eight-year-old boy left in the car. Mr. Cortolani followed them to the door and watched them drive away, and for the next half hour, until they came back, he kept looking at a watch that he took out of his vest pocket and furtively looked at. And when she came in, he scrutinized her with suspicious eyes. He frowned when the girl laughed merrily at something that Uncle Guido said in Italian.

When the party was over, families left in groups, most of them living close to one another and within walking distance. The men, although staggering a bit, were able to walk without problems. Uncle Guido offered the Cortolani family a ride home. Without hesitating, Mr. Cortolani accepted. He sat up front with Uncle Guido while his wife and daughter sat in the back.

It was after two and Joey could not fall asleep. He could still vividly recall Nicolina's soft lips upon his: his first real kiss. He could hear his mother's soft, muffled shrieks, her sighs of pleasure mingled with his father's grunting, animal sounds. And then they were done. He could tell by the stillness that followed.

He waited, his heart beating wildly. From his bed, he could see his parent's bedroom door, the white paint clearly visible in the darkness. Then, the door opened, and his mother appeared in the doorway. She was naked, and by the moonlight that flooded her bedroom, he saw her clearly. For just an instant, before she disappeared into the bathroom, he saw her, his beautiful mother, soft breasts swaying, the shadowy mound between her legs. It was the most beautiful sight he had ever seen.

He heard the toilet, the sink, then she reappeared. She seemed less concerned than normally, after their love-making. Usually, she wore a slip or a night-gown. Tonight, perhaps because of the wine coursing through her veins, she did not seem to worry about Joey seeing her. She did not even look toward his bedroom, as she normally did. As she entered her room, Joey could see the fullness of her hips, the soft shadows of her back. It was a sight he would remember for the rest of his life.

In the still of the early morning, just as daylight began to cast soft shadows in the bedroom, Lucia Nocelli stirred with thoughts of Guido and Clara Cortolani making intimate love. She wondered if the girl was truly virginal. The thought of Guido teaching the girl the ways of love made her warm inside, and she turned to Giovanni, his hard body relaxed in sleep. She touched him, as she had done hundreds of times during their marriage. And he reacted as he had always done. He turned toward her in his sleep, his arm flung over her hips. His hand slid over her even in his sleep. It came to rest on her buttocks. Lucia felt him harden, and she kissed his mouth.

For the second time that night, they made love. It was not unusual. It had happened that way many times before. It had happened that way when Joey was conceived. It had happened that way when little Jimmy was conceived. As her husband reached his noisy climax, Lucia smiled contentedly. Perhaps she would become pregnant again. She kissed her husband tenderly.

CHAPTER
11

Eight days later, on the 15th of August, the idol of almost every woman in America died. The "Sheik," Rudolf Valentino, died of a perforated ulcer. Or so it was reported. There were rumors that he had been killed by a jealous husband or lover, or someone jealous of his fame. Lucia Nocelli was positive that his death was not natural, or even accidental. "Someone has killed him!" she blurted as she and Angelina wept into their handkerchiefs. They sat in Lucia's kitchen.

Angelina had brought over the newspaper with the movie idol's picture on the front page early the morning after his tragic death. She had read it and interpreted it for Lucia. There were already stories and rumors of women committing suicide, Valentino's picture clutched in their hands. The whole country was in mourning.

"First it is Caruso, and now Valentino," wailed Lucia. "They do not like Italians in this country, I tell you, Angelina. I have seen it since I have come here."

"Oh, Lucia, that is not true," consoled Angelina, wiping away her tears. "I know it is hard for you who has just come here. It was so with my parents and my husband's parents when they first came over. But it is not so bad for my family now. Tony is a foreman and his brother is a policeman. And my nephew is going to college to be a lawyer. Everyone has a chance to get ahead in this country. We even have our house paid off."

"There is that bitch from the back-yard. I know that she hates us." Lucia's sorrow was turning to bitterness. "She has such an ugly mouth. How have you stood it so long?"

"She does not bother me because I can answer her back in her own tongue. It was the same when we first moved here. She used to hang out of her window and scream at my oldest son, the one who is married and lives in New Jersey. I would bring him in the house and just ignore her. Then, one day, I got them twisted and I screamed back at her in the same foul mouth that she used . . . only worse." Angelina smiled for the first time that morning. "I must have screamed for five minutes after she shut her window. I could see her neighbors laughing behind her back. I don't think anybody likes her, not even her husband. They say that he fools around with one of the neighbors. Anyway, she doesn't bother me anymore.

"No, she bothers me now." Lucia smiled wryly, Valentino forgotten for the moment. "Perhaps I should learn some good words."

"I'll bet you already know some," laughed Angelina.

Lucia Nocelli chuckled, letting it go at that. It was true. She did know some choice words. They were some of the first she had learned. She was careful not to use them, however. She had taught her Joey not to use them in the house by putting soap in his mouth. Not even her Giovanni used foul language in her house.

She served coffee and they sat silently for a time, each with her own thoughts. Then, Angelina, her cup drained, asked, "Are you all right?"

Lucia smiled sadly. "Giovanni will be cheated in bed tonight. I do not think I will feel like making love.

"There will be many women like you tonight. Lucky for me, Tony does not care about that too much. It is not a need that he must satisfy like your Giovanni."

"Does that not make you unhappy? I am so pleased when he wants me."

Angelina thought for a moment. "It used to be that way. With us . . . when we were young like you. Now, he hugs me and kisses me on the cheek, and I'm happy. I think he would rather talk about how well he's doing at work than make love. I don't mind it. It makes me happy just to see him happy."

"Then all this passion will disappear as we get older?" Lucia felt saddened.

"Oh, Lucia, it isn't that bad." Angelina touched Lucia's hand across the table. "We haven't stopped completely. We're not that old. But when we make love, we just lay in each other's arms afterwards and talk for hours. That is when I am the happiest."

Lucia never felt so close to anyone like she did at that moment. "I am so happy for you, dear Angelina," she said. "I wish it will be the same with me and my Giovanni in years to come."

"I'm sure it will be, Lucia." Angelina got up. "Do not cry too much over Rudolf. We have our own real life and blood men that we love. Now, if they should die, God forbid, then that is our tragedy. Then, we should cry. Valentino was only a picture on the screen for you and me."

Never had Angelina spoken with such eloquence. Lucia had gained a new respect for her this day. And when she had gone, she remembered her words and shed no more tears. She went about her house-work and tended to little Jimmy. How wonderful it would be if she became pregnant again before it was too late, she thought.

She didn't cry all day long. But when Joey rushed in, wide-eyed and told her that Valentino had died, she did burst into tears. "I know, my son," she said, wiping her tears. "He will not be forgotten soon." ʳ

Joey could not understand the reason for the tears. "Are you all right, Mom?" he asked.

"I will be fine," she said hugging him. "Sit down and I will make you a sandwich." She did not cry again until she saw pictures of the huge crowd that had gathered in front of the funeral parlor in New York, trying to get in to see the great screen lover for the last time. It was reported that some thirty thousand people jammed the street that day.

It was several weeks after Valentino's funeral that they saw the new neighbor for the first time. He sauntered down the street like a grandee of some rich, ancient family, one who had never one who had never needed to suffer from menial labor. He was immaculately dressed in a creamy silk shirt open at the collar. The light gray, felt hat was worn with the wide brim snapped down on one side of the face in the style made famous by the infamous Al Capone. He walked slowly, taking precise steps, his exquisitely carved cane making a tapping sound on the brick pavement with each step.

He looked neither to the left or right until he reached Lucia and Angelina who were enjoying the coolness of a bright September afternoon.

Then, he turned toward them and made a half bow while tipping his hat with his cane. And just as abruptly, he straightened and continued down the street. He stopped at the corner of Snyder Avenue and stood there, looking at the big, brown-stone houses across the street. He watched a trolley car rumble by, its heavy, steel wheels guided by the tracks. Then, he turned right and continued in the direction of Broad Street.

It wasn't until he disappeared, that the two women burst into a fit of laughter. "Now, we have a peacock on our street," said Lucia, almost choking.

"I wonder where he keeps his carriage? He must be a Duke or something." Angelina added her bit of wry humor. Mrs., Albano, from across the street, got up from her steps and joined them, her short, roly-poly body already convulsed by laughter.

"Hey, you two must be special people. I see the Count bowed to you." She spoke in Italian, although she spoke English as well as Angelina, "Lucia, I think he has the hot pants for you," she said.

"I must tell my Giovanni this. Perhaps he will be very jealous and give me nice things," said Lucia, grinning.

"If I know Giovanni, either he will laugh himself to death, or he will kill the peacock," responded Angelina.

"I think if Giovanni saw him as we just did, he would surely laugh himself to death." Lucia could not imagine her Giovanni feeling the least bit threatened by this peacock of a man.

"He is so different from his brother and his sister-in-law. They are simple people. They both work together in a restaurant. He is a cook and she is a waitress," said Mrs. Albano, happy that she could pass on what she knew of the new neighbors. "I brought over some sandwiches the day they moved in, and we talked, the wife and me. They have only been in the country less than a year, and they are renting the house next to the alley."

"The house next to the alley? I would like to be there when he meets the colored lady for the first time," laughed Angelina,

"Mrs. Furguson will probably laugh in his face. After that, she will probably stay in her house, like she always does. She bothers nobody. She doesn't even let her kids out to play," Mrs. Albano said.

"Where are they from?" asked Lucia.

"I think Sicily. I didn't ask, but the wife talks like a Siciliano."

"'Ah," groaned Lucia. "I hope he is not a gangster like Capone."

"Sh . . .," whispered Angelina, as though the man was close by, when in fact he had just turned into the street at the corner. He stopped for a moment, surveying the narrow street and the houses as though they were properties he intended to buy. Then, he made his way down the street.

Lucia started to get up, wanting no more encounters with the man. "Wait," whispered Angelina. "Maybe he will speak to us."

"Yes, wait. He will not stop if you go inside, Lucia, pleaded Mrs. Albano. "I want to hear what he sounds like. When I brought the sandwiches over to them, he took one and went upstairs with it. He didn't even thank me for it." With that, she went back across the street to her steps and sat down to watch. Against her better judgement, Lucia sat back and waited.

The man came slowly, his dark, intent eyes focused straight ahead, and for a time it looked as though he would make his bow and continue on. But, instead, he stopped, his eyes on Lucia. "Buon Pomeriggio (Good Afternoon)," he said. Then, in a beautifully modulated voice, he continued in a fluent, grammatically correct Italian. "I am Eugenio Casadante. I am your new neighbor."

They stared at him, Lucia praying that Angelina would not burst into laughter. At the same time, she felt her face turn crimson under his intense stare. Both were at a loss for words.

The man turned his head upward, as though looking down his handsome nose at them. "You are Italian, are you not?" He seemed momentarily puzzled.

"Yes," said Lucia lamely, answering him in Italian. She was surprised at how readily she understood him. She usually had trouble understanding Filomena, the Sicilian woman that Mrs. Albano had referred to.

"Ah, then I am correct. Only an Italian woman could be so beautiful. Are you married?"

Lucia nodded, not trusting her voice.

"It is a pity." Turning to Angelina for the first time, he continued. "Is it not a pity, Signora?"

Angelina could only frown. What Italian she knew made the man's Italian understandable, but she could not believe his outrageous behavior. He was actually flirting with Lucia,

"As you know, I live in the house next to the alley. It is only temporary, of course." The man now concentrated his attention solely on Lucia, his dark, handsome features always in a pose, always trying to impress her. "We are looking for a much better house . . . perhaps on Broad Street.

But we can wait. We are not here a year, after all. It takes time to get settled in a proper house."

Lucia wanted to tell him what a pompous ass he was, and to get on down the street where he belonged, but the eyes of half a dozen of the neighbors were on her, and she did not wish to make a scene, so she answered in a civil manner. "I am certain that you will find a house to your liking in time. We did not find our home until we were here some three years. We are here in this country twelve years. My friend, here, came as a child. You must excuse her if she does not speak more." Lucia was suddenly surprised at how well she spoke, using all the correct Italian she had learned. Almost all gone was the dialect from Abruzzi that she and all the paesanos(countryman) used. Puttana(whore), she thought. Are you trying to impress this man?

"Ah, yes, of course. It is always a pity when one cannot speak the tongue of their mother country. Everyone should speak Italian . . . the proper Italian, of course." He moved his hand in a grandiose manner. Gone was his stiffness of manner. He leaned forward, one foot on the bottom step. "Do you have children?" he asked.

"Two, "Lucia wished she were safely inside. The man was beginning to sound too familiar, and it was beginning to make her nervous.

"What a lucky person your husband is. I would be very fortunate to find a wife as beautiful as you." The man was totally ignoring Angelina as though she did not exist.

"There are many beautiful women in America. You should have no problem." Angelina, puta, Lucia thought. Why did you make me stay out here? Why don't you say something?

"I suppose you are right. I should have no problem. I am told that I resemble Rudolfo Valentino. Do you think so?" The man struck a pose, turning his profile to the two women.

Lucia forced a smile. God, how vain and obnoxious the man was. Handsome, yes. But not like her idol.

Angelina's ears perked up at the mention of Rudolf Valentino. In the best Italian she could muster, she said, "Yes, Lucia, he does indeed look like Valentino." She kept a straight face and smiled.

"Ah, thank you. It is a pity that he is dead. He should be remembered forever." While he spoke, he reached into the breast pocket of his jacket and drew out a small leather pouch. "I was in the jewelry business in Sicily, and when the great one died, I realized that here was something I could do to keep his memory alive." He opened the pouch and drew out a gold ring and a medallion on a chain, both with a fairly good likeness of Valentino on them. "I have gone to a specialist associate of mine," he continued, "and I have asked him to make me some jewelry with his likeness on them." He handed the jewelry, one each, to the women. "These are fourteen carat gold, as you can see. I am selling them at cost only because I think everyone should have something to remember him. I am making no money for myself."

The women had exchanged the jewelry and were looking at them carefully, Angelina looking behind each piece. "They are fourteen carat gold," she said, as though surprised.

"It looks just like him," said Lucia.

"I would like you lovely ladies to have one or both of these," said the man, leaning a little closer.

"As a gift?" laughed Lucia.

The man smiled, showing beautiful white teeth. "I would like to do that, but I have invested my own money just to have them made." He shrugged.

"How much?" asked Lucia. It would be nice to have something to remind her of her idol.

"I would need thirty dollars for either one."

Lucia's face sagged sorrowfully as she looked at her friend. "I could never afford it," she said. They handed him the jewelry, both shaking their heads sorrowfully.

"It is something you will cherish all your life." The man held the pieces in the palm of his hand, admiring them. "They are so beautiful."

"I am so sorry. Food and shelter for my children come first. My husband works too hard for his money." Lucia was genuinely sorry. She would have liked to have the necklace.

"I have the same thing in silver," the man said, trying to smile. He put away the gold pieces and brought out copies in silver. "You can have these for half the price of the gold ones."

"If I could not have the gold ones, I do not want any at all," said Lucia.

"But how can you go through life with nothing to remind you of him? I do not understand you." The man sounded almost rude.

"Perhaps it is better to forget." Lucia looked at Angelina. Her friend nodded in agreement.

The man put the jewelry back into the pouch. Suddenly, his brow was covered with beads of perspiration. He took a white, linen handkerchief from his pocket and wiped himself. "I am going to make you an insane offer." He spoke directly to Lucia. "But only because you are so beautiful, and because you are Italian. I will give you both for forty dollars."

"I cannot afford it. I am sorry."

"Ask your husband. He should be happy to buy them for you."

Lucia smiled at the thought. She was certain that her Giovanni would buy her the jewelry, if she wished him to. But now, she wanted only to get rid of the man as she saw Joey and Sammy turn into the street. They stopped in front of the Cohen store, talking and laughing. Then, Sammy went in and Joey was on his way down the street toward them. He looked puzzled when he saw the man. She got up. "I must go now," she said brusquely. "My son is coming home, and I must feed him."

"May I come to speak to your husband? I feel that I can convince him to buy these beautiful pieces for you."

"I am sorry, but my husband is much too busy at night. He is putting in the electric."

The man nodded approval. "Then, at least give me your name, Signora."

"My name? My name is Signora Nocelli. And this is my friend, Signora Richetti." She lives next door."

The man gave Lucia a smile that was supposed to make her heart flutter. "I am so happy to meet you ladies," he said. "Perhaps you both can come to visit with my sister-in-law. She has few friends in this country."

Joey climbed the steps. Lucia put her arms about his shoulders. "My son, Joey," she said, proudly.

"A handsome boy," said the man. "He has your beauty." Lucia's face crimsoned. The man was outrageous. He was flirting with her right in front of her son. "You are wrong," she answered. "He has the good looks of his father, Now, good day to you." She turned to Angelina. "I will see you later, Angelina," she said. With her arm still about Joey, they went inside.

Joey sat eating a sandwich. He watched his mother as she prepared supper. Her face, always beautiful when in deep thought, now seemed strained, grim. He knew she was angry. Had the new neighbor made her angry? "Do you know that man?" he asked.

"No, Joey. He came down the street and stopped to introduce himself. He lives in the house next to the black lady, and he was trying to sell us some Valentino jewelry."

"Did he upset you?"

"No, Joey. Do not concern yourself with him. He is a bragger, ignorant." She sat down at the table across from him.

Joey recognized the words. His parents had used them on occasion when speaking about a certain acquaintance of theirs, a loud-mouthed braggart who did not even realize that his bragging was so obviously seen as lies. And he remembered that they usually had a good laugh at the man's expense. Then, why was she upset?

They heard Angelina calling from her back yard. His mother went into the yard to the fence that separated the back yards, and in a moment there were shrieks of laughter from the women. "Such a conceited peacock," came from his mother. And, "Rudolf Valentino, indeed . . . he must be turning over in his grave over that one," from Angelina.

Joey smiled happily. The man was being ridiculed and that made him happy, because he did not like him. And he did not want his mother to like him. And when she finally came in smiling, he grinned at her. She sat at the table again, looking into his eyes. Then, she burst out laughing so hard that Joey joined in. When they had returned to normal, she got up and came behind Joey, her hands on his shoulders. "I know you will never be like that one," she said. She kissed him on the top of his head.

CHAPTER 12

Joey looked forward to the start of a new grade in school. Always eager to learn, the fourth grade brought new challenges, new courses. Best of all, he renewed old friendships, made new ones. All the families that had gone to the farms were back, looking sun-tanned and healthy. That meant that Freddie, Carmine and Johnny were back. Now, they could play some of the games where more than two boys were needed. They all had stories to tell about their summer. But it all seemed to start when school began.

The colored girl, Sarah was back in school, but kept clear of him and his crowd. She and most of the other black children played together. She gave him a cheery hello, however, whenever they met. Watching her, at times, he noticed that she was troubled, her pretty face sad. It was no wonder, he thought. Having Mrs. Furguson for a mother, living the way the family lived, not being able to go out except to school wasn't much to be happy about. He tried to speak to her several times, but she cut him short, acting nervous and afraid.

For the first time, Sammy was in his class. That made it all the more exciting. It also made Joey aware of how bright a student Sammy was. He was easily the smartest student in the class, excelling in every subject. And when Joey went to him for help with some arithmetic problems, Sammy suggested that they do their homework together. This they did, taking turns at each other's house.

This pleased Joey's parents, for it became obvious that Sammy was a great help to their son. It pleased Giovanni Nocelli especially. With the little schooling he had received in his little village, he had not been able to learn much more than simple addition and subtraction. So it was no wonder that he became fascinated by the problems that they did, as simple as they were. He would sit at the kitchen table with them, and watch them and listen intently whenever Sammy explained one of the problems to Joey. And he would shake his head in awe. "There is so much to learn. Does your father know all this?" he asked Sammy one night.

"Yes, sir, Mr. Nocelli. He was born here and finished high school. He wants me to go to college."

Mr. Nocelli nodded approval. "You are a smart boy. You will become a doctor or a lawyer, and your parents will be proud of you."

"I hope so," Sammy said.

Lucia Nocelli had been listening quietly as she brought out some cookies and milk. She felt a twinge of envy. Why was it that the Jewish people were so ready to send their children to college? Why not her Joey? None of the new immigrant that she knew had plans for their children's education. They would go to work as soon as they were of age, then marry and raise a family. "Would you wish to go to college?" she asked Joey.

Joey had never thought of college. Hopefully, he would go to high school, maybe even graduate. He had thought of becoming a policeman, but that was the extent of his dreams. He looked at his father, surprised. "Who, me?" he asked.

Mr. Nocelli, also caught by surprise, shrugged. "It is your mother's idea," he said.

Joey looked at his mother, saw her encouraging smile. "Yeah!" he shouted. "Hey, Sammy, maybe we can go to the same college."

"That would be great," Sammy said.

Outside, the kids were waiting for them to finish their homework and come out. "Yo, Joey," came the urgent cry, "ain't you done yet? We're goin over to the center."

Joey and Sammy gobbled up the cookies and milk and ran out to their friends. Joey had already forgotten about going to college.

Not so his mother. She looked into her husband's eyes for a reaction. "Do you think it is only a dream, Giovanni?" she asked. But Mr. Nocelli was staring into space and did not answer. "Are we wishing for too much?"

Giovanni Nocelli finally focused on his wife's lovely face. She wanted so much for her children. "Yes, Lucia, it is a dream. Dr. Fanchetti was the only one in our village who ever went to college. But we can make it happen. If Joey wishes to go, we will let him go."

"Oh, Giovanni," she cried. She came to him, put her arms about him and kissed his cheek. Her full breasts bore into his back. "I am so happy."

Caught up in her enthusiasm, Giovanni Nocelli turned his chair and drew her onto his lap. He buried his face in her bosom, kissed each breast. "There is much time before he is ready for college. In the meanwhile, I would like to go to school to learn the numbers like they were doing tonight. If I could do that and learn to speak and write in English, I could become a big contractor. I could have my own business. And Joey could go to the best college." He was whispering his own dreams to her even as he nuzzled her breasts.

"You can do anything you try, Giovanni," she whispered.

"Anything?" he asked playfully.

She felt him growing hard against her buttocks, she knew his needs. "I will see if Jimmy is asleep she said softly."

She kissed him and went into the living room, she came back: quickly, she whispered. "Will you carry Jimmy upstairs to his bed?"

There was an impulsive smile on her lips. "Joey will not be home for at least another hour.

CHAPTER 13

It was comfortable in the hide-out, in spite of the chilly October evening. It had drizzled all day long, and it was one of those days that the chill got down to the bones. Had it not been for the drizzle, they would have been hanging around a small fire and baking sweet potatoes with Carmine and the other boys.

They didn't say much. It was just the two of them. By mutual consent, they had decided that the other boys should not know about their secret place. They knew that the first time that they let them into their hide-out would be the last time that they would ever use it. For when Freddie and Carmine were together, they had a tendency to become extremely boisterous. And if that happened in the hide-out, they would be heard and chased out, and the hole in the ceiling possibly closed forever. That is, if the new neighbors found them out. God only knows what would happen to them if Mrs. Furguson heard them. Joey always shuddered at the thought.

It was still in the tiny space, the house on either side extremely quiet. The only light filtered through the hole in the ceiling. It came from the gas-lamp at the intersection of the two alleys and highlighted their faces. As usual, they sat facing one another, their backs against the wall of each house. They hadn't spoken for a good while.

"Look," Sammy said finally.

Joey looked at Sammy's face and saw that he had distorted his features. And the way that the light hit, he looked positively grotesque. "Don't," he said.

Sammy immediately relaxed the muscles in his face. "I was just thinking about Lon Chaney in that movie," he said.

"The Phantom of the Opera," Joey said. "Well, he looked nicer than you just did."

Sammy laughed. "Weren't you scared when the girl pulled away his mask while he was playing the organ?"

"You bet. I closed my eyes. I heard some lady fainted. I'm glad my Uncle Guido was with us. Don't you?"

"Yeah, he's swell/¹ agreed Sammy. "I would never have been able to see it if I didn't go with you and your Uncle Guido. You ever wish you could be like him when you get big? I know I would . . . always have money . . . a nice car . . ."

"Yeah, I guess I would," Joey agreed.

"Would you want to be a gambler?" Sammy asked. "I think I would. I think I would make a good gambler."

"Yeah, you would. But not me. You see how I get when I lose . . . even when we're playing for fun."

"I'll bet your Uncle Guido don't get mad. He's cool. You got to have a cool head to gamble." Sammy grew quiet, a contented smile on his face.

They were silent for a time, each dreaming his own dream. They did that a lot whenever they came up into their hideout. "Boy, we could scare the hell out of Freddie and them on Halloween," said Sammy, almost to himself.

"How?"

"Well, suppose one of us gets dressed like a spook and stays up her, and the other gets the guys to play follow the leader? Then he runs into the alley, and as soon as they follow him, the spook jumps down out of the hole in front of them."

Joey had to muffle the laughter. "That would be funny. The only trouble is that we would be giving away our hangout," he said.

"Yeah, that's right. Maybe we can do it at the end of the alley. As soon as they come into the alley, the spook pops out," Sammy said. "You can get a sheet and get dressed in your yard."

"What about if we do it just as you reach my back yard?" Joey was thinking about Mrs. Furguson. He did not want to make any fuss near her house.

"That would be all right. But I sure would like to scare the hell out of Mrs. Furguson too," said Sammy, reading his mind.

"Never mind. We'll do it near my house, if we do it."

As they talked, voices could be heard in the house where the new neighbors lived. The voices were muffled as though in another part of the house. They were sitting just about where the stairway would be. But suddenly, heavy footsteps could be heard running up the stairs, with others following. A voice could be heard shouting in Italian. "Brutto ladro (The ugly thief)" and "andare all'inferno (go to hell)," was readily understood by Joey. A door was slammed. Then there was a loud banging on it. It sounded like it might be the door to the rear bedroom of the house.

The first impulse was to get out of there. But something held them. Curiosity? For Joey, it was something deeper. He disliked the man who walked daily down the street as though he owned it. Mostly, he hated him because he made his mother so uncomfortable whenever he walked by. She seemed to sense it even when she was inside. She would stiffen at the slightest sound of his cane tapping on the brick sidewalk.

Without a word, he moved toward the loose bricks. It was darker because he was moving away from the hole where the light filtered through, but he found the spot, his fingers feeling the loose bricks. He put his ear next to the wall. There was silence at first. The shouting had stopped. Then, almost as clear as though he was in the room with the man, he heard the oily, obnoxious voice of the man he hated so. He did not understand all of the Italian words, but he understood enough to piece together what was said. There was a note of disdain in his tone of voice. "I do not like it when you call me a thief, dear brother," he said. "I am not a thief. I will go to work when I find a suitable position. I have not gone to the best of schools only to become a cook like yourself."

The banging on the door had stopped, and the brother's voice could be heard, though not as clearly. "At least I do honorable work. At least I work and pay the bills . . . my wife and I. But you . . . you have not earned a penny since we arrived in this country."

"I sell the Valentino jewelry, do I not?" "The Valentino jewelry . . . hah! What a disgrace. You are selling those cheap imitations, and cheating the people. And you say you are not a thief? I should turn you over to the police."

"I am not a thief." The man's voice sounded threatening. 1 am not holding a pistol at their heads when they buy them. They do not care what they are made of. They buy them because of their love and respect for the great Valentino. Now, enough of this. Get away from the door and leave me alone."

There were two more bangs on the door, then the sound of crying. "Che disgrazia(That misfortune)," the brother wailed. "Our parents must be turning over in their graves."

"If they are turning over in their graves, it is because of you and that pig of a wife of yours. After sending you to the best of schools, look at you. What have you made of yourself, a cook?"

"At least I am not a thief." The fight seemed to have drained from the brother. Now, there was a half-hearted banging on the door, but it sounded different. It sounded like the banging of a man's head. "Ladro(Thief) . . . ladro(thief) . . ." the brother wailed.

Now there was another voice . . . a woman's. Come, Attilio. Come down," he said.

"Yes, go down, Attilio. Go to your pig of a wife."

This brought a new tirade from the brother. "Animale . . . animale," he moaned.

"Come, Attilio," the woman beseeched.

The brother's voice became faint as he apparently went down the stairs. "Why don't you go away? Leave us and go away," came the cry of despair.

Then there was silence.

"Wow!" whispered Sammy. "What was that all about?"

Joey remained silent. He felt justified in feeling such hatred for this man. He was a disrespectful pig and a crook. It was lucky that his mother had not bought any of the Valentino jewelry. He must make sure that she never did. But how could he warn her without telling her where he had heard such a damning conversation. "C'mon," he said finally.

They were down in the alley and made their way to Snyder Avenue before either spoke. The drizzle had not stopped, and the fine moisture beat against their faces as they headed for St. Martha's center. "Did you understand what they were talking about?" asked Sammy.

"I didn't understand all the words, but I understood enough. The guy who thinks he looks like a movie star . . . well, his brother called him a crook because he's selling those medals and rings . . . and they're fakes. And the brother wants him to get out because he won't go to work."

"He tried to sell my mother some," said Sammy. "She told him she didn't know who Rudolf Valentino was." He laughed. "I don't think she was lying either."

"I wish I could warn my mother. But I can't say where I heard about it."

"Yeah," Sammy agreed. He thought a bit. "You can say that I heard my mother and father talking about it. You can say my father knew they were fakes as soon as he saw them."

"That sounds good. I think I'll say that."

"Ladro . . . ladro . . ." Sammy was saying the word over and over again, making it sound like a tune. "I'll bet that means crook."

"How do you know"

"It sounds like a crook. I'll have to teach my father, so he can call him that," Sammy said, laughing. "He already owes the store ten dollars. Every time he comes in for cigarettes, he tells my father that he'll pay him as soon as he gets this job in a jewelry store."

"Boy, I hope they move," said Joey. "I wish they never moved around here." The harmony of his little world had been disrupted. Moving was the only solution he could think of.

"Yeah," Sammy agreed.

CHAPTER 14

For weeks, whenever Uncle Guido came to visit, the topic of conversation was sure to focus on the coming Dempsey-Tunney fight. Uncle Guido had already gotten two tickets to the bout, and Joey had never seen him so enthusiastic. His father, on the other hand, was not at all enthused, and was doing everything possible to get out of it. But Uncle Guido was insistent. "This will be the greatest fight ever. Just to see the great Jack Dempsey . . . ." He argued his case by pounding the table with both hands.

"But I do not like to see two men fighting. Surely, you can get someone else to go with you . . . your lady friend perhaps."

"Who, the Irish girl? I don't see her anymore."

Lucia, who had been mending a tear in Joey's trousers, looked up, a hopeful smile crossing her face. "You are seeing Clara?" she asked.

Uncle Guido smiled sheepishly. "Twice," he said, the fight forgotten.

"And all is going well?"

Uncle Guido shrugged. "I don't know. Both times I took her out, I had to take her mother and father. I can't even talk to her alone."

"Hah! Those two. They think they are still in Italy," laughed Giovanni.

"Perhaps they know of your reputation," Lucia joked.

"I haven't even kissed her once." Uncle Guido looked furtively toward the living room where Joey was waiting for Sammy.

"And you will not until you are married . . . if I know those two," Giovanni chuckled. "But there are ways. When Lucia and I were courting, we were always in the company of her relatives. But we found ways to be alone . . . eh, Lucia?"

Lucia blushed prettily.

"I don't know what to do." And Uncle Guido began to unburden his heart. "For the first time in my life, I find a girl that I respect and even think about marrying, and I don't know how to act. In a way, I'm glad that her parents are always with us."

"Guido," Lucia said sternly, "you must only be yourself. I saw Clara looking at you. I am sure that she likes you, and she would like to be alone with you. You must find a way. Perhaps you can take her to the theater."

Uncle Guido almost spilled his wine. "Theater," he groaned. "I had to pay for four people and her mother even sat between us."

Giovanni laughed uproariously. "Thank God, we did not have a theater in our village. Guido, I feel sorry for you. Do you know what I would do? I would not go there anymore for a while. And when they wish to know why, I would tell them that this is America, and that they should forget their old ways. Tell them that they must allow you to see Clara alone."

"Do not listen to him, Guido," interrupted Lucia. "When you see Clara again, you must tell her that you wish to see her alone. She is a sensible girl. She will speak to her parents."

"Then, if they do not allow you to see her alone, you should leave her," snapped Giovanni. "What do those two think they have there?"

"Stop it, Giovanni. She is a good girl and would make Guido a good wife."

Suddenly, Giovanni slapped his hands together. "I know what you must do," he said. "Ask her to go to the fight with you. Remember, you have only two tickets."

"No." The response was quick. "No, I'd never take her to a place like that. There are mostly men, and there will be a lot of swearing. It's no place for a decent girl," Guido shook his head. "And don't try to get out of going to the fight with me," he added, stabbing his finger toward Giovanni. "Any one in his right mind would give his right arm to go see this fight. I could sell my tickets for ten times what they cost me."

Giovanni could not hide the tiny smile as he looked at his wife. "Is this not a friend?" he asked.

"It could be that he is out of his mind." Lucia kept a straight face. "Anyone who would rather take you and not his lady friend cannot be sane."

"You're right, Lucia. I am going out of my mind. That girl is driving me crazy. Why don't you talk to her and her parents?"

"I will see." Lucia had already decided to do just that. She knew how Guido must feel. Her Giovanni had threatened to leave her more than once because they could not be alone. But that was in the old country. She got up and left the men to themselves, feeling a satisfaction in knowing that Guido's eyes no longer followed her like they used to. He had been smitten by the girl, and now, his mind was only on her. And she would like to keep it that way. There must be no break-up between those two. She would have to speak to the girl . . . and her parents.

Sammy had just come in and Joey was getting ready to go out with him. "Be careful," she told him in Italian. "And say good-bye to your Uncle Guido." Joey ran into the kitchen, then was out of the front door with Sammy.

He is getting so big, she thought. Soon, he will not need me any longer. I will no longer need to protect him from harm. But I still have this one. She smiled tenderly at her youngest. Little Jimmy was in his little, red car. But he seemed exhausted. "Get me, Momma," he said.

"Is my baby tired?" she crooned. "Do you want a cookie?"

"I'm sleepy," he said.

She took him out of the car and cradled him, nuzzling his face. She carried him up the stairs. He felt so light in her arms . . . so frail. He was not at all husky like Joey. Soon, he too would grow up, and she would no longer be able to hold him in her arms. Suddenly, she wished that Guido would go. She knew that Giovanni would come to her. Little Jimmy would be asleep and Joey was out playing. They would be alone. Perhaps she would conceive again. Perhaps it would be a girl this time.

CHAPTER 15

The fight was over. The great Jack Dempsey had lost, and there was great sorrow in South Philadelphia. Everywhere, there was rage that the idol of everyone had been robbed of his championship. Already there was talk of a rematch. This time, Dempsey would put Tunney away, leaving no doubt in anybody'd mind about who the true champion was.

For Uncle Guido, it was the best of times. On a hunch, and as a result of the great odds that was being placed on Dempsey to win, he had bet on Tunney. Or, perhaps it was the fact that Joey had mentioned that Sammy thought that Tunney could win. At any rate, he was now over two thousand dollars richer. Giovanni had not been able to understand why Guido had been pulling for Tunney during the fight, when it was obvious that everyone in the drizzly Municipal Stadium was cheering for Dempsey. There was a moment when Guido squeezed his arm so that it hurt as the announcer announced the winner—Tunney. Guido leaped out of his seat. He had hugged Giovanni, drawing ugly stares.

Guido, accompanied by Giovanni, had just finished collecting the last of his bets from Rico Manelli, owner of the pool-room where Guido did most of his gambling. He had left ten dollars and announced that the refreshments were on him. At the height of the prohibition era, cheap bootleg beer and whiskey was readily available at the pool parlor. But only if you were a card member. The door at the bottom of the dark stairs was always locked to keep out undesirable people like the police, and only card carrying members had keys.

Their business done, Uncle Guido and Giovanni headed down Snyder Avenue. Only a short three block walk, Guido had left his automobile in front of Giovanni's house where Joey and Sammy sat in it, minding it. "I'm glad that's over," said the jubilant Guido. "I was afraid one of those guys wouldn't pay off. But I got every cent."

Giovanni shook his head. "This is a bad business that you are in, Guido. Everybody in that place knows that you have all that money. You are not afraid that they will try to take it away from you . . . maybe kill you?"

"Nan," laughed Guido. "I told everybody what a great fighter you were in the ring. I said you trained with Mickey Walker and Harry Greb, two very good fighters."

"You are crazy. I never fight in my life."

"I know, Giovanni. But they don't. They think you're my body-guard. Here." Guido was shoving something into his hand as they talked.

Caught by surprise, Giovanni took the folded bills, but stopped when he realized what it was. "What is this, Guido? You make me embarrassed."

"Take it, Giovanni. That is what I would have had to pay one of those guys to walk with me."

A trolley car screeched to a stop, its steel wheels causing sparks to fly. A man and a woman got off and the trolley was once more on its way. Several cars that had stopped behind the trolley continued on their way. One stopped and parked half way down the block.

Giovanni tried to hand back the money. "You do not need to pay me. I come with you as a friend. You insult me, Guido."

"Keep it. Buy something for Lucia and the kids." They crossed the Ten Street intersection, and Guido noticed the parked car up ahead. There was something strange about it. Since it had parked, no one had gotten out of it. "Giovanni, put that money away, quick," he said.

Giovanni recognized the fear in Guido's voice, and a shiver ran through his body. He followed Guide's eyes, saw the car, dark and ominous in the quiet street. "C'mon," hissed Guido. They started to walk across the street, away from the automobile. But, before they got to the middle, three men spilled out of it. They were big, burly men and looked like water-front workers.

"Hey, Guido. Wait a minute. We want to talk to you," shouted one of the men."

"Run," yelled Guido. They began to run, the three men chasing them. People suddenly appeared, staring. Some small boys began yelling, "Fight . . . fight" Guido and Giovanni made it across Nine Street and had reached the black-smith shop when Guido began gasping for breath. He stopped in front of the big, wooden garage doors of the shop, holding his hands on his chest, breathing hard and in obvious pain. Giovanni, some ten feet in front of Guido, stopped when he realized that his friend could no longer run. He came back just as the men reached Guido.

"Stay out of this, mister," the smallest of the three said, speaking to Giovanni. "This is between me and him." He turned to his two friends. "Watch him, you guys." The two men edged closer to Giovanni.

People had begun to gather about them, and Guido began to feel safer. These men apparently weren't after his money. "What do you guys want?" he gasped. "Who are you?" Then, to the crowd, "Somebody call the cops."

The man out-weighed Guide by at least fifty pounds. He approached him until the hapless Guido could smell the stench of cheap beer on his breath. He spoke in a low, growly voice, so that the crowd could not hear him. "You come fucking around my wife again, I'm gonna break both your arms and legs, understand?" he said.

"Who?" It was all that Guido could mumble.

"Fanny Coyle, that's who. She says you been sneakin around tryin to date her. Well, she's my wife, see. And I want you don't bother her no more."

Guido shook his head, acting completely bewildered. He mumbled something about not knowing she was married . . . about not meaning any harm. Thank God, the slut had not told her husband that they had been lovers. As far as he knew, Guido had only been bothering her for a date.

"Well, you know now, you dago bastard," the man grated.

"And just to make sure you don't forget . . ." And here, the man made a terrible mistake. He punched Guido in the face.

With a cry of rage, Giovanni rushed the man, bowling him over. Before anyone could move, he was on top of him, straddling him and pummeling him in the face. The other two men tried to drag Giovanni off, but he swung at them, hitting one of them in the crotch so that he let out a howl.

Guido kept screaming, "Call the cops . . . call the cops"

In the meanwhile, one of the boys had run down to Joey's house and told him that his father was in a fight. Joey ran in to tell his mother, then ran down to the corner, followed by Sammy. Lucia grabbed little Jimmy and ran next door to Angelina's house, screaming that her Giovanni was in a fight. Tony, Angelina's husband, his smashed nose indicating that he had once tried the boxing ring as a means of making a livelihood, put on a jacket and also ran to the corner. But, by the time he got there, it was all over.

Mr. Glatfelter, the blacksmith, lived over his shop, and he was disturbed by all the noise on the street below. He opened his window and saw the big crowd that had gathered. "Vat's going on?" he yelled.

"Help, Mr. Glatfelter," Joey yelled up at him. "They're beating up my father."

The window closed and seconds later the giant appeared, his massive biceps glistening under the rolled up sleeves of his shirt. Pushing Guido aside, he grabbed a man in each giant hand and dragged them of Giovanni. When they continued to squirm, he banged their heads together. Guido had stopped screaming for the police. He stopped Giovanni from further hitting the man under him. "Stop, it's over, Giovanni," he said. "Come on, let him up." Giovanni got up reluctantly, letting the man loose.

In the distance, a police siren could be heard. "Better get going, mister, before the cops get here." As he helped the man up, Guido spoke to him softly, reassuringly. "I promise I won't bother your missus again, okay, mister? Honest, I didn't know she was married," he lied.

The man glared at him through swollen eyes. "C'mon," he said to his friends. Mr. Glatfelter let them free and they hurried to their automobile and drove away before the police arrived. Mr. Glatfelter, satisfied that everything was under control, shooed away everybody. Then, turning to Giovanni, he peered at his cut lip. "You come in. I fix," he said.

"it is fine," said Giovanni, pressing a handkerchief to his mouth. "I wish to thank you for helping me," he added in his best English. He offered his hand and the giant took it.

"You got fine boy," he said, ruffling Joey's hair.

"Yes, thank you," said Giovanni.

"Thanks for helping out, Gus," said Tony, Giovanni's next door neighbor. "You must have scared the hell out of those guys." He shook the blacksmith's hand. "Come on, Giovanni, let's go get that lip fixed." He walked Joey and his father home while Guido spoke to the policemen who had arrived in a paddy-wagon. Nodding at Guide's explanation, they strolled back to the police vehicle, Guide's gift money in hand. They drove off without questioning anyone.

Later, seated about the kitchen table, Guido explained who the men were. And Giovanni shook his head, a sad smile causing his cut lip hurt. "To think that I fought to protect a whore-master," he said, looking at his wife. He spoke in Italian, looking about to make sure that Joey was not near. But Joey was outside basking in his father's glory. "Had I known that he was the girl's husband, I would have let them do what they wanted with you. And I would even help them cut off your balls."

"Oh, Giovanni. Tell him that you do not mean what you say," said Lucia.

Guido knew that his friend was only joking with him. He knew Giovanni would risk his life for him. It was more than he, himself, was able to do. He could not believe that he had not been able to do more: at least tear one of the men off of his friend. They were big men, to be sure, but he could have done more. Now, he could only apologize and relate to Lucia her husband's part in the whole incident. He thanked Giovanni over and over again. "And I want you to keep that money I gave you," he said at last. "You sure earned it tonight,"

Giovanni had forgotten all about the money. He took it out of his pocket. "No, Guido. Let us not begin again about this money. I did what I had to do because you are my friend. You do not have to pay me for my friendship," he said, laying the money down in front of Guide.

But Lucia had other ideas. Picking up the money, she unfolded it and counted the five twenty dollar bills. Her eyes lit up. "How much money did you win, that you can give Giovanni this much?" she asked in awe.

Guido was grinning. "Oh, at least twenty times that."

Carefully, she folded the money. "In that case, I will keep the money." She kept the money in her pocket-book.

"Lucia," Giovanni protested, "I will not take money from my friend."

"You are not taking the money. I am. It is a small price to pay for your cut lip. And since you are mine, I intend to get paid for the damage to my property. Is that not fair, Guido?"

"I can't argue with your reasoning, Lucia," laughed Guido. "I'm afraid she is right, my friend," he told Giovanni.

"Lucia . . . the money," roared Giovanni. He did not like to be embarrassed like this in front of his friend. Sometimes Lucia could be unreasonable.

Lucia went to her husband and kissed him lightly on the lips. He drew back in pain. "You see," she said, making her point. "You hurt so much that I cannot even kiss you. And if I cannot kiss you, then, I will have to be satisfied with the money."

Giovanni looked at his friend and shrugged. "What can I do with her? I would rather fight with those men again than argue with her."

Guido grinned. "I'm sure you will know what to do, ray friend." He got up to leave. "I think I'll go see Clara. And I'll lay the law down to her, just as you have done with Lucia."

"I hope that you will have better luck with her than I have with this one," Giovanni said, not quite meaning it, for he could feel Lucia's soft breasts pressing hard against his back. He knew he would be generously rewarded for the money safely in his wife's pocket-book.

CHAPTER 16

Sarah Furguson waited at the school-yard gate, her back to the stiff October breeze. She wore a thick, green sweater that bulged at her budding breasts. She smiled, strong, white teeth contrasting sharply with her honey colored skin. She shook her head and said something to another colored girl. The girl waved and walked off. Other children streamed out of the gate. It was the end of the school day.

Joey watched her, catching her eye, as he waited at the building entrance for Sammy. He saw her motioning to him and thought that she meant someone else. He looked about him, then pointed to himself. She nodded, laughing. He went to meet her.

She smiled prettily, as she always did when they met. As he came close, he could not help but note how she had grown over the summer. She was several inches taller than he was, and no longer looked like a small girl. She was on the verge of becoming a woman. "Hello, Joey," she said. Her smile grew even brighter.

"Hello, Sarah."

"You waiting for Sammy?"

"Yeah." Joey began to feel self-conscious. He felt all the eyes in the school-yard on them. He hoped she didn't want to walk home with him. He did not mind talking to her around the school, but to be seen walking down their street together . . . that was something else again. He did not know why he felt this way.

"Mamma wants you to come see her," said the girl.

"Your momma?"

"Lord, Joey," the girl giggled. "You sound like she's gonna eat you up."

The thought had occurred to Joey. "What does she want with me? She hollers at me every time she sees me."

"She wants to talk to you."

Mrs. Furguson knew about the hide-out. Joey was sure of it. He became defensive. "What does she want, Sarah? I don't go near your alley anymore." And he wasn't fibbing. He hadn't been up in the hide-out in weeks.

"It's nothing like that, Joey. She just wants to talk to you. She's not going to bite you." The girl laughed heartily. "Will you come?"

"To your house?"

"Of course, silly. Will you come?" she asked again.

"Yeah, I guess." Joey wanted to end the conversation before Sammy reached them. He was just coming out of the school building.

"I'll tell her. She'll be home from work by four. Bye, now." She was gone before Sammy reached Joey.

"What was that all about?" Sammy asked as they began walking home.

"Her mom wants to talk to me."

"Oh, oh. You think she knows?"

"How should I know?"

"You going?"

"I guess so. I'll ask my mom."

"That's smart," Sammy said, grinning from ear to ear. "That way she'll know in case she never sees you again."

"That's not funny, Sammy."

"Don't worry about it. If she asks you about it, just say that you'll never go up there again. If she doesn't, then we can still use it."

It wasn't until several days later that Joey finally went to see Mrs. Furguson. Joey had made it a point to ignore the invitation, even going so far as to evade Sarah in school. But one day, the girl ran after Joey, as he and Sammy walked home. She had her brother Hebert with her.

"Joey," she said, all out of breath, "Momma wants to know when you're coming to the house."

Joey suddenly became nervous. They were approaching their street. "Will she be home today?" he asked.

"She'll be home in a half hour."

"Okay, I'll come then." At the corner, Joey made a pretense of stopping at Sammy's house for something. Sarah and her brother made their way home.

As soon as they disappeared into their house, Joey went home. Milk and cookies awaited him, but he felt no hunger for them. "Why do you not eat your cookies?" asked his mother.

"I'm not hungry," he answered.

"Then, you are sick. You are always hungry when you come home from school." She touched his forehead with the back of her hand.

"I'm not sick."

"Then, what is it that bothers you, my little boy?" She sat across the table from him, catching his eyes by moving her head in front of him. It usually made him laugh, but he did not laugh now.

"Mrs. Furguson, the colored lady wants to talk to me."

"So? Have you done anything wrong in her alley? Did you fight with her little girl in school?"

"No. I don't know what she wants."

"I am sure that she means you no harm. Do you wish me to come with you?"

"No, Mom. I'll go. She'll be home soon."

"Do not be afraid. She is a good woman. She works and she does not bother anyone. I wish some other people were like her." She smiled reassuringly. "Go see what she wants."

Joey suddenly felt ravenous. Without a word, he ate up the cookies and drank the milk. His mother smiled. "you see, you were hungry after all," she said.

The moment the door opened, Joey's nostrils were assailed by the overpowering smell of kerosene. The little boy, Hebert, his dark eyes smiling mischievously, looked up at him. "You come to visit with Sarah?" he asked.

"I come to see your momma," said Joey.

"She not home."

"Well, I'll come back later." Joey was almost gagging on the offensive odor that seemed to be trying to escape through the doorway.

"Hey, wait, Joey," Sarah yelled from the kitchen. She came running in. She had changed from her school dress, now wore a printed, cotton dress that seemed too large for her. "Momma'll be home any minute." She drew Joey through the tiny vestibule, then into the living room where a kerosene heater stood in the middle of the room. It threw off an intense heat as well as the terrible odor, except that now, it did not bother Joey as much. Joey sat down on an old, worn sofa that had several tears in it. It was part of a set which included two other chairs of matching material. There was a rip in one of them, and the stuffing had begun to squeeze out.

"You gonna take your dress off for Joey?" asked the boy.

"Hush your mouth, Hebert, or I be washing it out with soap," hissed the girl.

"I can come later, if you want," said Joey, embarrassed.

"There's no need to do that. Hebert'll be nice. Won't you Hebert?" The girl grabbed the boy's ear and twisted it, making him yelp. "Now, you be nice while I go make sure nothin's burning." She went into the kitchen,

"She naked under that dress," said the boy. "And she got hair on her pussy, just like my momma," he whispered. "You wanna see her pussy?"

"No, Hebert. I come to talk to your momma. And I'm going to tell on you if you don't stop talking like that." Joey felt the soothing heat from the stove. He suddenly felt at home in the smelly house. A strange smell from the kitchen mingled with the kerosene smell. It was a cooking smell, but one that was totally unfamiliar to him, different from his mother's kitchen. It was even different from the fragrant smells from Sammy's mother's cooking.

Soon, the girl came back and sat on the arm of the chair across from him, her dress hanging loosely over her legs. The boy inched closer to her, snuggling close to her. The girl put her arm about him. "Were you a good boy in kinder-garden today?" she asked.

"Uh huh,"

"You like it?" asked Joey, remembering his unpleasant first days there.

"Yeah, I like it."

"You like your teacher?" Joey was grateful for the common ground in the conversation.

"Yeah, I likes my teacher . . . but I likes my Sarah better." And without warning, he picked up the hem of the girl's dress and lifted it high over her waist, exposing her brown legs and bare crotch. With a scream, the girl tried to take the dress out of his hands without tearing it, but the boy held on tenaciously, continuing the exposure as Joey looked on in wonder. She looked so different down there, so different from little Carmela from next door.

Finally, the girl punched her brother in the face, and he let go. Laughing gleefully, he ran off, up the stairs. "I'm gonna tell Momma on you, you little pig," screamed the girl. When she looked at Joey, she was clearly embarrassed. "You didn't see anything, did you, Joey?" she asked.

"No," he lied, the image of sparse, curly hair barely covering the dark lips of her vaginal parts engraved forever in his mind.

"That boy gonna drive me and Momma crazy," she said. She left to go check on the cooking. Several minutes later, Mrs. Furguson came in, her pretty face looking 'tired. "Hello, Joey," she said, with a big smile that reminded Joey of Sarah, when she smiled, and so totally different from when she yelled at him whenever she caught him in her alley.

"You wanted to see me?" Joey asked, nervously.

"You give this boy some cookies, Sarah?" she yelled into the kitchen, ignoring his question.

"No, Momma," the girl called back. "Hebert ate them all."

"That boy!" moaned Mrs. Furguson. "He's a mess." She had taken off her coat and held it in her arms. She looked at Joey with a disarming smile. "Your daddy makes that dago red, don't he?" she asked.

Joey looked at her with a vacant stare, not really knowing how to answer. The woman continued. "I hear he makes some good wine. Good wine is sure hard to find these days." She left him for a moment, to go into the kitchen, dropping off her coat on a dark dining room table. When she came back, she had a quart bottle and a brown paper bag. "Will you ask your daddy if he'll sell me some of that good wine?" she asked. I'll pay him a dollar for a bottle." She took a dollar from her pocket-book.

"I don't think my father sells his wine," Joey said, lamely. He knew that to be true. He gave a bottle to some of his friends during the holidays, but he never sold it. There seemed to be a law against it.

"Well, you just go on and ask him, Son." She put the bottle carefully into the bag, then handed Joey the bag and the dollar bill. When Joey hesitated in taking them, Mrs. Furguson said, "Go on, Joey. If your daddy don't want to sell me his wine, that's okay. You just bring back the dollar and we forget about the whole thing. I won't even tell your daddy that you been hiding up in my alley with your Jew friend. I won't even close up the hole." She was grinning broadly.

Joey took the bag firmly, put the dollar in his pocket. He had begun to tremble. The woman truly had magical powers Else how could she know? They had been so careful.

"Careful you don't drop that bottle." Now, her voice was soft, caressing, and it made Joey feel somewhat better. "You a good boy, Joey," she said, patting his head while leading him to the door. "If it be all right with your daddy, you bring it when it gets dark." At the door, she looked up and down the street, then let him out. Hugging the bottle tightly, he turned into the alley and walked hurriedly to his back yard. He sighed with relief when he saw that it was still unlatched.

At the supper table, Joey's parents discussed the situation. Joey ate quietly, not participating in the discussion, yet feeling like an important part of it. He had not mentioned anything about the hide-out when he had told his father what had happened. Only that Mrs. Furguson wanted to buy a bottle of wine.

They spoke in Italian, as was usually the case when they discussed important things. "The only thing that worries me is that it is not legal to sell the wine," said Giovanni. "The money is good. If I sell thirty bottles, I will have enough to make another barrel of wine."

"Then sell it. I am sure that the woman would not tell the police," said Lucia. "Perhaps she needs the wine to celebrate something, and she will never ask again. Surely, the police would not be interested in one bottle of wine."

"True," agreed Giovanni. "Guido has told me many times that people are selling wine and are even making whiskey in their bath-tubs to sell. He says that he could sell all of my wine for me if I wished to sell it. Of course, I would not get a dollar a bottle for it. The people who buy it must make money from it also."

"The woman is nice to you?" Lucia spoke to Joey.

Joey nodded.

"Then why do we not give her a bottle as a gift? You give it to others, and she is a good woman," Lucia said to her husband.

Giovanni looked thoughtfully at his wife, gave a little smile, then got up, took the bottle from the bag and went down into the cellar. He had just tapped the first of the new wine that he had made last autumn, and he was proud of it. It had turned out remarkably well, as his wines usually did. After he had filled the bottle, he sipped from it, nodded his approval. On the opposite side of the cellar stood four barrels of grapes fermenting. He sniffed at the mulch, dipped his finger and sucked the juice from it. After he had tasted his new wine, he had made the new batch with the same combination of grapes as he had used last year, except that he had replaced one crate of Muscat for the stronger Alicante grape. Now, it was up to God.

Upstairs, he put the bottle in the bag. "When you are through eating," he told Joey, "you will take—the wine to this woman, and you will give her back her dollar. Tell her that the wine is a gift."

"I can go now." Joey was pleased by his parent's decision. Making the wine a gift was sure to please Mrs. Furguson, they would be on good terms. He wasn't sure that he would ever go up in the hide-out again, however.

"Finish eating first, then you go," his father repeated. "And if somebody says anything, you say that it is a gift."

"I'll go through the alley."

"Good. Then no one will see you."

Joey hugged the bag tightly against his breast as he made his way down the alley. He trembled with excitement. What if someone entered the alley as he was about to come out into the street? What if the man who sold the jewelry happened to come out of his house and ask him what he had in the bag? Even the thought of keeping the dollar entered his mind. Mrs. Furguson and his mother had never spoken to each other, so there was not much chance that either would know what happened to the dollar. As far as anyone knew, his father had accepted the dollar for the wine. Now, Sammy wouldn't do it. He was smart enough to know that since Mrs. Furguson shopped at his parent's store, it could possibly slip out that the dollar had not been returned to her.

He peeped out of the alley. The street was deserted, everybody probably at supper. He quickly climbed the white steps and banged at the door. It was opened immediately, and once more he was assailed by the smell of kerosene. Sarah wore the same loose cotton dress. She let him in and quickly closed the door. And for a moment, they brushed against each other in the tiny vestibule. He felt her breast against his shoulder. They felt different . . . hard compared to his mother's softness, whenever she hugged him. The girl even smelled different.

"Momma," called the girl, as they entered the living room. Mrs. Furguson came down the stairs, dressed neatly in a flowery, green dress. She smiled happily when she saw the paper bag.

"You got me some wine?" she asked, reaching for the bag. Without a word, she took the bottle out of the bag, looked at the deep, dark redness and nodded approval. "Looks good. Can't taste it now. Gotta go to the church meeting," she said to Joey. The boy, Hebert, came in from the kitchen and looked on. "And don't you touch this bottle. You hear me, boy?"

"Okay, Momma." The boy stood eyeing the bottle.

"My father said you can have the wine as a gift," Joey said, holding out the dollar.

Mrs. Furguson looked surprised, then pleased. "Bless you, Joey," she said. "You thank your momma and daddy, and you go on and keep the dollar. And tell your daddy that I'd like to buy a bottle every once in a while. With the holidays coming up, I don't know where I can get me some good wine."

Joey was totally surprised at his good fortune, but he wasn't sure if it was right to take the dollar. "I can't take this, Mrs. Furguson. It's a gift." He held the dollar out to the woman.

"Oh, go on, Child. You put that money in your pocket." She took the money out of his hand and stuffed it into the pocket of his jacket. "I got to go to church meeting, now. Hebert, bring me my coat."

"Thank you, Mrs. Furguson," said Joey.

"What you want I should tell Leroy, if he comes," asked the girl,

"Jus' tell him I be home eight . . . eight-thirty." Mrs. Furguson put on her coat. It made her look bulky, almost twice as wide as Sarah.

"Good bye, Mrs. Furguson. Thanks again." Joey turned to leave. "Bye, Sarah . . . bye, Hebert," he said.

"You can stay for a while, if you wants," said Mrs. Furguson.

Joey saw the eager look in Sarah's face.

"Yeah, Joey, stay some," cried Hebert.

"I can't. I got to get home to do my homework. Sammy is probably waiting for me right now. We do our homework together," he explained. But Joey could not wait to tell Sammy about his good fortune. They would head right for the ice-cream parlor, if his father let him keep the money. It had been such a long time since he'd had a chocolate, ice-cream soda.

"Don't forget to thank your momma and daddy, hear me, Son?" was the last thing he heard as he closed the door behind him. Breathlessly, he reported what had happened, to his mother and father. They were still at the table, each with steaming cup of expresso before them. They listened, both faintly amused at Joey's excitement.

"That is a lot of money. What are you going to do with it?" asked his father.

"You mean I can keep it?" Joey could not believe his ears. He had fully expected his father to claim the dollar. It might have been different with his mother.

"It is a gift to you, is it not?" his father asked, looking sideways at his wife.

"I guess."

"Yes, Joey, it is a gift from the lady. And you can keep it."

"Can I treat Sammy after we're done our homework? He always treats me. And I'll keep the rest," Joey quickly added.

"That is exactly what I would do if I was an American boy with a dollar in my pocket," his father said.

"Thanks, Pop." Joey grabbed his school books and started for the door.

"Do not tell your friend about the wine," his father called after him. "Nothing about the wine."

"Okay." And Joey was gone.

Giovanni sipped at his expresso. Finally, he said, "It is strange that you said nothing."

"You did very well by yourself, my husband. I would have done exactly the same thing," she said. And the look she gave him could mean only one thing.

"Ah, you are indeed a lucky man, thought Giovanni, as he looked into his wife's eyes.

CHAPTER 17

The five boys were hanging around the fire when the huge, colored man walked up. Without a word, he picked up a piece of a wooden crate from the fire and lit a cigarette. "Thanks, y'all," he said, black face beaming. Without another word, he sauntered down the street, broad shoulders swaying. His black, fur-collared coat flapped open in the wind. All eyes watched him until he reached the alley . . . Mrs. Furguson's house.

"Wow!" exclaimed Freddie, breaking the ice. "That's a big nigger." None of the boys had ever seen any blacks except the Furguson family on their street. And here was this guy acting like he owned it.

"Aw, he ain't as big as Mr. Glatfelter," said Joey, referring to the big black-smith.

"Bet he's just as big," said Sammy. "Hey, I wonder if he's Sarah's father."

"Nah, I don't think so," said Joey. He remembered Sarah asking her mother about a certain Leroy. This must be Leroy.

"How do you know, smart guy?" Carmine, the oldest in the group, was more belligerent than the rest.

"Come on, Carmine. I just said that I didn't think so."

"Well, I think he is."

Sammy knew Joey better than the others. He had seen Joey speaking to Sarah in the school-yard. He had a feeling that he really knew who the big black was. "Why don't you guys bet on it?" he said.

Carmine took the bait. "yeah, Joey, I bet you a nickel that I'm right."

Joey was mad at Sammy for bringing the matter to a head, but he was angrier at Carmine. He was such a smart-ass. He thought he knew everything. "Put up your nickel, Carmine. You got a bet," he snarled,

Carmine wasn't so sure of himself now. "I only got two cents," he said.

"Okay, put up your two cents." Joey took out two pennies and handed them to Sammy. He was determined to make Carmine pay for being so smart. "Sammy holds the bets."

Carmine gave his two pennies to Sammy. "Okay, now how are you gonna prove it, smart guy?"

Joey was in his glory. "Well, I happen to know that he's goin¹ over to see Mrs. Furguson. And his name's Leroy."

"So what? He could still be her father," Carmine persisted.

"He's not her father. He's just a friend of Mrs. Furguson, Sarah told me," Joey lied.

"You're lying, Joey. Before, you said you didn't think he was her father. And now, you say you're sure he ain't."

"I heard her tell Joey," Sammy said, lying for his friend.

"Bull-shit," Carmine shouted. "You're both lying. Give me back my money." He made a threatening move on Sammy.

Sammy moved away from the fire, waiting for Joey to tell him what to do with the money. He put the coins in his pocket and raised his fist to fight off Carmine if he had to.

"Let's forget it, huh, Carmine," said Freddie. Johnny, Carmine's brother, and the smallest of the group, looked on, hoping they would stop arguing.

"Yeah, let's forget it," agreed Joey. "Give him back his money, Sammy."

Money in hand, Carmine still persisted in goading Joey. "Okay, I'll drop it, you nigger-lover. And I hope he screws your girlfriend." Carmine screamed with laughter. Jesus, that big bastard would rip her good," he yelped. "Would you want her for your girlfriend, then?"

Joey swung with all his might. But Carmine, though older, was not physically stronger than Joey, so he was already moving backwards and the blow missed. It sobered him up, however. "Aw, come on, sore-head," he laughed. "I was only kidding."

"Someday that 'kidding' is gonna get you in trouble," said Sammy, getting in between the two. "You got no right saying things like that. Next thing you know, you'll be calling him a Jew-lover cause he hangs out with me."

"Shit, Sammy, I hang out with you, don't I."

"Come on, you guys. Cut it out," said Freddie.

Peace was restored, but not until Joey had his last word. "Look, Carmine, Sarah's a nice girl. And you better cut out the smart-ass talk about her. It's none of your business if I want to talk to her."

"All right, let's forget it." Carmine took his sweet potato out of the fire and began blowing on it to cool it. Then, satisfied that it would not burn him, he began to peel off the scorched skin.

As the dying embers flickered and died, they huddled about, not saying much anymore. Joey had kept a close watch down the street. He saw Mrs. Furguson, in her bulky coat, going home from the other end of the street and felt a sense of relief. The specter of the big Negro ravishing the helpless Sarah stayed in his mind for some time. And for weeks afterwards, he would watch the girl at play, searching her face for signs of anguish, sadness, worry. But to his great relief, he received nothing but her bright, warm smile.

Joey became a regular visitor to the Furguson house. With Uncle Guide's guarantee that the police would not bother him if he sold a bottle or two of his wine to his friends, Giovanni began to send Joey to the house once or twice a week, saving the dollar bills in a small, tin, tobacco can. He hid the can in the cellar behind the wine barrels. He would make sure that he earned enough money for his next batch of wine.

Always, Joey went through the alley. And now, Mrs. Ferguson always made sure that the back yard gate was unlocked when he arrived, so that all he needed to do was get into the back yard then knock on the kitchen door to be let in. Sometimes, when Mrs. Ferguson wasn't there, he stayed with Sarah and little Hebert until she arrived. Sometimes, it was Leroy, the big black, who would come first. Joey would leave only when Mrs. Furguson finally arrived and paid him for the wine. He, Sarah and Hebert would stay in the kitchen while Leroy made himself comfortable in the living room, usually dozing off on the big sofa.

In spite of his big, toothy smile, Joey did not like the man. There was something sinister about him. Perhaps the impression had been stamped on Joey's mind when he had come into the house cleaning his nails with a knife with a gleaming switch-blade. Seeing Joey there, he had snapped the knife shut with a deliberate motion, all the while looking directly at the boy. Joey had been glad when Mrs. Furguson finally came home.

Then, Joey noticed that Leroy no longer came when Mrs. Furguson was not at home, usually on church-meeting nights. Even he was warned not to come until a certain time. The woman was always there when he arrived with the bottle of wine. Joey was disappointed at first because he could no longer spend any time with Sarah and her brother. But he felt a sense of relief when he realized that Sarah and the boy were no longer ever alone with Leroy.

CHAPTER 18

Thanksgiving was not a typical Italian holiday, but the Nocelli family had quickly adopted the traditional American holiday. This year was special. 'Uncle Guido had implored Lucia to cook an extra-large turkey, which he had supplied along with all the trimmings in order to make it a magnificent feast. The idea, of course, was to impress Clara Cortolani and her family, who would be invited. Lucia had agreed, and the Cortolani family had been wined and dined and had been introduced to America's most cherished holiday.

Throughout the sumptuous dinner, Lucia had noticed a sadness in Clara Cortolani's eyes in spite of the laughter and wellbeing that resounded about the table. And in Guide's eyes, there was a worried look. At times, it disappeared, but suddenly he would look at the girl, and the look would return. There seemed to be a barrier between the two.

After dinner, the men sat at the heavy, oaken dining room table, picking on toasted nuts and fruit while they drank Giovanni's best wine. It was much like the feasts of Easter and Christmas except that the Cortolani family had never eaten turkey before. Mr. Cortolani commented, between puffs of a cigar, that turkey meat was good, but he would just as soon have a good plate of home-made pasta with a sausage and meat-ball gravy. Giovanni was inclined to agree, but he didn't say so. They talked mostly of the old country: who had died . . . who remained.

Joey had gone out after the main meal was over, and little Jimmy had fallen asleep. The women were in the kitchen cleaning up and preparing coffee and slicing up a cake that the Cortolanis had brought with them. When Clara asked for the bathroom, Lucia led the way upstairs, saying that she wanted to check on little Jimmy.

When the girl came out of the bathroom, she was confronted by Lucia who led her into her bedroom. "What is wrong between you and Guido?" she asked.

"Is it so noticeable?" The sadness showed in the girl's lovely eyes.

"I see sorrow in your eyes, and Guido is miserable. I can tell. He is like part of my family."

"I am so sorry for him," the girl said softly.

"But why? What is it?"

The girl gave a deep sigh. "He wishes to marry me, and I cannot marry him."

"Your parents?" Lucia was prepared to be furious, to vent her anger on the girl's parents.

"No." The girl's eyes could not meet Lucia's. "They wish me to marry Guido. At least, they do not object. They think he is a fine catch."

"Well then? He was so happy when you were allowed to go out with him alone. He told us that your parents would not let you at first."

"That is true. And I like Guido very much, but I do not love him."

"There is someone else?"

The girl nodded. "I was in love with a young man from our town. My father did not like him, and that is why he brought me to America." The girl wiped the tears that the thought of her loved one brought to her eyes. "I have just received a letter saying that he is coming for me."

Lucia took the girl into her arms. "I understand," she said, knowing exactly how she felt. "Does Guido know?" she asked.

"He does not know the reason why I have refused him."

"Do you want me to tell him."

"No. I feel that I should tell him."

"Yes, I think you should. It will be hard. Are you sure about your sweetheart? Perhaps you should wait until he comes here to this country. Perhaps he will not like it here. Perhaps you will not feel the same about him."

"I have thought of that. That is why I do not want to tell him yet. Paolo and I were so much in love that it is hard to imagine that anything has changed. I cannot marry Guido and then find out that I still feel love for Paolo. Do you understand?"

Lucia nodded. "I understand, as any woman would," she sighed. "Come, let us go down. They are calling."

When they came down, Clara's mother had set the coffee and cake on the table. "I was showing Clara all the nice things that Giovanni has done with the house," Lucia said. "Soon, we will have electric . . . perhaps by Christmas."

"You have done wonderful things," Giovanni. I wish t our bathroom was new like yours," said the girl.

But when Lucia looked at Guido, his eyes were on hers, questioning. He knew they had talked.

He came back after driving the girl and her family home. Lucia had not told Giovanni about the conversation, and she waited, knowing that he would come back. The table had been cleared in the dining room, and now they sat at the kitchen table, the room still smelling of good things from the day's cooking. Giovanni picked idly of some nuts.

"You spoke upstairs?" Guido asked without preliminaries.

"Of course we spoke," laughed Lucia. "We would not be women if we did not speak."

"What is wrong? Tell me."

Lucia poured coffee for him, wishing she knew how to answer. "I promised Clara I would not say anything to you. She wishes to be the one to tell you," she said.

Giovanni smiled a sardonic little smile. "it is probably her stuff-shirted parents," he said

"No," said Guido. Her parents seem to have approved of me."

"They have?" Giovanni was genuinely surprised. Knowing the Cortolani family from the old country, he had assumed that nothing short of a doctor or a lawyer would be considered good enough for their daughter. "Do they know what you do for a living?" he asked.

"Yes and no." Guido shrugged.

"Then, that must be it."

"I don't think so," said Guido. "Everything was going so well. I know that she cares for me."

"Why don't you see her as quickly as you can, and talk it out," Giovanni said. "She said she would tell you."

"Please, Lucia . . . you tell me. I am dying for this woman, and I must know."

"Tell him if you know, Cara. It was you who brought them together." Giovanni could not see his friend in such a state.

"But Giovanni, I promised . . ."

"Guido, if Lucia tells you, you must promise that you will not let on that you know," Giovanni insisted.

"I promise."

Lucia looked at her husband, still undecided. But when he nodded reassuringly, she let out her secret. "Clara was very much in love with a young man from her village. And now, he has written that he is coming for her." She could see the pain in Guide's eyes. "She wishes to make sure if she still loves the young man or not. She wishes to be fair with you, Guido."

It was quite a while before any one spoke. Then, Guido smiled sadly. "Well, now I can understand about the other man. There has always been another man. But it was usually I who was the other man.

"Are you all right, Guido?"

Giovanni had never heard his friend reason so simply.

"I am fine, my friend."

"What are you going to do?"

Guido smiled reassuringly. "I'm not going to do anything rash, if that's what you're thinking. I will wait to speak to her. I will let her tell me all about this other man, as I promised. I will act shocked and surprised. And if they get married . . . who knows, I might be the other man in her life. This seems to be the story of my life. It always has worked great for me," Guido said.

"Yes, until the husband finds out," laughed Giovanni. He was happy to see that Guido was taking it so well. It almost seemed as though a huge load had been lifted from his friend's mind.

Guido joined in the laughter. "The only reason the Irish girl told her husband about me, was because I had left her for Clara. I'd bet a hundred dollars I could see her again if I wanted."

"Do not count on me to protect you from her husband again," said Giovanni, seriously.

"Do not make plans, Guido." Lucia touched his arm. "Perhaps Clara will find out that she no longer loves this young man."

"We'll see." Guido smiled glumly as he left.

CHAPTER 19

Joey heard the grinding, grating sound before he turned into his street. He knew the sound well, and he groaned. It was the coal truck. He hoped it was not at his house. But there it was. The body, black from many similar deliveries, was already raised at an angle, and the coal was sliding down a metal chute into Joey's cellar. A man was standing beside the chute, making sure that the coal kept sliding smoothly. Several children were standing nearby, watching. Little Jimmy was staring out of the parlor window.

Joey stood on the top of his steps. He watched as the coal slowly emptied out of the truck. The truck was still almost full. From out of the window where the chute fed the coal into the cellar, a wave of dark air billowed out. Joey ran into the house yelling for his mother. She came running down the stairs, money for the coal in her hands. When Joey told her of the black air coming out of the cellar, she hurried outside and spoke to the man. Immediately, the man pulled a lever, and the coal stopped sliding down the chute. The man waited patiently as Joey and Lucia began bringing out pails and pots full of water. As one was delivered to the man, another was being filled in the kitchen sink. The man resumed unloading the coal, now pouring water on it as it slid down the chute. The black air no longer billowed out of the window, and soon the coal was completely unloaded. The dust in the cellar would not be so bad.

When Joey went down into the cellar a half hour later, the dust had settled. It lay on the dirt floor, on his father's work table and on the wooden contraption that his father was building for the church. Joey didn't know what it was except that it looked like a large table with long, wooden bars on each side of it.

The clean-up job wasn't as bad as it could have been, thanks to Joey's quick thinking. And it certainly wasn't as bad as last year when the coal had slid and rolled all over the cellar. He had had to shovel almost half of it so that it was in a neat pile. Since then, his father had built a coal-bin which held the coal together. Not even two shovel-fills of coal had escaped. He had dusted the wooden contraption and the work table and was sweeping the floor when Sammy came down the steps. "Need any help?" he asked.

"Yeah, hold the shovel for me," Joey said. He had swept the dust into one small heap. Sammy held the shovel against it and Joey proceeded to sweep it up.

"What's this?" Sammy asked, looking at the wooden contraption.

"I don't know. We'll ask my mom when we go up," Joey answered.

"You have a neat cellar. Mine is filled with all kinds of boxes of stuff we sell."

"I know." Joey had been down in Sammy's cellar once. He had been fascinated by all the cardboard boxed of various sizes and shapes. There was barely room to walk between the rows that were piled almost to the ceiling. Each box was labeled in large letters: toilet paper, soap, etc.

"What's in there?" Sammy pointed to a door in the back of the cellar. It was in the center of a wooden partition that was covered with old pieces of linoleum, roofing paper and an old rug that made it almost air-tight.

"That's my pop's wine cellar," Joey said proudly. He went to the door and opened it. He pressed the button on the new light switch that his father had just put in, and an electric bulb lit up the tiny room. The sweet, pungent smell of mash assailed the nostrils of the boys.

"Wow!" said Sammy. "This is great." He looked in awe at the wine barrels that line the room, into the barrels with the mash. Tiny bubbles, escaping from deep in the bowels of the barrels, came to the surface with a faint pop. "It looks like puke," he said after a while.

"That's the new wine. We have to squeeze it and put the juice in those barrels over there. We squeeze it in this thing." Joey pointed to the wine press that reached to the ceiling joist, to the round wooden container with slats a quarter inch apart. "The wine seeps out between these cracks and into the pail down below when we put the mash in. I get to squeeze it every day," Joey said. He was proud of his expertise. It wasn't too often when he could show off like this with Sammy. The Jewish boy was so smart.

"Can I help you when you get to squeeze it?" Sammy seemed genuinely fascinated.

"I guess. I'll have to ask my pop."

"What does it taste like?"

Without another word, Joey took the glass that his father used to taste the wine. He opened the valve gingerly so that none of the wine spilled to the ground. He filled the glass, then he handed it to Sammy. Sammy sipped it, made a wry face. Then, he sipped it again, drinking half the wine in the small glass. He handed the rest to Joey. "This is not as sweet as the wine my father drinks on our holidays," he said.

Joey finished the remainder of the wine. "Want some more?" he asked.

"Better not." Sammy's grin belied his words.

Joey filled the glass again. Just as quickly, they emptied it. Sammy agreed that it was the best wine he had ever tasted. "My father gets his wine from this man who sells us all our religious stuff. It's already koshered by our rabbi."

"We don't have to do that." Joey was filling the glass again. He spilled some of the wine, but no longer worried about it. There was plenty of wine in the barrel.

"We better not drink anymore. We're liable to get drunk," giggled Sammy. His head was as light as a feather. He sat down on an empty crate the grapes had come in.

"You're right, Sammy. This'll be the last," Joey agreed. He sipped from the glass, and suddenly it tasted terrible. His stomach seemed to turn over. He handed the glass to Sammy. Sammy sipped from it, then put it down on the platform that kept the barrels off the floor. "I don't want any more," he said. His face had suddenly turned pale, and the grin was gone. "I think I'm gonna be sick."

Joey was suddenly moved to action. Not here! Not sick in the wine cellar! He just knew his father would be very angry. His father had never laid hands on him before.

But for something like this . . . there was no knowing what he might do. "C'mon," he screamed, his own stomach suddenly, temporarily stabilized.

They rushed upstairs, Joey leading Sammy by the hand. Out into the back yard they went, as the shaken Lucia looked on. Joey opened the door to the out-house and Sammy rushed in just in time.

Lucia heard the retching, horrible, disgusting sound. It made her wince. Her son's eyes seemed to bulge out of his head, as he implored Sammy to hurry up. Too late. With a gush, the torrent of vile liquid splattered against the out-house wall, then ran down to the brick pavement in disgusting rivulets. Steam rose from the small puddle and mingled with the chilled air.

Lucia was already filling up a pot of water as she anxiously watched her son. He seemed to be staring at the mess, wondering what it was. Then, his body jerked, and out came another spurt of the vile stuff. By the time the pot was filled, she had her coat on. She carried it out and set it down on the ground. "Are you done?" she asked in a flat tone of voice. She inspected his clothing. There was one small spot on his knickers, near the left knee.

Joey was frightened. He nodded, shivering. He knew he was as close to a beating as he had ever been.

"Go upstairs and clean your mouth out. And clean that." She pointed to the spot on his knickers.

From inside the out-house came Sammy's plaintive voice. "Joey, can I come out?" he asked. He sounded worried.

"Are you done?" Joey repeated his mother's question. He felt a lot better now, except for the terrible taste in his mouth.

"Yeah," came the answer.

"Come on out. My mother's here." Joey felt that he should warn Sammy. "And watch where you step."

"I know." The door opened and Sammy came out, a sheepish grin on his face. He looked directly at Lucia, not knowing what to expect. He was relieved when she shook her head and smiled. Her eyes were full of understanding, and Sammy was reminded of his own mother. She smiled like that when he was in trouble.

"Take him upstairs with you, and clean yourselves," she said.

She was in the kitchen cooking when they came down. She had already cleaned up the yard, then had gone into the cellar and put everything back in order. The glass was placed exactly where he always kept it. She scuffed some dirt over the tiny puddle of wine on the floor. She surveyed the rest of the cellar. Joey had done a fine job.

"Come back," she called, as the two headed for the front door. Joey grabbed Sammy by the arm, and together, they went back to the kitchen. As they stood there, she looked at them. She came close and sniffed at Sammy's clothing for any sign of his debauchery. Finally satisfied, she backed off, and in her best English, she said, "Don't you never do that again." Her face wore a frown until they left.

CHAPTER 20

The winter was a harsh one. It snowed right after Thanksgiving, and it seemed that the snow never disappeared from the ground. And Giovanni seemed to be home from work more and more. Carlo Fabrizio, the contractor that he worked for, had not been able to land an inside job for that winter, and although it sorrowed the old Italian, he had to send his men home when the ground was so frost-hardened that it was impossible to dig, or so—cold that bricks could not be laid. And if the walls of a building could not go up, there could be no inside work. His crew of some twenty men had been whittled down to a skeleton crew of five of which Giovanni was one. Carlo liked Giovanni because he could do so many different things. He could work along as a helper with the carpenters, laborers, even brick-layers. He had helped pour concrete and finish it off with a trowel. He had even learned how to drive one of the trucks, although he was not allowed to do so. He was a man of many trades. It was well known that Giovanni had put in a brand new bathroom in his own house, and was just finishing putting in electricity. This was not a man who was let go.

However, if the work was not there, or if the weather made work impossible, there was nothing that Mr. Fabrizio could do but send his men home. And it seemed that this winter, Giovanni had begun to lose one or two days each week. He fretted about it as the family savings began to dwindle, but he did not stay idle. He worked about the house on his days off, finishing up his electrical project, patching up all the holes he had

had to make in order to run his wiring. Then, of course, he worked on his project for the church.

What the boys had seen in the cellar, was the rough frame for a stand that would carry the statue of Our Lady of Mount Carmel in the procession in Her honor. It had to be strong enough so that four men could carry it and the statue on their shoulders, one on each corner, yet not be too heavy for the men. And, of course, it had to be made so that it could be dismantled and stored in the basement of the St. Nicholas of Tolentino Church.

Ever since Giovanni and his family had begun to attend the St. Nicholas Church instead of his own parish church, he had been called upon to repair the old stand every time they used it. Finally, he had decided to build a new and sturdier one. It was his secret project. No one at the church knew of it, and the next time the stand was needed, he would offer Monsignor Bellaci the new one. He knew his offer would be accepted and appreciated. Perhaps, as a result, he would be made an honorary member of the sodality in spite of the fact that he did not belong to that parish.

He was contemplating what sort of design he would use to trim the rough stand. It had to be a work of art, but not too garish. It had to be simple, but not plain. It had to seem as though it was part of the statue, as though the "Lady" was floating on it. He sat on a stool and stared at the stand and sipped from a glass of his new wine. He heard Lucia calling from the head of the stairs.

"Giovanni, it is Guido."

Guido came down the stairs. He had to duck slightly on the last step to avoid banging his head on the header joist. As usual, he was dressed for the evening, complete with stiff collared white shirt, tie and coat. He stepped gingerly on the dirt floor in an effort to protect the new shine of his patent leather shoes.

"So, what brings you here, Guido?" Giovanni looked at his friend. This was not one of the nights that he usually came for supper. It was even too late for that.

Guido shrugged. "I came to see how you were. I heard that Carlo does not have much work for the winter."

"You have heard right. It has not been like this since we arrived here. Mr. Fabrizio keeps us on the payroll, but only from day to day. If the weather is bad, we come home." Giovanni went to the foot of the stairs, called for a glass, then went into the wine cellar and returned with it full of wine. He handed it to Guido.

"Do you need money?" Guido was staring at the stand in the middle of the cellar, and he asked the question absent-mindedly.

"No, we have saved some money."

Guido seemed to have lost interest in the conversation. He sipped the wine, still staring at the fabrication. He lifted on one of the out looker pieces of lumber. It came up easily. "What the hell is this?" he asked.

Giovanni explained about the stand and what it would be used for in the procession. Guido nodded in understanding, "And how are you gonna get it out of the cellar?" he asked, puzzled.

Giovanni smiled. "Hey, Guido, you must know that it will come apart. Then, it will be put together again at the church."

Guido smiled sheepishly. "of course I knew that. I was just teasing. But I did hear of a man who built a boat in his cellar. It's still-there." They both laughed.

"Would you be interested in making some money on the side, Giovanni?" Guide's voice had lowered instinctively. He glanced furtively at the stairs.

"I could always use some extra money, especially now." Giovanni's voice had also become almost a whisper. He did not pretend to think that Guido's offer would be a nice one, or even a legal one. He did not want Lucia to hear. Perhaps you wish me to be your bodyguard again," he said, wryly,

"Nothing like that, Giovanni," Guido was peering into the glass of wine, at the ruby, red coloring. "I told some of my friends about the great wine you make. They would be willing to buy all you will sell."

Giovanni was relieved. He was not sure what kind of an offer he was expecting, but what he heard was not at all offensive. Actually, he was pleased that his wine could be so much in demand. "My wine? And how much would they give me for my wine?" he asked.

"I could get you six dollars a gallon."

Six dollars! Giovanni was overwhelmed. A quick calculation showed that he had almost a thousand dollars' worth of wine ready to sell. He had paid only a little more than three thousand dollars for his house. How could this be. Of course, it had to be illegal. "Who would pay me this much for my wine?" he asked in awe.

Guido chuckled. "When something is hard to get in this country, then people are gonna pay a lot of money for it. Prohibition's made it hard to get whiskey and beer and wine. Companies are not allowed to make any of it to sell. So, the little people like us make it. Some people make gin in bathtubs, and some make beer. People like you make wine."

Prohibition had meant little to Giovanni. He had never been much of a beer or whiskey drinker. As long as he had his wine, he had been content. "Of course, it is illegal to do this, is it not?" he asked.

"You have much to learn, my friend," said Guido. Some of our most prominent people are doing this . . . only on a much bigger scale. Of course, it is illegal. But when the people want something to drink, somebody has to get it for them. These people are becoming millionaires."

"I can believe that . . . at these prices."

"You'll do it, then?"

Giovanni made a wry face. "Guido, if I sell my wine, then I will not have it to drink. I know it would help to earn me some money, but I do not need this. I will find some other work. We will not starve."

Guido stared at his stubborn friend. The man had a gold-mine here in his cellar, and he refused to take advantage of it. Maybe he should have spoken to Lucia first. "I'll tell you what I'll do, my friend," he said. "I'll tell my friends that you'll only sell five gallons at a time. At six dollars a gallon, you can make yourself a quick thirty dollars whenever you need it. Maybe, when they see how good it is, they'll offer you more."

Giovanni was suddenly interested. He liked this new option very much. At least, they would not starve this winter. "That sounds very good, Guido. It is something that I can live with," he said. "Will you come for the wine?"

"No, Giovanni. Here's what'll happen. I'll bring you an empty five gallon can. You fill it up and have it ready. Then, I'll bring a man with me when it gets dark. He'll take away the wine and leave you an empty can. He'll be the only person you will deal with from then on."

"What of the money?"

"He'll pay you cash. You just tell him when to come for the next batch."

"Okay, Guido." Giovanni mimicked his friend. "You explain to your friends that I will sell my wine only when I need to."

"Okay, my friend." Guido was pleased. He was sure his friends would be pleased. It was a good policy to be on the good side of these people. There was no knowing when he might be in need of a favor. Of course Sam Maglione, the man who would be doing business with Giovanni, was not in the upper echelon of the mob that controlled the liquor policy in the city. As a matter of fact, he was just getting his feet wet, having just been admitted into the organization. At the moment, he was no more than an errand boy. But Guido was comfortable with him and trusted him to be fair with Giovanni. He had played poker with him on several occasions, and he knew he was shrewd and was ambitious. He would go far in the organization. He was a good person to know.

Two evenings later, the first bit of business had been completed. Guido had not come the evening after they had talked, and Giovanni had brushed it off as a hare-brained scheme and was rather relieved. But he had come the next night with a strange man and two five-gallon cans. The man was about the same height as Giovanni, but not as muscular. He was smartly dressed in a gray, tailor-made business suit. Rather handsome in a rakish way, it was his eyes that caught the attention of anyone who looked closely. They seemed to smile even when serious, a sort of mocking look that made him appear sinister at times. "John," he called his friend by his Americanized name for the stranger's benefit, "this is Sam Maglione. He will be the only one you do business with. If anybody else comes, you don't know what they're talking about. You understand?"

The man offered his hand. His eyes looked less sinister, less menacing when he grinned. "Good to know you, John," he said. "I hope we can do some business together."

Giovanni felt the strength of the sinewy hand, and he wasn't sure if he liked the man or not. A glance at Lucia gave him a feeling of misgiving. She was staring at the man, questioningly, almost fearfully. She managed a smile when Guido introduced her. The man nodded, his eyes showing only respect for her.

"You have the money, of course," Giovanni asked before he even made a move to go into the cellar with the cans.

The man smiled. He turned to Guido. "Your friend is a good business man," he said. He took out a wallet and counted out thirty dollars, handed it to Giovanni.

Without another word, Giovanni folded the money and put it into his pocket. Then, he took the two cans and went down into the cellar. The man turned to Lucia. "Signora, may I have a glass. I would like to taste your husband's wine. Our friend, Guido has spoken so well of it." He spoke in Italian, and Lucia understood his dialect so easily, that she was tempted to ask him from what part of Italy he was from. He could have been from her own home town. She went to the cupboard and brought back two glasses. But when she attempted to fill the glass with the wine from a bottle on the table, he stopped her. "If it is all the same with you, I would like to taste the wine that I am buying." His smile was disarming, and Lucia was beginning to like the man. "And you, Guido. Would you like some?" she asked in Italian. She was already pouring when he said he would like some.

"You are from Abruzzi, are you not, Signora?" the man asked. He had also recognized the dialect she spoke.

"I am from Monteparaiso. It is near Vasto," answered Lucia, now completely taken with the man. "You must be from near there. I understand you so well."

"That is a compliment, Signora, since I have been here in America since I was eight. But, I do remember the name of your town. We came from Vasto." The man sat down at the table. He felt at, home, here with this beautiful woman.

"Guido is from our town, also. He came here as a boy, but I can barely understand him when he speaks in Italian. He has forgotten almost all of it," said Lucia. She turned to Guido with a reproachful look.

The man turned to Guido. He spoke in English. "I never heard you talk in Italian, Guido."

"Now, you know the reason."

Giovanni came through the cellar door, five-gallon can in hand. He was frowning as he set it on the table. "It is not good to leave the wine in this can. You must put it in bottles as quickly as you can with as little air as possible. If you do not, it will spoil." Giovanni was speaking to Guido in Italian. He was surprised when the man spoke up in Italian.

"Capiso, (I understand) you, Giovanni. If you wish to speak in Italian, then we will do so."

"He comes from Vasto, Giovanni," said Lucia.

"Oh, I am pleased." Giovanni smiled for the first time. "But, I prefer that we speak in English. I am trying to learn my new language," he said.

"Okay, John. Do you mind if I taste the wine?"

"Of course not."

The man unscrewed the cap of the can, then tipping it gently, he poured some of the wine into his glass without spilling a drop. He looked at the rich, red color, sniffed at it, then sipped it, letting it roll about in his mouth. Finally, he swallowed it. He drank the rest from the glass. He nodded approval. "It's as good as you say, Guido," he said. "Let's hope it doesn't change," he added, the meaning quite clear.

Guido laughed. "John would kill anybody who watered down his wine. He's too damn proud of it to do that. You got no worry, Sam."

The man nodded. "You should be proud, John. It's good wine . . . one of the best I've tasted."

"Thank you."

Sam Maglione screwed on the cap to the five-gallon can. The wine was better than he had expected. There was no doubt in his mind that he would need more, once the customers of his club tasted it. And when his partner, Vince Pertucci, got to taste it, he would sure in hell want more of it. He was already complaining about the quality of the wine he was getting from another source. Somehow, he would have to make a better deal than the one he had with these people. "When can I come for more?" he asked. Christmas and New Years are right around the corner, and I can use all you sell me."

Giovanni looked at Guido. He showed concern.

"I told you, Sam. John only wants to sell his wine when he needs the money," Guido protested. "He wouldn't be selling at all if he was working steady."

"Sure, sure. But think it over, John. The customers are going to be crazy for this stuff when they taste it. Maybe you can sell me some more for the holidays."

"I will think it over," said Giovanni.

"Good. It's been a pleasure doing business with you," Sam Maglione said. He shook hands with Giovanni, nodded to Lucia, then headed for the door, the wine in his strong grasp.

Guido remained in the kitchen for a moment. "Everything all right?" he asked. He looked at Lucia, then at Giovanni.

Lucia didn't look happy, Giovanni merely nodded. "Good night, then." he said. He went to the door. Then, while Sam Maglione waited inside, Guido went out to the car and started it. Making sure that there was no one in sight, he motioned to him. In a moment, they were gone.

Giovanni counted the money, then gave it to his wife. "It is good money for my wine," he said.

"Yes, I know," she agreed. "But do you think it is right?"

"It will help. It is almost a week's pay."

"Yes, it will help," Lucia said. "He seems to be a nice man. But, he frightens me . . . his eyes . . . ."

"I think he will be fair. Hopefully, I will not need to sell him anymore. If only we got busy again."

It was only two nights later that Sam Maglione returned. He had an empty five gallon can with him. "John, I need more wine," he said without any preliminary talk.

"But we have an agreement. I am to sell you the wine only when I need the money," Giovanni said stubbornly.

The piercing eyes sought Lucia's aid as she stood behind her husband. To no avail. She was as resolute as her husband. "Okay, John. Think it over. I"ll leave the can here, and I'll check with you in a couple of days." The smooth voice was apologetic. "I'm sorry to bother you, but you must see my predicament. Your wine is so good, and I have none left. My partner has even agreed to give you a dollar a gallon more." The man waited to see if the new offer had any affect.

Giovanni only smiled. "You must understand, Mr. Maglione, I cannot sell my wine like a business. It is for my own pleasure and my friends."

Sam Maglione bid them good night. "Maybe, I'll have better luck next time," he said as he left.

Giovanni didn't work the next two days, so that when the man came again, he had worked only two days for the week. Sam Maglione was offered one can of wine. But without too much persuasion from the man,

Giovanni agreed to fill the other can. There was little small talk, and when the man left with the wine, he smiled with satisfaction. "Maybe I'll be lucky again," he said. After he had left, Giovanni counted the money again. He could not believe it. Sam Maglione had made good his promise to pay him seven dollars a gallon. He handed Lucia the seventy dollars.

The very next night, he came again. At first, he pleaded that he needed the wine, that he could use three times as much, that every one of his customers asked for it. Then, as Giovanni balked, the soft voice took on a sinister tone. His eyes narrowed and seemed to pierce right through the two. He lashed at them, speaking in Italian so that there was no chance of misunderstanding him. "Guido said that you would be easy to do business with. But I see that you are no different from all the other people that come from the other side. You are too thick-headed for your own good. You will never make good in this country." Then, sensing that Giovanni had become tense, his muscular hands twitching, and Lucia seemed frightened, the man's voice softened. "Signora, I am sorry if I have frightened you, but your husband has a chance to make some good money, and he doesn't take advantage of it. Sell me seven five gallon cans a week and he would not have to work all winter." Then, he turned to Giovanni and spoke in English, "It's cold out there, John."

Lucia felt her husband tremble. Although the same height as the man, he was more muscular and heavier. He could easily throw him out bodily, as he seemed on the verge of doing. She put her hand on his arm and he seemed to relax. She was glad that Joey was not there to see his father so angry.

Without a word, Giovanni picked up the two cans that Sam Maglione had brought with him and went down into the cellar. When he returned, it was obvious that they were full. He set them down on the floor. "Here, take the wine. But, this is the last of it. Do you understand, Mr. Maglione. There will be no more wine. Pay me and go." He held out his hand for his money.

Sam Maglione looked at Giovanni, then at Lucia. He seemed surprised at the outcome. His face had turned livid and violent thoughts rushed through his mind. Stupid, dago bastard, he thought. They come here and they want everything on a platter. He had the urge to slip on the iron knuckles he carried in his coat pocket and smash the grim face of Giovanni. He felt like smashing the two cans of wine against the wall.

His eyes focused on Lucia. God, she was a beautiful woman. But she looked scared, like she was going to scream. This is where he drew a line. He felt himself relaxing. And as he did, he could see that she was relieved. Without a word, he counted seventy dollars from his wallet and handed it to Giovanni. "I'm sorry you want it this way, John," he said, his voice, friendly. "I really hope you change your mind." Picking up the two cans, he made his way out.

Lucia and Giovanni stared at one another without a word until they heard the roar of the car outside. When they could hear it no longer, Lucia spoke. "I thought he was going to attack you. He had something in his pocket."

"I am glad that it is over, Cara. I should never have started it.

CHAPTER 21

G iovanni was puzzled by the strained manners of the others when he went in to work on Monday. The four men had been talking among themselves . . . not laughing and joking as usual. They were suddenly quiet when he entered the large garage that housed the trucks and equipment. He greeted them and they nodded solemnly. "The boss wants to see you in the office, said Tomasso, the foreman.

Giovanni's stomach turned. Something was not right. Usually Carlo Fabrizio was in the garage with the men, supervising the preparation for the day's work. The weather was not too bad . . . workable. And why was he not out here in the garage. Lay-off? "What is wrong?" he asked.

Tomasso shrugged. "He's in there now," he said.

Giovanni headed for the door at the back of the garage with a great deal of apprehension. Never had he been called into the office, except on the day he had been hired. His hand trembled as he turned the knob and opened the door. He nodded to his boss.

Carlo Fabrizio seemed to have aged beyond his sixty years. He looked as though he had not slept all night. The large, glass ash-tray was already filled with cigarette butts, smoke still curling up from some of them. It was odd, because the contractor usually smoked cigars. The old man spoke without looking at him. He spoke in Italian. "I will have to let you go, Giovanni," he said. "You know that things are not going well. The ground is frozen and there is no work."

Giovanni was not surprised. By this time, he had begun to fear the worst. "But Signer Fabrizio, I am content to work as we have been doing . . . two . . . three days a week. I have never complained."

"I am sorry, Giovanni. I cannot keep you. 1 will give you a week's pay. And perhaps the new year will be better." Carlo Fabrizio took an envelope from a desk drawer and handed it to Giovanni.

Signer Fabrizio, be honest with me. Will there be a job for me when the weather is good? If not, I will begin to look for another one."

"Yes . . . yes, of course," the contractor lied. But then, he looked Giovanni squarely in the eyes. "No," he said. "There will be no job for you. I am sorry, Giovanni, but that is the way it has to be."

"But why? I am one of your best workers. I have never asked for more money. I am always here when you need me. Why will I no longer have a job?" The simple truth had not yet dawned on the simple man.

Now, the kindly contractor spoke to Giovanni as he would to a son. "Giovanni, what did you do to those people?"

Giovanni shook his head, his face reflecting complete ignorance.

"Two men came to my house last night," Carlo Fabrizio continued. "I know them well. They are members of La Mana Nera . . . the Black Hand"

"La Mana Nera?" Giovanni stared in disbelief. The name brought fear to his heart. What did these people have to do with him? He suddenly sat down in a chair, his legs suddenly grown weak.

"They told me to lay you off or else they would bomb my garage, my trucks . . . even my house." The old man's face was flushed. "What the hell did you do to these people?" he implored with his hands.

At last it all came to him. Sam Maglione and the wine It had to be that. With his voice trembling from fear, he told the contractor about the wine, leaving out only the fact that Guido had brought Sam Maglione into his home. He would deal with Guido later.

Carlo Fabrizio listened closely, now lighting up a cigar, as he usually did, instead of a cigarette. Giovanni finally finished, and they sat in silence. The contractor showed no emotion, except that he appeared slightly relieved. He puffed on his cigar, taking tiny puffs and letting the smoke curl about his nose. Finally, he said, "Would you like my advice, Giovanni?"

Giovanni nodded, fully expecting the contractor to tell him to go to the police.

"Give them the wine. Give them all of it, if they want. Give it to them even if they don't pay you."

"But signer Fabrizio, you have tasted my wine. You know how good it is. What will I give you at Christmas? What will I give my other friends? It is not right."

"My son, I give you this advice as a father. If I had it in my power to do so, I would order you to give them the damn wine. They are animals. They would not hesitate to blow your house up . . . hurt your wife . . . your children . . . Is it worth it?" The contractor's color had come back to normal. Now, he was the father figure and confidant that he normally was to his men. "You see, Giovanni, the wine means nothing to them. They can always get it somewhere else . . . even though it is not as good. But these people . . . these animals . . . they cannot have anyone say that they got the better of the organization. They must hold people like you and me in fear of them. Otherwise, how can they stay in power?"

Giovanni listened carefully. At first, the only thought in his mind was to wring Sam Maglione's neck if he came to his house again. But the thought of harm coming to his wife and children changed all that. So, he listened carefully. Carlo Fabrizio made sense. He had heard many stories about these people in the short time he had been in America. La Mano Nera(The Black Hand) was not an organization to displease. He sighed. "Will there be work for me if I do as you say?" he asked.

"Giovanni, get in the good graces of these people, and I am sure that we can go on as before."

"And you do not think that I should go to the police?"

The kindly old man held his two hands in front of his face as in prayer. "Please, Giovanni. For your sake and mine . . . do not even think of it. We would both be destroyed. Take this week's pay and have a good holiday. After the new year, come back and we talk. In the meantime, sell them the wine. At the price they are willing to pay you, you will have a nice little bit of money. Use it well. In this country, you need money to make money."

Giovanni stood up. "I will make sure that you get some of my wine before they do, Signor Fabrizio," he said, "Buona Festa (Good feast), and thank you for your advice. They shook hands warmly and Giovanni left the garage, a sober and wiser man. He went by several places where he thought he might find Guido. When he could not, he went home.

Lucia was not surprised when she saw him come into the house. Another day lost. But today, there was a grim look on her husband's face that she had not seen before. She knew that there was something more troubling him. "What is it, Caro?" she asked.

"I have been laid off." Giovanni sat down wearily at the kitchen table.

Lucia sat across from him. "Because of the weather? Soon it will be warm again, and you will go back to work. We can sell some of the wine."

"It is because of the wine that this has happened."

"The wine?"

Giovanni nodded. "Because I would no longer sell the wine to Sam Maglione, he sent two men from La Mana Nera to Signor Fabrizio's house and threatened him. They told him to lay me off or they would bomb his shop and home. The poor man could do nothing. He gave me a week's pay."

La Mana Nera!" Lucia's face had suddenly turned pale. She made the Sign of the Cross. "Santa Maria, what will we do?" she gasped.

Giovanni got up, went to the cupboard, picked out a cup, then filled it from the coffee-pot on the stove. He blew into the steaming cup until he could sip the coffee. "Signer Fabrizio said that I should sell them all the wine they want. Only then will we be at peace with them. He said they would not hesitate to harm you and the children."

"Poor man. To think that he has been threatened because of us. "Will he let you go back to work?"

"He said that I must make my peace with them, then I should go back to see him."

"Then, that is what you must do, Giovanni. Sell them the wine at whatever price they will pay you. We must find Guido and tell him to speak to that man."

"I have looked for him. He is not easily found." Giovanni sipped the coffee thoughtfully. "You know, Cara, I have been doing much thinking since I left Signor Fabrizio. If I sell all my wine, there will be enough money to buy one of those houses that we have been looking at . . . the ones with the porches. Perhaps it is fate. We will not even have to worry about moving all my wine."

"Yes . . . yes. It is fate. Grazia Dio (Grace God)," exclaimed Lucia. Her face had regained its color. "Everything will turn out right, will it not, Giovanni?" she asked.

"It will, Lucia. I promise." And Giovanni looked at his wife, at the transformation right in front of his eyes. Her face was flushed, and never had she looked so beautiful. Her nipples were prominently pressed against the cotton dress she wore. "You have nothing on underneath. Why?" he said softly.

"I knew you would come home," she answered, her body trembling.

"Joey is at school?"

"Yes, and Jimmy is asleep."

Giovanni came to her side, kissed the top of her head. He passed his hand down her arm, then cupped one of her heavy breasts. She turned up her mouth and he kissed it. "Shall we go up to see if he is still asleep?" he asked.

"Yes." It was almost a gasp. Her legs were so weak that Giovanni had to help her up.

Guido and Sam Maglione came to the house two nights later. At the sight of Guido, Lucia became furious. "You!" she screamed, pointing at him. "Get out! Get out of my house. I do not want you in my house."

"Lucia!" Giovanni tried to calm her. Guido was stunned. The smile he had come in with had disappeared.

Lucia turned on her husband. "How can you call this person your friend when he has caused us all this trouble.

I would rather be friends with Mr. Maglione. At least I know what kind of person he is."

Guido tried to approach her, to apologize, to reassure her that he never, for a second, thought something like this would happen. He had only tried to help them out of their financial difficulties. But Lucia would have none of his entreaties. The last two days had been nightmares. They had not been able to find Guido, and her mind had been in a turmoil. Questions had plagued her and her husband. What if Mr. Maglione was already planning to demolish their home? Was Joey safe? Her Jimmy? Giovanni? How could they get word to him? And here they were in her home as though nothing was wrong . . . and that stupid smile on Guide's face . . . . Reaching for a broom, she went after Guido, hitting him on the head and shoulders.

Guido turned his back and protected himself as best he could until Giovanni took the broom away from her. By then, Guido was safe in the vestibule with the door closed behind him. He was visibly shaken, as could be seen through the single pane of glass in the door.

And suddenly, Sam Maglione was laughing, a deep, chuckling laughter that shook his slender frame. "By God, I'm glad I didn't have to deal with you, Signora," he said.

Lucia glared at him.

"You have to forgive him, Signora." Sam Maglione's voice became a soothing, almost hypnotic sound in the room. "He only meant to help you and your husband. He came to my place and asked if I could use some good wine. Well, you know, people drink water if you flavor it good enough. The only trouble was that I didn't know how good your wine was. My customers are demanding more and more of it." He shrugged.

"Why did you have to frighten us like that?" Lucia's face reflected the bitterness she felt.

"Lucia . . . arrestare(stop)," implored Giovanni. "It is enough."

"It's all right, John. Let her get it out of her system." Sam Maglione had taken control of the situation. "Signora, you and your family were never in danger. You have a good friend in Guido. And since he is a friend of mine, so are you friends of mine."

"But you made Mr. Fabrizio lay me off. You frightened the poor man half to death," Giovanni interrupted.

Again, Sam Maglione shrugged. John, it is our way of doing business. Perhaps, the two men that visited him used words that were too strong . . . too threatening. Carlo Fabrizio is well respected in our community. He was in no danger."

"Lucia, can I come out?" It was Guido, and he called out from the safety of the vestibule.

Lucia went to the door and opened it. Guido came in, smiling sheepishly. "I am sorry, Lucia. Forgive me," he said.

I am sorry, also, Guido." Lucia lifted her face and he kissed her on the cheek. "We thought you had already been killed or beaten up when we did not hear from you. We were so frightened; we did not know what to do." Giovanni went to Guido and embraced him. They kissed each other on the cheeks. All was well between them once more.

"Once more, I apologize . . . to everyone," said Sam Maglione.

The men sat around the table, then, and worked out an agreement, Lucia busying herself with little Jimmy, but never out of earshot. "How much wine are we talking about," the club-owner asked. He was all business, now, and he spoke in Italian so that there was no chance of Giovanni misunderstanding.

"There are four barrels. Of course, one is started, and I would like to keep one for myself," replied Giovanni. He felt more at ease, speaking in Italian. Now, he could speak his mind freely, say exactly what he wanted to. And he could understand exactly what Sam Maglione wanted. When he heard them speaking in Italian, Guido got up and drew Lucia into the living room, where they spoke quietly.

Sam Maglione was impressed with the great amount of wine involved. The most he had ever gotten from people like Giovanni were two barrels. "Giovanni, I am not one to quibble," he said. "Let me have the three full barrels, and you keep the one that is started. For this, I will give you one dollar more a gallon. Of course, it must be as good as this one." He sipped from his glass, nodding approval.

"Mr. Maglione, that is impossible. You must remember that what you are drinking and what I have been selling you is the last of my old wine . . . the wine that I made last year. The three barrels that you wish to buy is not yet three months old. It is good enough to drink, but I do not think that it will taste as good as the wine I have been selling you."

Sam Maglione's eyes suddenly turned fierce, and they locked with Giovanni's. "Then, the new wine will not taste like this?"

Mr. Maglione, what can I say? If you drink my new wine now, it will taste good. If you let it stay for a year, it will be excellent."

Sam Maglione's eyes became less fierce. "We will see," "Would it be possible to taste the new wine?"

"Not tonight. The barrels are not yet tapped. You can taste it when you come for it. Of course, if it is not suitable for your needs, you need not buy it."

Sam Maglione broke into a tiny smile, and his eyes became shrewd, sinister. Giovanni's last remark had rung a bell, alerting him. The man didn't care whether he sold his damn wine or not. Maybe the thought of sabotaging the whole deal had even entered his mind. "Giovanni," he said,

"I am sure that the wine will meet my approval. You take too much pride in it, and I know you would not do anything irresponsible to spoil it."

"Spoil my wine, Mr. Maglione? I would die first."

"Then, it is a deal."

"Eight dollars a gallon?"

"Shouldn't we wait until we taste it . . . say tomorrow night?"

"Of course." Giovanni knew that the man before him would be pleased with the new wine. He, himself, had tasted it when he stored it in the barrels, and it had tasted good enough to drink even then. "One thing I must insist on, Mr. Maglione," he said. "You must not keep the wine in the tin cans for long."

The man laughed. "Giovanni, let me tell you something," he said. "I don't even have time to put the wine in the bottles, and it is gone. Now, I will have to ask you to be patient. I will send people with four or five cans at a time. It is impossible to take it all at once."

Giovanni nodded. "That will be fine. However, there is one thing that I will insist on. I will deal only with you. You must come whenever we do business.

Sam Maglione frowned. "That is not always possible. I have a business to run, you know. But I will do this. I will let you meet my partner. Then, it will be either him or me that you will deal with. And your money will be on the table here, before the wine leaves your house. Is that satisfactory?"

"That will be fine."

They stood up and shook hands. Then, they went into the living room. Guido was already on his feet. He looked into Giovanni's eyes, saw the smile and knew that all had gone well. Sam Maglione spoke to Lucia. "Signora, I am happy to have met you. You are a good woman. I am sorry to have caused you all this worry. And I will speak to Carlo Fabrizio and tell him that it was all a big mistake." Turning to Giovanni, he said, "Giovanni, if you ever need help, you know where to come." Then, nodding to Lucia, he was gone, following Guido down the steps.

"He is not such a bad man," mused Lucia.

"He is a fine man," agreed Giovanni, "as long as he gets his way."

CHAPTER

22

J oey and his father had just finished trimming the fragrant, majestically formed Christmas tree. It was Christmas Eve, and from past experience, Giovanni had learned that if he waited until the last moment, he could get a tree for almost nothing. He had even found them abandoned, the owner gone home for La Festa di La Vigelia . . . the Christmas Eve meal. This tree had cost him fifty cents. But it was the most beautiful tree he had ever found.

Lucia was in the kitchen making final preparations for their own Vigelia meal. It included baccala in a salad with mushrooms and black olives in olive oil, linguini in a delicate clam sauce and stuffed calamari with peas in a thick tomato sauce. Then, there was the tiny, crisp smelts that melted in the mouth and brown rice. A bowl of fruit and a bowl of toasted nuts stood on a shelf. There could be no meat eaten on this night.

When the door-bell rang, Giovanni called to Joey. "It is probably your Uncle Guido. Go open the door." Joey went eagerly, for he was certain that there would be gifts. He opened the door and was greeted by the beautiful, laughing face of Fanny Coyle. She promptly grabbed him and gave him a resounding kiss. Nothing had changed. From the car came Uncle Guido's voice. "Hey, hold the door open. It's cold out here." Then, Uncle Guido struggled up the steps, a large object in his arms. Giovanni was there to help him when he came in. Together, they placed the object on the sofa, and for the first time, Joey realized what it was. "A radio!" he shrieked. Lucia hurried in from the kitchen. Together, the Nocelli family stared at the beautifully finished dark wood, at the rich fabric of the speakers with the finely latticed moldings, the dials. It reminded Joey of the domed shape windows of the church.

"Oh, Guido," moaned Lucia. Giovanni could only shake his head.

"Now, we can see if your new electricity works, John," said Uncle Guido, grinning from ear to ear. He had been calling his friend by the Americanized version of his name since he had introduced him to Sam Maglione the same way.

"Are we gonna keep it?" Joey asked.

"Sure, you're gonna keep it," said Uncle Guido. "It's too heavy to take out again."

"Oh boy!" Joey was beaming. The Fishbaums were the only people he knew who had a radio. Of course, there was the radio that blared out on warm days from one of the houses behind them, but he didn't know them.

Lucia hugged Uncle Guido. "Grazia," she said in a husky voice. He kissed her cheek. Then, Giovanni hugged him. "You are crazy, but how can I thank you?" he said.

"I think there'll be thanks enough when we sit down to eat," Uncle Guido answered. Then, going to Fanny Coyle's side, he proceeded to introduce her to Lucia and Giovanni. Lucia instantly grew a liking to the smiling, friendly face, and soon the two were setting the kitchen table while the men set the radio up on the end-table next to the sofa. Fortunately, Giovanni had placed a receptacle on the wall behind it for a future electric lamp.

Uncle Guido plugged the radio cord into the receptacle, then, with a great flourish, he turned the top knob. The room was instantly filled with an unearthly chatter until Uncle Guido turned the volume down and began turning the selector knob. And after a lot of screeching and chattering, they heard the Christmas music. everybody applauded. Little Jimmy stood in front of it and stared at the box that the music came out of.

They left it on while they ate, hardly reacting to the fading, erratic sound, and when Joey was finished eating, he went to it. He was quickly warned not to fool with it, by his father. Little Jimmy joined him.

At the table, the grown-ups picked on fruit and nuts. Fanny Coyle, her Gaelic features radiantly beautiful, remained mostly quiet. But the adoring look that she bestowed on Uncle Guido was not lost on Lucia. It made her like the girl all the more. Uncle Guido, it was learned, had stopped seeing Clara Cortolani when it became evident that her heart belonged to the young man who had come to America for her. Fanny Coyle had divorced her husband and had moved in with Uncle Guido, and for the first time in months, he looked healthy and contented. He seemed to have put on weight.

"Is everything okay with Sam," asked Uncle Guido at one point in the conversation.

"He has already taken a barrel," Giovanni laughed.

Several hours later, Joey lay awake, waiting for the inevitable sound of the front door opening and closing several times. Through the large, round grill in the floor, through which rose the heat from the kitchen and warmed his room, he could hear the whispers and laughter as they brought in gifts for him and little Jimmy. It had been that way last year and the year before. Santa Clause . . . Uncle Guido had not forgotten them.

Giovanni brought in the new year with shots fired into the air from a pistol he had bought for five dollars from one of the men at work who had been laid off as soon as the bad weather set in. Several other men in the street were also firing into the air, the flashes clearly seen in the darkness. Off in the distance, other shots were heard, as well as the clanging of pots and pans.

Angelina and Tony, from next door, came over with little Carmela and her brother, Nunzio. All the grown-ups kissed each other and wished one another a happy new year, toasting it with wine. After listening to the radio a while, the children grew restless. Nunzio wanted to go home.

"Don't you wish to eat?" asked Lucia. She was already preparing a quick sauce of garlic and oil and crushed dried pepper. In another pot, the water was coming to a boil for the pasta. In a few minutes, they would be enjoying pasta a aglio e olio (garlic and oil), washed down with Giovanni's best wine.

The children wanted none of it. They had already gorged themselves with Lucia's delicious filled cookies and pizzelle, an anise-flavored waffle pressed very thin. When Angelina handed Carmela the key to the house, Joey asked if he could go with them. Angelina looked at Lucia, who nodded. "All right, Joey, you can go. But, you better be good," said Angelina, looking directly at her daughter. "There's root—beer in the ice-box. You can play lotto." She escorted them to the front door and watched as they entered the house. "Keep the door locked," she called. "Don't open it until me and your father comes home."

As soon as they entered the house, Nunzio said he was tired and went to bed. Joey and Carmela went into the kitchen, still warm and cozy from the coal stove. The impish face was flushed as she served Joey a glass of home-made root-beer and cookies. She sat across from him and looked at him as though she had waited forever for this moment. "I feel like we're married people, Joey. Don't you?" she giggled. "You wanta kiss me? Everybody kisses each other on New Year's Eve." In the gas-light, the eyes in the tiny face glowed.

The exquisite feeling, he had felt when he kissed Nicolina Flaviano came rushing over him. "What about your brother?" he asked, lowering his voice, as though the grown-ups next door could hear them through the walls.

"Don't worry, Joey. We can't get caught. My mother has to wait for me to open the door." Despite her bravado, Carmela's voice had lowered perceptively. "Wait, I'll go see if my brother's sleeping yet." She tip-toed up the steps, and in a moment was down again. Joey could not believe that Nunzio was still asleep in spite of the loud creaking of the stairs. Subconsciously, he was hoping that he was still awake. He didn't feel right about this thing they were about to do. Of course, it wasn't as bad as what they had done that morning in his back yard. They were only going to kiss. They had kissed at his birthday party.

"Come here, Joey," Carmela called from the darkness of the parlor. She was checking the lock on the front door. Her parents would have to ring the doorbell to get in.

Joey met her in the middle of the parlor. He could see her by the dim light that filtered in from the kitchen. She did not look so tiny, only an inch or two shorter than he was. "Happy New Year, Joey," she said.

"Happy New Year, Carmela." Joey suddenly felt her lips, wet and splashy, on his. Her hands were about his waist. "Open your mouth a little," she gasped. When he did, her warm, tiny tongue darted in and her lips remained glued to his for what seemed like a terribly long time. Her plumb, childish body was pressed tightly against his. Finally, out of breath, he pulled away. "Did you like it," she whispered.

"It was okay."

"Want to do it some more?"

"Okay." Joey had liked the feel of her baby fat body more than the kiss. He would try to put his tongue in her mouth this time.

She tugged at his hand and he followed her shadowy form to the sofa. He saw her lay down. "C'mon, Joey, get on top of me," she whispered.

"Why?" He had never heard of people kissing while laying down. They always stood up in the movies.

"I saw my mother and father in bed doing it. You want me to show you how they do it."

"Kissing?"

"No, silly. They were doing what big people do to make babies." The girl giggled.

"Will we make a baby?"

"No, silly." Another giggle. "We're too little."

Joey was only slightly hesitant. Would they wake Nunzio up with the groans and moans? He laid down on top of the girl as she spread her legs to accommodate his body. He waited for her to begin sighing and murmuring like he had heard his mother do. But nothing happened except that her mouth found his again. Again, they kissed until he ran out of breath. "Did you like it?" she asked.

"Is that it?" Joey wasn't at all impressed.

"I guess," the girl replied. "Of course, they're naked under the covers and they move a lot and make a lot of noise."

"Why do they make noise?"

"I don't know."

Joey got off the girl, suddenly feeling the chill where their bodies no longer touched. It still remained a mystery, and he was glad. He would wait until he was grown up like his father before he learned to make babies. As they waited in the kitchen until Carmela's parents returned, he wondered who he would have his babies with . . . Carmela or Nicolina Flaviano?

On New Year's Day, Lucia fixed a nice platter of leftover food, stuff that Donna Catarina could easily chew. She found a bottle of her husband's now precious wine and went in to visit the old woman next door. She had not been in to see her since she had brought in a nice Christmas meal for her, and she felt a sense of guilt because she had not looked in more often.

The door was unlocked as usual, and the moment she entered the house, she felt the chill, almost as cold as the outside. "Donna Catarina," she called. There was no response. She went through to the kitchen. The remains of the Christmas meal remained on the table, the bottle of wine empty. The door to the cellar was locked, therefore, she could not be down there. Lucia went upstairs, filled with anxiety. The poor woman must be sick. She went directly to the bedroom. She was trembling from the cold.

Donna Catarina lay in her bed, her crazy-woman face serene and at peace with the world. Lucia could not remember ever seeing her without her wild eyes shining fiercely, insanely. Now, they stared straight ahead, calm in death.

Death must have come recently for there was no smell or signs of deterioration. Lucia looked at the body of her neighbor without fear, for she had seen death several times in her family. She had seen her brother buried when the child was not quite six months old, and her mother several months later. Her father died just before she married Giovanni and came to America. She crossed herself and left to inform her husband.

CHAPTER 23

J oey knew that something was worrying Sarah when he saw her in school, one day late in January. The bright, toothy smile no longer greeted him. Rather, she seemed to shy away from meeting him head on, always seeming to be heading in the opposite direction when they met in the halls or in the school-yard. After school, she seemed to disappear as soon as the bell rang.

One day, however, she approached Joey when he was alone in the school-yard. "Momma wants to know can you bring another bottle of wine?" she said, glancing furtively about her.

"I can't, Sarah. I told your mother that my father couldn't let her have any more. It's almost all gone, then he won't have any for himself. Besides, I already brought her a bottle this week." It was only because Lucia had intervened in the black woman's behalf that she was getting a bottle a week. Giovanni had wanted to stop it altogether since he had made the deal with Sam Maglione. By now, the club-owner had taken just about all the wine he had bargained for. He and another man had been making nightly visits, sometimes two and three, always taking with them three or four five-gallon cans of the precious wine. Only one barrel was left to Giovanni, and that was already almost half empty. Giovanni had already told Joey that he should tell the woman that there would be no more wine.

Sarah seemed relieved. "I'll tell her," she said, moving quickly away.

Sammy found him a moment later. "I seen you talking to Sarah," he said. "You find out what's bothering her?"

"No"

"You want to know?"

They had moved to a corner of the school-yard, away from the milling, screaming children at play. Joey became evasive. "You can tell me if you want," he said.

Sammy hesitated only for a moment. He knew Joey was concerned. "That black guy that used to go there to visit . . . well, he moved in. He lives there now." Sammy saw the look of surprise and anguish on his friend's face, and he wanted to stop. But he couldn't. He blurted it out, feeling the same anguish as Joey. "I think he's bothering her."

"You mean like Freddie was saying?" For the first time, Joey felt the chill of the cold, winter day.

Sammy nodded.

"You're lying, Sammy. How do you know?" Joey cried.

"I was up in the hide-out the other night . . . the night it was warm. And I heard them." Sammy looked around, then continued. "Leroy . . . that's his name . . . was trying to sweet-talk Sarah into unlocking her bedroom door. She was crying and telling him that she was gonna tell her mother if he didn't stop fooling with her. He finally stopped . . . telling her that he was only kidding."

Joey wiped his runny nose with the sleeve of the new jacket he had gotten for Christmas. He had been unaware that Sammy had been going up into the hide-out. It must be a couple of months since he, himself, had been up there. "How do you know he moved in with them?" he asked.

"Oh, he came into the store to buy cigarettes, and he told my father to charge it to Mrs. Furguson because he was living there. And when Mrs. Furguson came in, she said it was all right." Sammy looked at his friend. There was more, but he didn't know if he should tell him or not.

From inside the school building, a bell sounded, muffled because it was inside and the doors and windows were shut. Recess was over. They started back to class, Joey, plainly agitated. "Joey." It was something that Sammy didn't want to burden his friend with, but he had to let it out, else he would explode. "Joey . . . he told her he would kill her and her mother and her brother if she told anybody," he said.

Joey went up into the hide-out twice in spite of the chilling cold in the coming weeks, but heard nothing. He watched the girl, scrutinizing her for a tell-tale sign that something more had happened. But there was no change in the girl's behavior. He began to feel better. Perhaps Leroy had stopped tormenting her.

His relief was short-lived, however. A week later, after a week-end that left the city crippled with eleven inches of snow, Sarah failed to attend school. Joey wasn't concerned at first. He, himself, had not gone in the Monday after the storm. A few students had struggled in, only to be turned back. He went in Tuesday, upon his mother's insistence, only to find that half the class still had not attended. He did not see Sarah. Nor did he see her the rest of the week. And when she came in the next Monday, she seemed to be in a trance, failing to answer to her name when he called to her in the halls. Joey looked carefully for signs of abuse, but found none, the light chocolate skin of her face smooth and without bruises. But something had happened. He was sure of it. He tried to speak to her, but to no avail. Every time he tried, she turned away, her eyes avoiding him.

That Friday, she spoke to him. She appeared to be in a better state of mind than she had been. "You bringing some wine this evening?" she asked. Several weeks had passed and Mrs. Furguson had not asked for any.

"I'll see, Sarah. My father is trying to save some for himself. He don't have much left."

"You tell my momma when you come?"

"Okay, Sarah, I'll tell her." Joey had already told Mrs. Furguson, the last time he had delivered her wine. He would do it again, if his father let him take any more. He wanted to tell the girl that he knew of her plight, that he would tell her mother. But before he could say another word, she was gone, running back into the school building. The last thing he remembered, was her dark, sad eyes looking into his . . . trying to tell him . . . beseeching his help.

That night, right after supper, he took the bottle wrapped in the brown paper bag. "Do not forget to tell the lady," reminded his father. "That is the last wine that I can send her."

Without a word, Joey went out the back door and up the alley. The snow had been trampled into a thin blanket of ice, and there were moments when he avoided slipping by holding on to the fence boards with one hand. He heard an out-side toilet flush and was grateful that his family no longer had to come out into the cold to go to the toilet It was only two years ago that he did.

The gate to Mrs. Furguson's back yard was locked. It was usually unlocked when he had to deliver the wine. He continued down the alley toward the street, looking up at the hole to the hide-out as he passed. He wondered if Sammy was up there. He doubted it. It was too cold. The street was dark and deserted when he came out into it. He quickly climbed the steps of the Furguson house. And before he could ring the bell, the door opened and Mrs. Furguson's honey-colored face greeted him. She held a finger to her mouth, indicating for him to be quiet. She had closed the door leading into the living room, and they remained in the vestibule. From inside, came the sound of snoring. It could only be Leroy, it sounded so loud.

Mrs. Furguson took the bottle from Joey and handed him a dollar bill. "Sarah says you're not gonna bring me no more," she said in a whisper.

"My father's got no more to sell." Joey matched her tone of voice.

"You tell him I'll give him two dollars."

"All right, Mrs. Furguson . . . I'll tell him." Joey turned to leave. The tiny cubicle was beginning to stifle him, the smell of kerosene coming mostly from her clothing. He needed some fresh air.

"Wait, Joey."

Joey turned back.

Mrs. Furguson's face was sternly set as she listened attentively. The snoring had stopped for a moment, then, with a loud, ripping snort, it continued. Satisfied that Leroy was still asleep, she turned back to Joey. "You been up in your hole, lately?" she asked, her voice still a whisper. When Joey hesitated, she spoke reassuringly. "I won't punish you if you been."

Joey nodded. Strangely, he felt no fear of the woman.

"You hear anything whilst you up there?"

Joey shook his head.

The woman stared at him, her dark eyes only now beginning to frighten him. "Don't lie to me, boy," she growled.

"I'm not lying, Mrs. Furguson.

The woman's piercing eyes bore into his. "Joey, you like Sarah, don't you? She a good friend of yours. If somebody try to hurt her, you would tell me, wouldn't you?" she said.

Joey nodded, too frightened to speak.

"Maybe your friend, the Jew-boy, heard something."

"Like what, Mrs. Furguson?" Joey knew what she wanted to know. Should he tell her? What if Leroy made good his threat to kill them all?

The woman hesitated only a moment. "Hebert tells me that somebody fool with my Sarah up in her bed-room. He hurt her so bad she cry." Mrs. Furguson had not mentioned Leroy's name. Did she know who it was? Joey's mind was in a turmoil. If only he could get out. Then, suddenly, Mrs. Furguson face was no longer frightening. Now, it showed the anguish of a mother whose child was in danger. "Please, Joey, tell me if you know something,"

Now, it was Joey who listened for the snores. They came in a regular, steady cadence. "Mrs. Furguson, I did hear something," Joey lied. He did not want to get Sammy involved. "About a month ago, I heard Sarah crying in her bedroom and a man was trying to get in. She told him to go away. He finally did go away, but he told her he would kill all of you if she said anything to anybody."

Mrs. Furguson seemed to collapse. Her eyes filled with tears. "My poor baby," she cried. Without another word, she opened the front door for Joey, and he darted out.

That night, Joey woke up with a sweat. The black giant was in his room, a large kitchen knife in his hand. Had he already killed his family. He let out a shriek. In an instant, his mother was in his room. "Joey, what is wrong?" she asked. "Did you have a bad dream?" She was sitting on the edge of the bed, touching his forehead, tucking him in.

"I'm all right, Mom," he said, no longer trembling. "I just had a bad dream."

"Go to sleep, Caro," she said. "Good night."

"Good night, Mom."

It was a reoccurring dream and went on for weeks.

CHAPTER 24

After Mrs. Furguson let Joey out, she remained in the vestibule for several minutes. Her first impulse was to go to the kitchen, take the largest knife she could find and slit Leroy's throat as he lay, snoring away what could be his final moments alive. She came out, finally, and stared at the huge black. He completely covered the sofa, so that one of his legs was bent at the knees while the other straddled the arm of the sofa and hung over at least a foot. On his back, the snores came at regular intervals, the grating sound drowning out the steady hum of the kerosene heater. Even now, the sight of him caused a shiver of sensual pleasure to run up and down her spine. He was her man. She had decided that when she had let him move in.

Actually, he was a good man, tender to her and her children when sober, which was usually the case. He worked steadily, loading and unloading trucks for a wholesale fruit and produce firm along Delaware Ave. And he handed most of his pay over to Mrs. Furguson. Besides, he brought home bags of fruit and vegetables once or twice a week. Things had been wonderful for the Furguson family since he had moved in. Mrs. Furguson had not missed a month's mortgage payment since he came.

Now this.

Was it possible that it was all imagination? She pondered the thought, as she walked to the kitchen, still thinking of the knife. Sarah sat at the table, the heat of the coal stove at her back as she did her homework. Looking at her sweet, virginal face, deep in thought with a math problem, it was hard to believe that such a thing had happened to her. She had not said a word, But Mrs. Furguson had seen the sadness and sometimes fear that was reflected in her eyes. And when she had asked her daughter what was wrong when she had missed the whole week of school, she had answered that she had been bleeding down there. And Mrs. Furguson had been relieved and saddened. Like herself, her Sarah had gotten her period at the age of twelve, Poor baby, as though she didn't have enough problems, now she had to worry about becoming pregnant.

It was Hebert who had told her that Leroy had tried to hurt Sarah. Pie had heard him pounding on her bedroom door, and he had heard Sarah crying. He was frightened, he told his mother, but he had climbed up the stairs and had punched Leroy on the legs until he had finally picked him up bodily and carried him downstairs after threatening to kill everybody if they told. Mrs. Furguson had found him asleep, the empty wine bottle at the foot of the sofa.

Now, Hebert sat across from his sister, making childish drawings on one of Sarah's old copy books. He felt secure with his mother home, so he drew pictures of a house with a little boy, a bigger girl and a momma standing outside. Mrs. Furguson went to the cupboard and put away the wine. She would have liked a glass of it, but she put it off. She had to think clearly. She went to the stove and warmed her back, trying to get rid of the chills that had been running up and down her back since she had talked with Joey. She looked down upon her children with much sadness.

Why, Leroy? she questioned. You such a good man. I know you love my children as much as I do. Why you talk about killin us all? I know you don¹ mean it. But you scarin hell out of them. And I don't like it when my children be scared. 1 don't know what to do about you, so I goin¹ to speak to my good Lord Jesus. He tell me what to do.

Without a word to her children, she went back into the parlor. She sat heavily on a chair facing Leroy asleep on the sofa. With her back to the vestibule wall, she looked out through the window. There were still small piles of snow from a week ago. Ice was forming on the corners of the window panes. In the light suppled only by the kerosene heater, Leroy looked peaceful and at ease . . . vulnerable.

It would be so easy to cut his throat, she thought. But she had already ruled that out. She knew the good Lord wouldn't want that. Besides, the thought of Sarah and Hebert witnessing such a sight made her stomach turn. She had seen too much of it around her old neighborhood. It wasn't a pretty sight.

She got up, suddenly feeling exhausted from the weight of her problem. She went into the kitchen and sat with the children. Sarah looked up from her homework, saw her mother's troubled face.

"What's wrong, Momma?" she asked.

"I be talkin' to Joey. He tell me Leroy try to hurt you. Hebert tell me the same thing." Mrs. Furguson saw the look of fright in her daughter's eyes, but continued relentlessly. "I gotta know, Sarah. I gotta hear it from you."

"He was drunk, Momma. He never bothers with me when he sober. He good to me and Hebert when he sober. Ain't that so, Hebert?"

The boy nodded somberly.

"You want me to throw him out?" Mrs. Furguson's face was grim.

Sarah knew that all that was needed was her word, and Leroy would be out in the cold before he could completely wake up. She also knew that her mother worshipped him, and he really was good to them, had been especially helpful and remorseful since the incident. He had gone out of his way to make it up to her. He had apologized and bought toys for Hebert and nice clothes for her at Christmas.

"Don't throw him out, Momma." Hebert spoke up without looking up from his drawing, to which he had added a stringy looking man figure. "He gave me some nice presents come Christmas. He say it be Santa that bring 'em, but I see when he bring 'em in and hide "em."

A tiny smile crossed Mrs. Furguson's face at the memory of the boy's face, when he had received the toys. It quickly disappeared. "What you want me to do?" she asked Sarah.

"I think he be all right, longs he don¹ get drunk," Sarah answered.

"You sure?"

"Yes, Momma." Sarah saw the tiny look of relief in her mother's eyes and was glad.

"You gotta promise to tell me even if he look at you wrong. You hear me . . . both of you . . . ?"

"Yes, Momma," Sarah said quickly.

"Hebert?"

"Yes, Momma."

Mrs. Ferguson went to the cupboard, took out the bottle of wine and uncorked it. She poured some into a glass and drank it. Then, she emptied the rest down the drain. "There be no more wine in this house," she vowed, looking at her children. She felt better already . . . a lot better.

Leroy rolled over, causing the sofa to creak. There was a smile on his face. He had heard the conversation at the table, and sighed with relief. It was cold out there.

CHAPTER 25

It was the last Saturday in April, and Joey was still in bed. Giovanni had long since left for work and little Jimmy was already downstairs riding about in his little, red car. Ordinarily, Joey would be up and getting ready to make his rounds of lighting the gas jets for Sammy and the other Jewish people. Lucia had already called up the stairway twice, and Joey had answered, "Okay."

On her third call, she climbed the stairs. This was unlike Joey, and she was now concerned. When she entered his bedroom, she found him asleep. But this was not the sound sleep of a healthy child. His breathing was labored, and his face was flushed, as though with fever. Following the instinct from years of caring for her children, Lucia touched his forehead. Fever. There was no doubt about it. She had felt that clammy hotness too many times. But somehow, she knew that this was not some ordinary cold fever. Joey's body was drenched with cold perspiration. And he was mumbling something about lighting the gas.

For a desperate moment, she thought of getting Donna Catarina. She would know what to do. But, even as she flew down the stairs, she realized that the poor woman was dead and would never help anyone ever again. She went out into her back yard and climbed the first two rungs of the ladder so that she could look over the fence. "Angelina," she called.

Her neighbor came out quickly. This was their favorite means of communication, and there was a warm smile on her face. But when she saw the look of fear on the lovely face of her friend, she forgot about the sugar she was going to borrow. "What is it, Lucia?"

"It is Joey. He has a fever."

In a moment, Angelina was at the front door and upstairs in Joey's room.

"If only Donna Catarina were alive," moaned Lucia in Italian.

But Angelina shook her head. "No," she said. "The old lady wouldn't be able to help him. We must get a doctor.[11]

"But Giovanni has gone to work . . . . [11]

"I will send my Tony. Keep him covered."

Doctor Vittorio Lavanturio was a short, stout man with thick glasses and a fat, ruddy face. His gray, sparse hair seemed to be matted down on his head, and his scalp gleamed through. It was said that he was close to seventy, yet he took time out from his office practice to make house-calls. He came quickly, his office only a block away in one of the big brown-stone houses on Snyder Avenue.

In Joey's room, he worked methodically, almost expecting what to find after his first look at the boy. He took his temperature and checked his chest with an old stethoscope that he took out of an ancient leather case, as Lucia looked on. He had asked Angelina to wait downstairs. With a wide, flat, wooden compress, he held the boy's tongue down and looked at his throat. He frowned. The grayish color 'of the throat and tonsil meant one thing. He probed gently about Joey's throat, felt the tiny swelling of his neck glands.

Diphtheria, he sighed. Another case. He would have to report it to the Health Department.

Lucia heard the sigh and knew that all was not well. But she watched, praying silently, while the doctor injected her son. He had not awakened through it all.

Downstairs, the doctor washed his hands carefully, then sat at the kitchen table.

"Is it bad?[11] Lucia asked in Italian. She knew that the doctor, who had studied medicine in Italy before coming to America, loved to speak in Italian whenever he had the opportunity, even though he had become quite proficient in speaking English.

148

The doctor finished writing out a prescription before he spoke. He looked at Angelina, ignoring Lucia's question. "Did you touch the boy at all?" he asked her in English.

"No," she answered slowly, trying to remember. She was certain she had not checked the boy for fever. It had been obvious, just by looking at him, that he was very ill.

"You're sure?"

"Yes, I'm positive."

"Good. You go home and don't come into this house until the boy is completely well. And don't tell anyone that you were here. Do you understand . . . not anyone. Otherwise they •will have to quarantine your house also. The boy has diphtheria."

"Diphtheria", the word struck fear in Angelina's heart. She had lost a niece to the dreaded disease only a year ago.

Lucia watched closely, not quite understanding the exchange. But when she saw the look of fear in her friend's eyes, she cried out, "Chi e?"

Angelina burst into tears. She wanted to go to her friend . . . to comfort her, but she dares not.

"You had better go now," said the doctor, firmly. "And if you feel anything at all, call me. Do you understand?"

When Angelina had gone, the doctor turned to Lucia. He suddenly felt tired and thought of retiring and going back to Italy. He looked at the lovely, frightened face of the woman before him, and he knew what it was that kept him here. These people, mostly alone in this strange country, needed him. "Signora," he began, now speaking in his best Italian. "Your son is a very sick boy. Luckily, we caught it early, and I think he will recover. He is a strong boy. But you must give him his medicine as I prescribed it. I will go to the pharmacist and come back with it. Then, it is up to you and God. Your son has diphtheria."

Lucia gave a tiny scream—Now, the full realization of the deadliness of the dread disease came to her. Diphtheria had meant nothing to her at first. Now, she remembered the name. Diphtheria . . . the sickness that had taken Angelina's four-year-old niece. She made the Sign of the Cross.

"I will have to report it to the Health Department," the doctor continued. "They will put a sign on your door. This means that no one can come in or out."

"And my Giovanni? How can I help my son without my husband?" she asked.

"I am sorry, Signora. If you husband comes in that door, he cannot leave to go to work until the boy is well . . . until the quarantine is removed from your door."

"How long?"

"It all depends on the boy. Perhaps one month . . . maybe two or three."

"Dio aiutami a(God help me."

"I am sorry, Signora."

Little Jimmy had been sitting in his little car, riding about in the living room. He drove into the kitchen. "Is Joey sick?" he asked.

"Yes, son," answered the doctor. "And I want you to promise me something."

"I promise." The boy got out of the car and came to his mother. She hugged him.

"I want you to promise me that you won't go near your brother until he gets better. Do you know why?"

The boy nodded. "If I do, I'll get sick."

"That's a smart boy. "Don't even go in his room." Turning to Lucia, he spoke in Italian. "Does he sleep with his brother?"

"No, he has his own bed in the middle room."

"Good. We have no problem there," said the doctor. "Now . . . about your husband. You must decide if he is to come home or sleep somewhere else. Do not forget . . . if he comes in that door, he cannot leave. He could easily spread the disease. The Board of Health wants to prevent this from happening. That is why they put up the quarantine sign . . . to protect others."

"Then, he cannot even come in to see his son?"

"I am sorry. If he is seen coming in and out, and the neighbors report him, he can go to jail."

This brought forth a burst of tears. How could she manage without her Giovanni? Little Jimmy said, "Don't worry, Momma . . . I'll help you."

Doctor Vittorio Lavanturio stood up, patted the boy on the head. "That's the good boy. You help your mother when she needs you. And don't forget . . . don't go near your brother." Then to Lucia, in Italian. "Be sure that the boy does not go near him. And you must wash your hands whenever you go near him. I cannot stress this point enough.¹'

Lucia nodded.

"And don't worry about him. He is strong. He will get well. You must be strong. As I said before . . . it is up to you and God." Then, he chuckled. "If you do not feel well however, you may pray to God, but be sure to send for me. Now, let me go get this medicine." The good doctor left then, wondering about God, and the way he played with people's lives. Here was this little Jimmy, so sickly looking . . . you would think he would be the sick one. He had seen Joey doing errands for the Jewish families, and he had seen him at play. He was as husky, as healthy as a young animal. And he was the one who was sick. Perhaps this was one of the strange ways God did things. Had it been the little fellow who was up there in that bed, he doubted very much if he would survive. At least, the big boy had a fighting chance. Now, he would have to pray that the little fellow didn't come down with the disease.

Giovanni saw the large, ominous looking paper that was pasted on the glass of his front door. "Che diavolo (What the hell)," he muttered, thinking it was a prank. He could not read what it said. He tried to open the door, found it locked. He cursed. Never before had he found his door locked when he came home from work. Lucia was always waiting for him. She was always home making supper. He rang the bell, then pounded on the door. He was getting angrier by the moment. Finally, he saw his wife, her eyes swollen from crying, looking over the edge of the quarantine sign. But she did not open the door. Instead, she was trying to say something, while shaking her head.

"Che diavolo," he muttered. He pounded on the door again. "Lucia," he shouted, "have you gone mad? Open this door." He cursed himself for not carrying a key. He had never carried one, in all his years married to Lucia. She always had one in her pocket-book, and she was always home or with him, so there had never been a need to carry one. He vowed to carry one from now on.

Lucia was trying to tell him something. He watched her lips closely, but could not make out what she was saying. It was only Angelina and her husband who prevented him from breaking in the door. Hearing the shouting and banging, they and several of the neighbors had come out. Angelina explained the reason for the sign on the door and what it meant.

"No," argued Giovanni. "I will not stay locked out of my own house. I wish to see my son. I wish to be with my family."

The neighbors shook their heads sorrowfully. Tony, Angelina's husband, finally convinced him to come into their house and talk. Giovanni looked through the glass pane of the door, at his teary-eyed Lucia, and he almost broke down and cried. He put his hand against the glass and she put hers opposite his. He went into Angelina's house with a heavy heart. That night, he slept on Angelina's sofa. It was the closest he could get to his family.

Joey's fever-wracked body had begun to fight the dreaded disease from the moment that Dr. Lavanturio had injected him with shots of antibiotics and antitoxins. Even as he slept fitfully, strange and weird dreams tormenting him, it coursed through his body doing wondrous things, causing immune agents to rise and fight the dreaded bacteria and toxin. Dr. Lavanturio came every day until the series of injections were completed, and after a week, the good doctor smiled with satisfaction. Joey recognized him one day and asked him what he was doing there . . . a good sign. His heartbeat had settled back to normal. His fever had all but gone. "He is well on the way to recovery Dr. Lavanturio told Lucia one day. Now, he must rest. His body must do the rest."

"Grazia Dio (Grace God)," Lucia said. She made the Sign of the Cross. "I have prayed every moment since he became sick," she said.

"I am sure that He has helped." The doctor had finished scrubbing his hands and sat down at the kitchen table with a sigh.

"Do you wish for coffee, Doctor?" Lucia asked. He had accepted coffee before.

"Mrs. Nocelli, I think I would like to celebrate today. I understand that your husband has some excellent wine. Perhaps a glass of wine would be more appropriate."

Without a word, Lucia went down into the cellar and brought back a bottle of wine. She placed it before the doctor, then placed a glass beside it. The doctor poured the wine, filling the glass. He drank half of it, licked his lips, then held the glass up as though for a toast. "God does so many wonderful things, but some are indeed miracles," he said. "Today, I have witnessed two of his best works . . . . Your son's recovery, Signora . . . and this very fine wine." He finished the glass of wine.

Lucia was ecstatic. "Then, my son is better? Can he go to school? What of my husband?"

Dr. Lavanturio smiled sadly. "No, Signora. The law requires that there be two or three months of quarantine to make certain that no one else gets the disease. Even though he is well, he may still be carrying the bacteria. I am afraid that the quarantine must remain on your door until the doctor from the Board of Health sees that there is no more danger to anyone. Only then will it come off and your life will once more become normal."

"Doctor, I have promised the Lady of Mt. Carmel that I would follow her in the procession with my husband and my two sons if Joey gets better. Do you think the sign will come down by then?"

The doctor thought a moment. The celebration wasn't until the middle of July. There was at least two and a half months to go. "Signora," he said, "continue to pray to Her. I think the Lady will make it happen." The doctor got up. "I must go now," he said.

"Doctor, is it not time that I pay you?" She had said the same thing the last four or five visits but always he had waved his hand.

"Your husband came to my office last night to ask about Joey and he paid me. He also promised me a bottle of his wine." The doctor was smiling gently, and Lucia didn't know if he was telling the truth or not about being paid.

"Then, I will fill your bottle to take home."

"No, no. I did not drink too much, as you can see. I will take this. Tonight, I will eat my supper and I will enjoy the rest of it and I will feel like King Umberto, himself."

"You are sure my husband paid you?"

"Do not worry about the money, Signora," he said. "Just stay well so that you can take care for your family." On his way out, the bottle of wine safely tucked in his little leather bag, he passed little Jimmy in his red car. He turned back and stood before him. How do you feel, son?" he asked.

"I'm fine."

"He has not been in his brother's room since Joey got sick," Lucia said. "He's a good boy. He listens to me," she added proudly.

"That's the good boy. Do you think you can get out? of your car so that I can give you a quick check-up? You have to have one every week to be able to drive a car."

The boy looked at his mother.

"Do as the doctor tells you," she said.

The boy got out of the car, and together, he and the doctor went back to the kitchen. He sat on the kitchen table just like he had done the last time.

"Okay, you know what to do," said the doctor. "Stick your tongue out at me."

The boy did so with a grin. This part was fun. But not when the doctor stuck the stick in his mouth. It almost made him gag and throw up the last time. The doctor already had the wooden compress ready and he checked his throat, then touched his forehead and neck, nodding all the time. It was almost like a miracle that this puny, little fellow was not sick like his bigger, huskier brother. "He is doing fine, Signora. Just keep doing whatever it is that you are doing and soon I will not need to come again," he said to Lucia. "And you, young man . . . you can drive your car for another week." He had turned to the boy and helped him off the table. "You listen to your mother, like a good little boy, and soon you will be able to play with your brother again."

"I always do," said the boy, going back to his car.

Doctor Lavanturio saw the proud look on the beautiful face and wished he was thirty years younger. He sighed, gathered up his leather case. "When I come back again in several days, I hope to see Joey much better. Maybe, he'll be able to come down. He must not go out, of course," he said as he was leaving.

Ah, Giovanni, what a fortunate man you are to have such a beautiful wife, he mused as he walked back to his office. Thirty years ago, he was also fortunate. He too, had had such a wife. And tonight, he would get drunk with the wine he had safely in his bag, and he would dream of his own beautiful wife who had died so many years ago. He would dream of a young, dark-haired beauty with eyes as dark as black olives and skin like a ripe peach with breasts as soft as . . . . He sighed once more.

154

CHAPTER
26

J oey came downstairs regularly now, his strength almost fully recovered. And every day, Lucia heard the same lament. "Why can't I go out? I'm better now." Lucia exerted great patience, hugging him fondly, for she was no longer afraid of contacting the dread disease. "It will not be long, now, my son," she would repeat. "First, they must take away the paper from the door. You would not want them to arrest your mother, would you?"

Joey's only consolation was the daily visits of Sammy and the other boys. They came almost every day after school and sat on his step or played in front of his house while he sat on the arm of the chair next to the window and looked out. It was Sammy who came every day, and he brought brand new cowboy cards with the chewing gum still in the package. They talked of school and baseball, and Sammy predicted that this was the year that Babe Ruth would break his own record of fifty-nine homers. And the Yankees would win the American League Pennant and the World Series, as well. But look out for the Philadelphia Athletics in a couple of years. It was 1927.

The other boys came around only occasionally, which was just as well, as far as Joey was concerned. There were things that he and Sammy shared that the other boys could not be a part of. There was a special bond between these two that had never developed between Joey and any of the others. Perhaps it was the way Carmine referred to the Jewish families whose gas he turned on every Saturday morning while Joey was sick. He called them kikes, but not when Sammy was around. But, no, it went even before that. For some reason, which Joey never realized, or even thought about, he had never gotten close to any of the other boys. At any rate, it had not even occurred to Joey that the really big reason was that Carmine and his brother, Johnny and Freddie were always gone during the summer to pick fruit and vegetables on a farm. Carmine reminded him one day when he told him to hurry up and get better so he could have his gas job back, since they would be leaving for the farm as soon as school ended.

It was late in May and the boys were hanging out outside the window while Joey looked out. It was a beautiful, crystal clear day and his mother had allowed him to open the window. Freddie was throwing a ball against the brick wall of the house while he stood at the curb and caught it as it bounced back. "Thirty-one . . . thirty—two," he intoned, counting a point every time he caught it on the bounce. Once, the ball hit a tiny bump in the brickwork and it bounced back on the fly. "Fifty-two," he shouted in glee, counting five points for the fly ball. He continued. It would be a hundred before he missed and lost his chance. The older boys could usually go to two hundred and more before missing.

They first heard the faint hum of the engine in the distance. At once, everything grew still. Johnny, who was now throwing the ball, stopped doing so. All eyes looked upward. Suddenly, the plane, a newly developed mono-plane, appeared above the row of houses along Snyder Avenue. Flying fairly low, it quickly disappeared over the roof-tops. But it stirred the boys into hysterical action.

"Lindy . . . Lindy . . . ." the boys screamed as they waved their hands. Joey poked his head out of the window so that he could follow the flight of the plane. Only Sammy remained calm. After the excitement had died down, he shook his head. "That wasn't Lindbergh," he said. "He's still in France.

"How do you know, smart guy. Maybe he already came back," argued Carmine.

"Nah, he couldn't be back so fast." And Sammy was right. It was two days after the historical flight of Charles A. Lindbergh, and "Lindy" was still being showered with praise by the people of France. But, by now, the whole world was aware of the historical, almost impossible flight, and children and even grown-ups were reacting in much the same way as Joey and his friends. Even now, a grateful nation was preparing a ticker-tape home-coming parade in New York City. For the moment, Babe Ruth and Jack Dempsey and the other heroes of the day were forgotten. The features of the jubilant Lindbergh were on every front page in the world. He and the Spirit of St. Louis had accomplished such a tremendous feat that ordinary people only dream of. And suddenly, Joey no longer dreamed of being a policeman. Now, he dreamed only of being an aviator.

Giovanni had missed the warmth of Lucia's body from the first night he had to sleep next door on Angelina's sofa. It had been difficult for him to understand the reasoning for him having to be apart from his family, and both Angelina and Tony had tried to explain that the city was trying to protect the people that he came into contact with. The quarantine was the legal way of doing it. Giovanni never fully understood how any law could keep a family apart, but he resigned himself to the fact that it had to be that way . . . that he could not be with his wife or his children until the paper came off his door.

In the meanwhile, he spoke to Lucia across the wooden fence that separated Angelina's back yard and his own. It was usually after dark and they spoke quietly. His only joy was the news that Joey was responding well to the medicines and injections that he received. And after the first week, when Joey was able to look out of his bedroom window, he spoke to his son, giving him courage and love. He ached to hold to hold his wife and once reached over the fence to touch her, but she moved back. "No," she said. "It would not be fair to Angelina if you would pass the disease on to her family."

"But you are well, Cara," he insisted.

"I thank God for that . . . that I can take care of Joey and Jimmy. The doctor thinks that it is a miracle that the little one has not caught it," she added, trying to get her husband's mind on other than his needs. It worked and they talked for an hour.

It was three weeks later, and on a night of the full moon, they saw each other's features clearly, almost as though it were day. Lucia looked at her husband across the wooden fence and saw the love and yearning, and her heart went out to him. If only she dared. If only she could let him come to her. Her body felt strange, sensuous. And the moon was full. It was well known among the mid-wives that women are most fertile on the full-moon. She reached up and touched his out-stretched hand. "I will leave the gate open tonight," she said softly. "Will you come when everyone sleeps?"

"Yes . . . yes, are you sure?" he gasped.

"The good doctor has assured me that all signs of the sickness is gone, but we must still obey the law. You should not come into the house, but tonight I must lay in your arms. I must feel your strength."

"Then, I will come to you, Cara."

"Be careful that you are not seen."

Joey heard the sound again. With the full moon lighting up his room, he went to the window and looked down into the yard. He looked into the back yards across the way. All the lights were out in the houses. It was almost one, by his alarm clock and surely everyone was asleep. There was the sound again, the same sound he had heard for the past several weeks. Someone was trying the latch to the gate. He could not see anyone, since the wooden fence along the alley was over six feet high, but suddenly, the gate swung open and a shadowy figure came into the yard. Carefully, silently, he replaced the latch and slid the slide bolt into place. He looked furtively about him, at the upper windows. It was then that Joey recognized the figure. His father 1

He ran to his mother's bedroom. She was not there. He ran down the stairs to open the kitchen door for his father. But there was his mother, in a long, cotton night-gown, already opening it. She turned when she heard him, her face all lit up with a secretive smile. "You must not tell any of your friends that your father has come to see you," she said.

Then, his father was in the room, holding his mother, kissing her face and neck and shoulders. "Giovanni," she giggled, "there is Joey." And suddenly, Joey was swept up in a crushing embrace, making him wince. Then, he was being held at arm's length. "Joey . . . figlio mio(my son) . . . you look so good." Giovanni spoke in Italian, but Joey understood him.

"I feel good, Pop," he said in English.

Then, there was another bear-hug, but it was mostly to hide the tears in Giovanni's eyes. "I am so glad . . . so glad," he cried.

"Now, you must go to bed, my son," Lucia said softly. They followed Joey to the stairway, his father with his arm about his shoulders. Then, his father kissed his cheek and watched as he climbed the stairs.

Joey heard them far into the night, down in the living room. He heard the tinkling giggles of his mother, then the moaning and incoherent whispering. He heard the hoarse groaning of his father, his mumbled "Lucia . . . cara . . . cara . . ." And Joey knew that there was more to making love than that which he had experienced with little Carmela on New Year's Eve. He finally fell asleep, feeling safe and secure in the knowledge that his father was home again. When he awakened to go to the toilet, it was still dark. He looked into his parent's bedroom. His mother slept soundly, her face lovely in tranquil exhaustion. There was a tiny smile on her face.

His father was gone.

Joey returned to his bed, somewhat troubled. He had heard the sound of the gate latch several other times, while he was sick. But the door had been locked by the slide-bolt. Tonight, the bolt had been left unlocked in order to let his father in. Had it been his father, those other times? Had he been checking to make sure that it was indeed locked? He finally fell into a troubled sleep, wondering if he should tell his mother or not. He did not want to worry her. But suppose it had not been his father?

CHAPTER 27

Leroy Davis walk home from his job on Front Street, and his feet never touched the brick pavements. It was a little after seven and it was still light. His shirt stuck to his body, for the June day had been exceedingly hot and humid. And to make it worse, a late truck had kept the men working later than usual. Had it not been for a bottle of cheap wine that his helper had managed to get, they might never have gotten through the day. Now, it was over and he made his way home on wobbly legs.

Joey saw him as he passed his window, large, white teeth bared in a silly, drunken grin. He stumbled on a loose brick and stopped to apologize to it, then continued on his way.

The sight of him made Joey wish he could get out of the house so that he could go perch himself up in the hide-out and listen for any trouble. He hoped Mrs. Furguson was already home. He could not understand how it was possible that Leroy was still living in Sarah's house after what he had told her mother.

Leroy made it to the Furguson house, fumbled with the keys that he kept on a ring, and finally found the right one. After some more fumbling to get the key in the lock, the door finally opened, but only because little Hebert had opened it from the inside. The boy took one look at the grinning, drunken face and ran to the kitchen to warn his sister.

"Why did you let him in?" hissed the girl.

"I don't know, Sarah," said the boy, fearfully. "I opened the door, and he pushed it in before I see what he look like."

They huddled together in the kitchen as Leroy stumbled through the house, into the kitchen. "Hey, Sarah . . . hey, Hebert," he greeted them with a sheepish grin. "Don tell yo' momma, I drank me some wine. I don't get drunk . . . ! just be feelin good," He tried to stand up straight, his huge body wavering.

"We won't tell Momma, Leroy. Just you go lay down on the sofa. We won't tell Momma . . . ain't that so, Hebert?" The girl was trying to hide her fear from her brother.

"We not telling Momma nothin¹," said the boy.

"You two good chillun . . . like my very own." Leroy came closer. He was sincere, not wanting to harm them in any way. But as he came closer, the children could see only this huge, drunken monster of a man menacing them. He could break their tiny bodies with hardly any effort at all. And the incident when Leroy was last drunk was not forgotten. It was vividly recalled by them.

"Don't you come any closer, Leroy," cried Sarah as she held her brother. They were trapped in a corner of the kitchen, and they were getting more and more frightened.

"I ain¹ gonna hurt you two none." Leroy was right in front of them now. He reached out a huge, muscular hand and touched the girl on the head, fondling the dark hair.

With a scream, Sarah pushed Hebert so that he rushed past the unsteady figure. She tried to get by him also, but Leroy had gripped her hair and was now hurting her without realizing it. "Please, Sarah . . . I ain't meanin' no harm," he begged. "Don¹ scream like that." Now, there was fear in his voice.

"Please; Leroy . . . please let me-go." Sarah's head was already twisted in such a fashion that any sudden move could easily break her neck.

Instantly, Leroy let go and the girl started to edge past him. With a look of relief, Leroy moved back to let her get by.

But it was too late. Mrs. Furguson had stormed into the house, finding the front door wide open. "What the hell that door doin¹ open?" she yelled. She was met by Hebert, tears streaming down his face.

"He hurtin¹ Sarah," he screamed. "Leroy got Sarah in the kitchen."

When Mrs. Furguson burst into the kitchen, Sarah was already out of Leroy's grasp, but the fear was still reflected in her features. She ran, sobbing, to her mother. Leroy looked on, his mind unable to grasp the situation that he was in. He grinned foolishly. "I ain' drunk, Pearl, Honest, I ain' drunk. I jus feelin good, is all. He swayed, leaning against the kitchen sink for support.

Ignoring him, Mrs. Furguson spoke softly to her daughter. "You all right, child?" she asked.

"Yes, Momma."

"You sure?"

"He didn't mean me no harm," Sarah replied.

But Mrs. Furguson had seen the fear in her little girl's eyes. There was no need for her children to be afraid of this man, ever again. Her voice was like the voice of doom, like a sentence. "Leroy, you get out of here . . . you hear? I don't want you scaring my children anymore," she said.

"Oh, Lordy . . . don' say that, Pearl. Say you don' mean it, Pearl." Leroy's eyes were wide with fright.

"I warned you about getting drunk." Mrs. Furguson stood, up to the big Negro, her eyes blazing with fury. "Now, you go on and get yourself out of here."

"Oh, Lordy, I think I gonna be sick." Leroy began to make retching sounds in his throat.

"Not in my kitchen, you don't." Mrs. Furguson rushed to the giant, grasped his arm and led him, stumbling and staggering, into the back yard and into the out-house. "You get rid of that slop in there," she said in a steel-edged voice. "Then, you march out that gate and don't never come back. We're through!" She came back into the kitchen, locked the screen door with a hook and eye lock, then locked the kitchen door. "Make sure the front door be locked," she told Sarah. "He not gonna bother you no more, honey."

An hour later, when they had finished an uneasy supper, Mrs. Furguson went into the yard and looked into the outhouse, for they had not heard from Leroy since she had led him there. It was dark, but from the kitchen light she could see the giant practically wedged in the small compartment. He was sitting on the toilet seat and sound asleep. For a split second, Mrs. Furguson felt a tug of compassion, but it disappeared quickly. Best she get rid of the man before he really did get to hurt her children. He was so big and strong that he could hurt them even by horsing around with them.

She shut the door to the out-house, for the night air had become chilly. She hoped Leroy would not cause any. trouble when he awoke. She did not want to have to call the police.

She did not know what she would do if he tried to get back in.

CHAPTER 28

Coincidently, later that same evening, a robbery was committed at Mrs. Levine's house. They had gone next door to the Fishbaums in order to listen to a comedy show on radio, something they did on a regular basis, and when they returned home, they found that their home had been broken into. The thief had evidently climbed a gas-light post next to the Levine back-yard fence and had gotten into the yard. Then, by breaking a small glass pane next to the lock, he had gotten into the house. The thief had concentrated on the master bedroom, finding several pieces of jewelry in a small jewelry box that was hidden under some of Mrs. Levine's fine underwear, but only after ransacking many of the other drawers. Mr. Levine immediately went back to the Fishbaum's house and called the police on their telephone.

Twenty minutes before a paddy-wagon full of policemen swooped down on the big, brown-stone house on Snyder Avenue, Sammy was looking out of the bedroom window that looked out on the wide avenue. Being the last house on the block, his bedroom had this side window that overlooked Snyder Avenue, beside the one in the rear of the house. Across the wide street, he saw the Levines coming out of the Fishbaum's house and enter their own, just next door. He looked at the clock on the bureau, becoming aware of the loud tic-tocing for the first time. Not being able to see the numerals in the darkness, he brought it to the window, and from the moonlight shining in, he was able to see what time it was: a quarter after ten. Exactly like last Wednesday. You could almost tell what time it was by the return of the Levines from the Fishbaums. He smiled smugly. If he were a thief, he would know exactly what time to rob the house across the street. On Wednesday and Friday evenings, between seven and ten, a burglar would find the Levine house empty. The Levines would be next door listening to the Fishbaum radio.

The Snyder Avenue trolley rumbled by on its way to Front Street. It made a stop on Eight Street to let a passenger off. Sammy moved to the rear window. From there, he could see the man more clearly if he came toward his house. He waited idly, curiously, wanting to know who was coming home at this time of night. Not too many people did, not in this neighborhood. He had seen Joey's father go into the alley twice. Maybe that's who it was. But, Mr. Nocelli never came on the trolley. He was mildly disappointed when the man crossed the street and continued out of sight behind the buildings on Eight Street.

But now, another person, a weird, shadowy figure in dark trousers and jacket came into sight from alongside of the last brown-stone house across the street. A flowing, dark cloak seemed to cover his head and shoulders. He looked furtively up and down the wide street, then hurriedly crossed it in a diagonal line, heading straight for the alley.

Sammy eased back into the darkness of his room, watching the man, trying to recognize him. But the cloak hid his face. Only once, when the man turned and looked in the direction of the Levine house did Sammy get a glimpse of his features, but it happened too quickly and the lighting was poor at the moment when the bright moon hid behind a cloud. Then, the man disappeared into the alley, his hurried foot-steps growing fainter as he made his way down the alley. Sammy listened carefully, hoping the sound would end abruptly, and he would be able to determine about where the person entered into one of the back yards. But it continued until it was out of earshot. He would have to ask Joey if he had heard the footsteps when he saw him next day.

He was just getting ready to get into bed, when he looked out and saw Mr. Levine rushing out of his house and ring the Fishbaum's door-bell. He seemed greatly agitated, banging on the door when no one appeared immediately. It wasn't long, however, before Mr. Fishbaum came to the door. He listened intently, then allowed Mr. Levine to go in. A moment later, Mrs. Levine came out on her porch and began screaming for her husband to come back because she was afraid to be alone in the house.

Suddenly, Snyder Avenue was a bedlam, with neighbors from everywhere going on to the Levine's porch, some in pajamas and others in robes. Mr. Cohen, already for bed in a long nightgown, was already putting on a robe when he came into Sammy's room. "Stay with your mother," he ordered. "I'm going to see what's wrong." Sammy saw his father cross the street and go up on the porch, joining the neighbors who were swarming about Mrs. Levine. She had stopped screaming.

Sammy watched the scene with his mother. She had also put on a robe and stood by his side, an arm resting on his shoulder. Every once in a while she shuddered, but said nothing. And it wasn't until the police came in a paddy-wagon and Mr. Cohen came back, did Sammy and his mother learn about the robbery. After watching for a few minutes, they left his room. "Go to sleep. You have school tomorrow," his father said.

"Yes, Poppa," Sammy said. He moved away from the window.

"Good night, Samula," said his mother, using her pet name for him. She kissed him lightly on the cheek.

"Good night, Momma," he said, fiddling with the bed. But as soon as he heard the loud creaking of his parent's bed as they settled in for the night, he went back to his post by the window. A small group of men and women still remained in front of the house, and a policeman was sending them home. They began to disperse and soon they were gone. From inside the house, two men in uniform and one in street clothing came out on to the porch. Sammy recognized Sgt. Petrone, mostly because of his great height. He stood almost a head taller than the two men in uniform. He spoke to the men and pointed to the corner of Eight Street. They nodded and made their way toward the corner. They walked slowly, looking at the pavement and on the porches, as they passed them, looking closely with their lanterns. Finally, they disappeared from sight, turning into Eight Street, in the direction that the man in the cape had come from. Sammy knew that there was an alley behind the row of brown-stone houses, and it led into Eight Street. They would probably search the whole length of the alley for clues. He wondered if the man he had seen was involved. They probably wouldn't even believe him.

What . . . a man in a cape?

CHAPTER 29

Uncle Guido was outside, on the pavement, speaking to Lucia through the open window. He had just handed her a bag of food, something he had been doing since Joey became sick. When Joey came to the window, Uncle Guido stuck his hand out, and he shook it. "You look great, Joey," he said. "It won't be long now; we'll be going to see some baseball games. I'll find out when the Yankees are coming to town. Is that okay with you, Joey?"

"Sure, Uncle Guido. Can we take Sammy?"

"Sure, why not." Turning to Lucia, he asked, "Did you hear about somebody robbing one of the brown-stone houses last night?"

"Doctor Lavanturio?" Lucia asked in hushed tones. "He lives in one of them."

"No I think it was one of the Jew families. The poor people were next door, listening to a show on their next door neighbor's radio," Uncle Guido answered. Joey was 'quick to realize who it might be. He knew that the Levines sometimes went next door to listen to the Fishbaum's radio. "Was it the Levine's house?" he blurted out.

"I don't know, Joey."

"What—time was it?" Joey became excited. "I heard somebody walking real fast down the alley last night."

"I don't know any of the details, Joey." Uncle Guido looked down the street as he heard a door close. The tall frame of Sgt. Petrone was leaving one of the houses. "Hey, here comes my friend, Sgt. Petrone. He must be

167

on this case. You be sure to tell him what you heard, Joey." He waved to the detective.

Sgt. Vito Petrone reached Uncle Guido with long, resolute strides. He was wiping, the sweat-band of his felt hat, then he wiped his face and neck, for at eleven o'clock, it was already hot and humid. The two men shook hands, Uncle Guido having to look up at the pock-marked face that otherwise might have-been considered good-looking. "Been good, Guido?" the detective asked, smiling. He looked appraisingly at the shiny automobile parked in front of the house.

"You know me, Vito," Uncle Guido quipped. "You investigating the robbery?"

Sgt.—Petrone nodded his head, looking at Lucia and Joey for the first time, his height allowing him to look straight into the window. He nodded to Lucia, his eyes resting on her lovely face. "Are these friends of your, Guide?" he asked.

"Mrs. Lucia Nocelli, the wife of my best friend," said Uncle Guido. "Lucia, this is Sgt. Petrone . . . a good friend to have."

Lucia nodded, her smile radiant.

"John Nocelli and me go back a long way. We both came from the same town in the old country," continued Uncle Guido, He turned to Joey. "And this is Joey, my God-child," he said, proudly.

Sgt. Petrone stared at Joey, and the face registered. "I've seen you before," he said, pointing a finger at the boy.

"You came to talk to the guys at St. Martha's," said Joey, excited that the detective had remembered him. He noticed people along the street looking over at them, and he suddenly felt important.

"You were the one who wanted to become a policeman."

Yeah, that was me. But I changed my mind. I want to be an aviator now."

"Like Lindbergh?" All of a sudden, every kid he knew wanted to be an aviator.

"Yeah but I still could be a policeman, couldn't I?"

Joey was anxious to turn over his information.

"Are you the one who's sick?" the detective asked, glancing at the quarantine on the door.

Yeah," interrupted Uncle Guido. "He's had diphtheria."

"Is he allowed to be talking to people like this?" asked Sgt. Petrone with a frown. He had impulsively moved several steps away from the window.

Uncle Guido spoke quietly, moving close to the detective. "The doctor said that as far as he's concerned, the boy is all better. He sent a report to the Department of Health, but you know them. That damned quarantine should be off that door right now."

"You're sure?"

"Dr. Lavatories' office is right there on Snyder Avenue. You can check it out."

"Yeah, I know where. I'll see what I can do." The sergeant was well familiar with the foot-dragging in the health department. They were quick to stick on a quarantine, but taking them down was like pulling teeth.

"I appreciate that, Vito. And I know my friend, John will appreciate it more. He hasn't been with his wife in all this time, Uncle Guido said. He spoke honestly, for not even he knew that Giovanni had disregarded the quarantine more than once.

"We'll have to do something about that," Sgt. Petrone grinned.

"He's got some good wine."

"I know all about his wine. Now, why don't you beat it, and let me do my job?" The detective was still grinning when he shook hands with Uncle Guido.

Uncle Guido turned to the window. "I've got to go, Lucia. Sgt. Petrone says I'm holding him up." Then, to Joey, "You tell the sergeant what you told me . . . okay, Joey?" He waved his hand. "I'll see you later." Then, he was off, wondering at the back of his mind, how Sgt. Petrone knew about the wine. The man knew everything.

Sgt. Petrone loosened his tie as he turned back to the window. And the first thing that he thought of was how incredibly beautiful the woman was. He stared at her, almost rudely. Had the boy not been there, he would have told her so. Sgt. Petrone was not a flirt, but these things needed to be told.

Looking at the wholesome beauty of the woman, he thought that here was the nicest thing that had come out of this investigation. For the past week, he had investigated two burglaries, last night made the third. The previous two had been grocery-stores, and except for twelve dollars that had been in the cash register of one of them, only food had been stolen.

There had been no leads to go on except that they all had been within a four block radius, and they all had been broken in from the rear.

There had been a lead in last night's burglary. The woman, Mrs. Levine had given him three names of people who had been in her house in the past several months and who lived in the vicinity. Joey Nocelli's name was one of them.

"Do you speak English?.[11] he asked Lucia.

"Yes, but I do not speak well." Her voice was crystal clear, as beautiful as her face.

Sgt. Petrone smiled. "I had not heard you say a word since I have been here. You should speak more. You speak very well."

"Thank you." Again the brilliant smile.

The detective almost groaned. God, he thought, how could a man stay away from a woman like this? He, himself, would have probably ripped that damned paper off the door, and they would have to drag him out bodily. But back to business. Enough of these private thoughts. It was too damned hot for that. "Mrs. Nocelli," he said, "did you see or hear anything strange last night?"

"No." Lucia was thankful that there had been no need to lie. Had he asked about the night before, she would have had to, since Giovanni had come to her and had been with her till dawn.

"You sleep in the front bedroom?" Sgt. Petrone pointed to the second floor of the house.

"Yes."

The detective nodded. "None of the grown-ups heard anything because they sleep in the front bedrooms. But, almost everybody who sleeps in the back say that they heard somebody walking in the alley." Sgt. Petrone seemed to be talking to himself. He appeared to be bothered by the heat. He wiped the sweat from his face and neck and wondered why the woman looked so cool. Probably worked in the fields in the old country. His mother and father had done so, and this kind of weather didn't bother them in the least. "Mrs. Nocelli," he said in desperation, "could you get me a glass of water?"

Lucia looked startled. She did not want to leave Joey alone with the policeman. What if he told of his father's visits? He had seen, his father come into the house . . . and from the back. "Joey, go get a glass of water," she said. Her heart had suddenly begun to pound. What if Angelina told? The policeman had yet to go there.

Sgt. Petrone's trained eye saw the woman's discomfort. Her face had suddenly become flushed, and for the first time he could see beads of perspiration on her forehead. And he guessed what had excited her. It was an old story. In most cases of quarantines, the husband, who had to earn a living, had to live outside the quarantined house. And in most cases the man had sneaked into the house to be with his family. The sergeant knew of these practices, and he had always looked the other way, as long as no one reported the person. John Nocelli probably was no different, not with a wife like the woman staring at him with the eyes of a frightened doe. They probably had not even told Guido that he had been to see his wife. Guido was many things, but he was not a liar.

"Mrs. Nocelli," he said soothingly, "I wish you would go get the water and take your time. I want to ask the boy some questions and he seems to have something to say to me. I assure you I will not ask him anything about your husband. All I'm interested in is to finish what I have to do and get out of this heat."

Lucia looked steadily into his eyes, finally deciding that he could be trusted. "Would you like some wine?" she asked. "It is cold from the ice-box.

Sgt. Petrone rolled his eyes. "Signora, wine would kill me in this weather," he said. At forty-five, he knew that he had high-blood pressure. He did not need wine today.

"What did you want to tell me, son?" he asked Joey when they were alone.

"Nothing, I guess. You already know about the footsteps in the alley."

"That's right. A lot of people heard them last night, but only on this end of the block. You know the little alley in the middle of the block . . . the one that comes out into your street? Well, nobody heard anything on the other end. It almost seems like somebody turned into that alley, came out into the street and went into one of the houses. What do you think?"

"Gee, I don't know. He could have gone in from the back yard if he left his gate unlocked." Joey's eyes were wide with excitement. To think that Sgt. Petrone was confiding in him.

The detective nodded. "That's right, Son. But suppose the person lived across the street. He would have to come out of the alley to get to his house. Your friend, Carmine lives right across the street from the alley, doesn't he?"

"Carmine? You don't think Carmine did it?" Joey was shocked. "He's only a kid like me."

Sgt. Petrone hated this part of his work. He saw the shock and fear in the boy's eyes, but he went on relentlessly, "He's been lighting the gas for Mrs. Levine and some of the other Jewish families on Saturdays, hasn't he? When you got sick, he took over the job, right?"

Joey nodded. "But he didn't go steal from her. His father would kill him." Joey remembered Carmine telling him of a beating his father had given him for stealing a dime out of his mother's pocketbook. "Besides," Joey continued, "Carmine would be running. He always runs. And he wears sneakers. The person I heard wore regular shoes."

The detective smiled to himself. The kid would make a good cop, very observant. And he liked the way he was defending his friend. "You can tell the difference?" he asked, amused.

"Sure, 1 can." Joey's voice was beginning to get louder with excitement.

"Lower your voice, Son. I didn't say he did it. But if you were a policeman, wouldn't you be asking questions like that? I even have to ask you if you were out of your house last night, even though you're quarantined. You're a suspect just because you were in Mrs. Levine's house." Sgt. Petrone spoke quietly, trying to calm the boy down before he asked him point blank. "Did you go out of your house last night, Joey?"

"No," Joey answered quickly. He wished he could say that Carmine and the other guys were with him, listening to his radio. They had done so on several occasions, sitting on his steps while he had the radio volume high enough so they could hear. For some reason they had not gathered their last night. "I didn't do it and neither did Carmine," he continued. "But I'll bet you I know who did do it."

"Who do you think did it, Joey?"

Joey looked back toward the kitchen, saw that his mother was still there. Outside, across the street, Mrs. Spinola sat on her steps breast-feeding her baby. Both the baby and her breast was hidden by a large towel. There were others watching them, but she was the closest. All the kids were in school. Still, he lowered his voice. "There's a colored guy who lives in Mrs. Furguson's house, next to the alley. I'll bet he did it. He could have left his gate open, and nobody could have seen him get in or out."

"Mm, next to the alley, huh. What makes you think he did it?"

"Because he's mean. He tried to hurt Sarah . . . that's Mrs. Furguson's daughter. And he told her he would kill them all if she told her mother."

"Kill the whole family?" Sgt. Petrone suddenly felt the sweat pouring out of his body. He wished Mrs. Nocelli would come with the water. But now, he could hear a child's voice inside asking for something to eat. He wiped his face and neck like he had done a hundred times already. Joey had hit a raw nerve. It was one thing to apprehend and sometimes to shoot at a criminal. He had done so a dozen times during his police career. But to him, child abusers were the worst criminal of all. He hated them with a passion.

If it were up to him, he would put them away and throw away the key . . . after he did them some special personal harm, especially if rape was involved. "How old is this Sarah?" he asked.

"She's twelve years old."

Sgt. Petrone stared at the boy. "That is a serious accusation, Joey. How do you know this?" he asked.

Too late. Joey knew he had just put himself into a tight corner. How was he to explain the hideout . . . the talk with Mrs. Furguson. "I just know," he blurted out.

"That's not enough, Joey. Like I said . . . that's a very serious accusation. You could send a person to jail, and all I'd have is your word for it. Are you going to tell me how you know?" He watched the boy intently. For the first time, he looked frightened. "I walked through that alley early this morning, Joey," the detective continued. I saw a hole in the ceiling . . . just big enough for a kid your size to get through. I used to have a place something like that for a hang-out when I was your age. I'll bet you heard something up there. You can hear a lot that's going on in the houses on either side of that alley. You probably heard some things in the other house, too."

"The people in the other house moved out about two weeks ago," Joey said.

"Then you did hear something in the colored house?"

"Yeah," admitted Joey.

"And you are telling the truth about this man?" And suddenly, the robbery became secondary to the detective. He hoped that somehow, the guy was the thief, that the crimes were connected. "What's the man's name, Joey?" he asked.

"Leroy." Joey was ecstatic. At last he was able to do something to help Sarah. "I don't know his last name," he said.

When Lucia finally came with the water, there were small chunks of ice in the large glass. She had chopped several pieces from the large block that cooled her ice-box. She had little Jimmy in tow. He munched on a piece of bread with jelly on it.

Sgt. Petrone drank the water gratefully. He must have lost at least that much liquid in the past hour. He was done with Joey, and he had decided to skip the dozen or so houses on this side of the alley. He was anxious to question this Mrs. Furguson. The name rang a bell. "Your son has been very helpful, Mrs. Nocelli. If he still wants to be a policeman when he gets older, I'll make sure he gets the chance." The detective felt good inside when he saw the beautiful smile of gratitude on her face. "In the meanwhile, I'll see what I can do about that quarantine."

"Please, I thank you very much. I wish to walk in the procession of Our Lady of Mount Carmel. I wish to thank her for Joey. I prayed to her every night, and she has made my son well."

"I'll make sure you get your wish, Mrs. Nocelli." Sgt. Petrone knew the date. The festival was in his parish. He remembered when he had been an altar-boy at St. Nicks. It had been a long time ago.

CHAPTER
30

Mrs. Furguson had slept on the sofa, just in case Leroy tried to come into the house again. She had been awakened by the ringing of the doorbell while it was still dark, and fearing a noisy scene outside, she had quickly let him in. Leroy was completely sober and almost in tears. He also smelled terrible from spending the night in the out-house. All he wanted to do, he begged, was to wash up and change so that he could go to work.

She watched him closely as he washed up and changed at the kitchen sink, the muscles of his upper body rippling. Her body warmed up to his huge body, and she actually thought of letting him make love to her . . . for the last time. There would be time, and the kids were asleep. 'But she knew that once he touched her breast, all her resolves would disappear. The giant was a course but tender lover, in spite of his size. She knew that she would forgive him and let him remain her lover. Sorrowfully, she made him coffee. Had it been another woman, she could have forgiven him. If only he had not touched her little girl.

Finally cleaned and dressed, Leroy smiled happily. His woman was making coffee. Everything would be just fine. "Come payday, I be sure to buy you and the kids something fine," he said.

"Sit down, Leroy," Mrs. Furguson said sorrowfully.

Leroy sat down and she brought him the coffee, like always. "When you come here this evening, I'll have all your clothes together for you. Then you be gone from here," she said.

"Aw, Pearl, you don' mean that. Say you don' mean it." Leroy's happiness was short-lived. "I ain't gonna touch the children no more. I swear. No more drinkin neither."

"Sorry, Leroy. You just can't be trusted. Twice now, you try to fool with my Sarah. And she just a child. I can't take no more chances. You gotta go."

Leroy broke down completely, tears streaming down his face. "Please, Pearl . . . ! love you and them kids like you all be mine. Please give me one more chance."

"Sorry, Leroy. I give you one chance and you screwed up. Maybe, in a little while, you come to visit with me. But you can't be livin' here no more." Mrs. Furguson was finding it easier to deal with the situation than she thought possible. Never really having control of her life in the past, she felt now, that this was really the right thing to do, the only recourse she had. Leroy had to go. But once he left the house, she would not mind him spending the night in her bed once in a while, just like it had been before. All she had to do was to make sure that he was sober. He could be controlled when sober. fie was a good lover, too.

Leroy was a defeated man. Mrs. Furguson hated to see this proud man, with all his swagger, looking so pathetic, but she had to be firm. "Finish your coffee, Leroy," she said. "I want you out of here before the children wake up."

Leroy finished his coffee and stood up. "Maybe, after a while, I maybe move in again? We be married, huh, Pearl?" Mrs. Furguson's cotton robe had parted, and a honey-colored expanse of her breast came into view. Tiny specks of perspiration dotted her cleavage. Leroy knew that Pearl wore nothing under the robe, always sleeping naked. And she had always been there for him. All he had to do was touch her breast. He moved toward her, his eyes riveted on her body.

"Don't try nothing foolish, Leroy." Mrs. Furguson pulled the robe together at her throat,

"Jus' one last kiss, Pearl. You know I always gets one last kiss before I goes to work in the mornin'."

"Not this morning, Leroy. Best you go now." There was a tiny quaver in her voice. Perhaps it was the thought of his hands on her, of her weakness for him. Whatever it was, her voice betrayed her, and Leroy sensed it. Hot dog, he thought. A quickie . . . right here on the kitchen floor. He made his move, grabbing the woman and trying to kiss her.

It was probably the biggest mistake of Leroy's life. Mrs. Furguson fought him. Fearing to awaken the children, she fought with a silent fury, kicking, scratching, trying to knee him in the groin. She had reverted to the ways of the streets, her means of survival. "Let me go, motherfucker," she hissed,

Leroy relaxed his hold on her, fully realizing that he had misjudged his woman, and with a mighty surge, she pushed him back and opened the drawer of the kitchen table. When she turned, she held a long bread-knife in her hands. Leroy took one look at the knife and began backing toward the front door, his eyes riveted on the twelve-inch blade.

Mrs. Furguson followed him slowly, the knife pointed straight out in front of her. "You screwed up again, Leroy," she said, her voice as cold as the steel blade. "You come back tonight, your clothes is in the yard. You get em, then get out. And I don't never want to see you again." Leroy backed out through the vestibule door, then the front door without once taking his eyes off the knife.

When Sarah came down, an hour later, Mrs. Furguson was sitting at the kitchen table having coffee. "Is Leroy gone?" she asked.

"Leroy won't ever bother you again, child. He won't be living in this house no more."

"Is he out of the toilet?"

"You can use it if you want. But if you don't need to . . . don't. I want to clean it out. No knowing what he did in there."

"It's all right, Momma. I used the pot."

"I used the pot, too, Momma," said Hebert, coming into the kitchen.

"That's a good boy." Mrs. Furguson patted the boy's head, "Sit down whilst I make breakfast."

When they were gone, Mrs. Furguson went out to the out-house. She was surprised that there was no mess. Leroy had obviously slept through the night. Still, she flushed the toilet, then went into the kitchen and filled a bucket several times and splashed the inside of the out-house and the surrounding brick pavement. She would wait until it all dried out, then she would use it. It would be too late to go to work. To hell with it, she thought. She had to be home when Leroy came for his clothes. She sat down and had another cup of coffee. She wished she had some of John's dago red.

CHAPTER 31

S he woke up with a startle. She was still at the kitchen table, in her robe, an empty cup of coffee still on the table, and someone, was ringing the doorbell. That son of a bitchin' Leroy, she thought. "Better not be you, fucker," she said out loud. She took the long bread knife out of the table drawer, laid it down on the drain board of the sink and covered it carefully with a dry-rag. "If that son-of-a-bitch corners me, I'm gonna have his cock," she muttered. The thought amused her. The door-bell jingled again, insistently.

When she peeped out along the edge of the curtain, she felt instant relief. It was a white man, probably a salesman, but he looked familiar. She opened the door, holding her robe closed at her throat. They stared at each other for several seconds before the man spoke.

"Well, well, if it's not Pearl Furguson." There was the tiny smile that made you forget the pock-marked skin and made him look ruggedly handsome.

"Well, I declare . . . Officer Petron. What you doing out of uniform?" Mrs. Furguson needed to talk some nonsense. Deep down, she felt a pang of remorse. She hoped that Leroy hadn't done anything foolish or desperate. She did not want that guilt on her conscience.

"Sgt. Petron, Pearl. I made detective."

"I always knew you would. Jake always said you were a good, honest cop."

"Enough of that crap, Pearl. You going to ask me in, or you going to watch me fry out here?" The fiery sun had peeped over the roof-tops and now beat down unmercifully. Sgt. Petron's shirt was wet with perspiration.

Mrs. Furguson opened the door wide, then squeezed against the wall to let Sgt. Petrone in. Then, she shut the door and locked it. The detective let out a sigh of relief. "Thanks, Pearl," he said. "Must be twenty degrees cooler in here."

"Take your jacket off."

"Good idea." He surveyed the room as he took off his jacket. "You did all right for yourself, Pearl," he said. "I was glad to see you get out of that neighborhood. Anybody bother you here?"

Pearl Ferguson sat down before she answered. She knew what the detective meant. He had shown plenty of concern when he used to stop in at Big Jake's saloon, asking Sarah how things were in school . . . if anybody bothered her. Living on the edge of an all-white neighborhood near South Street, the child went to an almost all white school, and "anybody" meant the white kids. "Nobody bothers me or the kids," she said. "They mostly Italian folks, just come over from the other side. They minds their own business." "Glad to hear that. You said kids?" "A little boy . . . Hebert. I didn't even know I was pregnant when Big Jake took off. He was born here in this house. An old Italian mid-wife delivered him. He looks a lot like Big Jake . . . light, straight hair and light eyes." Mrs. Furguson was feeling just fine, for the first time that day. She crossed her legs and allowed the robe to slip open so that a knee was bare. She always did like to flirt with the big cop. He was pretty naive in those days. But she always had the feeling that if she had not been Jake's woman, Officer Petrone would have made a move on her. "You hear anymore of Big Jake?" she asked. "I never did get a chance to thank him for leaving me enough money to take care of us for a while. Everything happened so fast after he had to close down because of Prohibition. Then, he had to sell the property to the mob . . . ."

"The last we heard, he was in Chicago. We lost track of him after that. Seems like he just disappeared."

"Them folks sure know how to make people disappear." Mrs. Furguson's laughter was deep, husky, and Sgt. Petrone recognized it for what it was. Just like in the old days. He felt the warning signal. He was reacting just like he used to . . . what was it seven . . . eight years ago. Better get down to business. He sat down in the chair across from her.

"Pearl, I'm not here on a social visit," he began. "One of the big, brown houses on Snyder avenue was robbed last night, and I'm just asking questions around the neighborhood. I had no idea you lived here."

"No need asking which one, cause I don't know nobody up there." Mrs. Furguson was on instant alert. She knew that Leroy would be an automatic suspect. She would have to be careful how she answered the detective's questions. She could probably send him to jail if she answered wrong.

"I've been questioning people all along the alley, and it seem like some of them heard somebody walking down the alley right after the robbery. They heard the footsteps between here and Snyder Avenue, but nobody heard anything beyond right here. Now, it's possible that somebody came through the little alley alongside your house and out into the street." Sgt. Petrone watched idly as the house-coat opened up a little at the throat. He remembered the woman kidding the customers at Big Jake's about how she never wore anything to bed. Big Jake had laughed, affirming her announcement with a nod of his head. The detective wondered if she was now naked under her robe. "Pearl," he continued, pushing aside the thoughts that were trying to take over, "did you hear anybody walking through your alley a little after ten last night?"

"No, I didn't. But maybe Leroy did."

"Leroy?" Sgt. Petrone dead-panned. He didn't miss the grin that flitted across the girl's pretty face. She still looked good.

"Fella been living with me."

The detective was surprised at the pang of jealousy he felt. He was sure he didn't show it. "What makes you think he heard anything?" he asked.

The woman burst out laughing. "Cause he spent the night out in the out-house, is why." Suddenly serious. "Least, I think he did."

"Want to tell me about it?" The detective suddenly saw Leroy in a new light. Perhaps Joey was right. The black man could very well be a prime suspect. But he didn't press the woman for information. He still wasn't sure how she felt about her lover. She was being a little too open about him . . . offering information too freely. It was almost like she was trying to implicate him in the burglary.

Mrs. Furguson sighed and the robe opened up a little more, exposing more of the cream colored breast. "Leroy is a good man. He been good to me and the kids. But once in a while, he gets drunk and, well he try to fool with my Sarah."

"Sarah?" Sgt. Petrone's voice reflected his anger. The boy, Joey, had told him the truth, but he had not been quite sure what the boy had meant. There was no mistaking what the girl's mother meant. "And you let him get away with that, Pearl?" the detective said bitterly. He remembered the sweet-faced little girl who used to sit on his lap, and he became furious with the woman. "You press charges and I'll make him rot in jail," he snarled.

"I told you he's a decent man except when he gets drunk." The woman's voice was flat. "He try to fool with her once and she locked herself in her room. He fell asleep and don¹ even remember what happen. So, I give him another chance. Then, last night, he try again and I throw him out. He so drunk he fall asleep in the out-house."

"What time did he fall asleep?"

"About six . . . maybe seven."

"And he was there all night?"

"I went out about eight—thirty, and he was sleeping like a baby. I went to sleep after that."

"You sure it was about eight-thirty when you went to look, Pearl?"

"Well, I ain't sure exactly. But I know I went out just before it got dark. I wouldn't be able to see him if I wait till dark." Mrs. Furguson laughed. "Lord, he so black."

Sgt. Petrone couldn't help chuckling. "You sure are something, Pearl," he said. But, he quickly became serious. "It's possible he woke up and committed that burglary. Have you seen him since then?"

"I let him in this morning to clean up and change. Then he went to work. He stink like a toilet."

"You gonna take him back in?" Sgt. Petrone wasn't sure why he asked. Was it his protective attitude for the girl, Sarah, or was he just plain jealous of Leroy and the thought of him making love to Pearl Furguson?

Pearl Ferguson was also wondering why he asked. "Nope," she said. "I told him his clothes be in the back yard when he come back from work. He ain't comin' back in this house.

"Good girl." Sgt. Petrone sounded relieved, for whatever reason. "I might have to take him in for questioning." He looked closely for her reaction.

"You do what you gotta do, detective."

"You sure? I'm not saying we're going to arrest him. He might be out in a day . . . maybe an hour. Aren't you afraid he might come back and make trouble for you?"

"No. I know Leroy. He come crawlin' around for a while, then he find himself another woman and he forget all about Pearl."

"I doubt that."

"Well, it sure won't do him no good to not forget, cause when he fool with my Sarah . . . that's it."

"Want me to take him in for child-molesting?"

"No," Mrs. Furguson said, emphatically, "I don't want the police asking my children no questions . . . no lawyers neither."

Sgt. Petron got up. "I'm going to pick him up . . . . let him cool off for a couple of days. He didn't show you any jewelry, did he?"

"Hell, Leroy ain't shown me no jewelry ever since I first know him."

"There were several pieces of jewelry stolen."

The woman suddenly got up, and the effort caused the robe to open almost to her thighs. Without trying to adjust it, she hurried into the kitchen. When she came back, she held a pair of pants and shirt at arm's length. "They the clothes he had on last night. You can tell where they been."

Sgt. Petrone held his breath, but they didn't smell that bad. He had smelled worse odors than that through the years. He went through the pockets. They were empty.

"Maybe he throwed everything down the toilet . . . drunk as he was." Mrs. Furguson laughed. She was sure Leroy hadn't committed the burglary. It made her feel good that she held no bitterness toward him. She was not a vindictive person.

"You don't think he did it, do you, Pearl?" It was more a statement, rather than a question.

"No. He's a good, hard-workin' man. He's not a thief."

"I don't think he is either. I'm gonna pick him up anyway. And I'm gonna warn him not to fool with you or the kids anymore. That okay with you?"

"I appreciate it, detective."

"Where does he work?"

"Do it have to be at work? I don't want him losin' his job." Mrs. Furguson stood up, showing real concern.

"Now, you don't want me picking him up her in front of the kids, do you? He might get rough." Sgt. Petrone stood appraising her without pretense. With the robe held tightly against her body, he could see her every contour. Her hips had become fuller since the last time he had seen her. Her breasts had always been large. They appeared to have retained their firmness.

"You right, detective." She proceeded to give him the name and address of the company that Leroy worked for. When she was done her eyes looked into his. A tiny smile hovered over her lips. "Well, detective . . . what do you think? Have I changed much?"

The detective nodded approval. "The years have been good to you, Pearl. You know you'll always look good to me." He grinned. "By the way, do you still go to bed naked?" When the woman looked blank, not understanding, he chuckled. "Remember, you used to tease the guys by telling them you always slept naked. Did you mean it?"

"Oh, yeah, I remember." Pearl Furguson giggled. "I ain't put anything on but this old robe since I got up this morning. You a detective. Why don't you find out?" She took a step closer.

Sgt. Petrone laughed out loud. "You're something, Pearl. I don't have the time, but I'll bet you don't have a stitch on under that robe."

"Take you but a minute to find out, detective."

Sgt. Petrone took a step closer. At arm's length, he reached for the lapels of the robe. The woman released the robe, where she was clutching it against her breasts, and her hands relaxed at her sides. The detective drew the robe open. He gasped. Never in his wildest dreams had he realized the wild beauty of this woman he had known for so long, but had never really seen . . . had only fantasized about. Her body, several shades lighter than her face, was flawless, the shade of honey. Her hips were no longer boyish, as he remembered them. Her breasts were full, still firm, with just the faint beginning of a sag. He brought the lapels together. "You are as beautiful as I ever imagined, Pearl," he said.

"You gonna stay?" The woman's voice was a husky whisper.

"Sorry, Pearl. I'm looking for a burglar . . . remember."

"You married?"

"No."

"Come visit me, then."

"I'll do that, I promise. I would like to see Sarah again. She must be quite a little lady." Sgt. Petrone looked good and long at this woman he had yearned for and was now available to him. He almost changed his mind and decided to stay. Instead, he drew closer and kissed her cheek. But the woman moved her head and turned her lips to him. She had to stand on her toes to reach him. Sgt. Petrone's hands slid up and down her hips as though to make sure they were real. When he finally pulled away, his voice was hardly audible. "I've been wanting to do that ever since I first saw you in Big Jake's," he said.

"I know," she answered.

"You knew?"

"Women always knows things like that." Mrs. Furguson pulled the robe tight about her again. "And I want you to know something, Sgt. Petrone." She stared him in the eyes for a second, trying to decide whether she should divulge her secret. "If it wasn't that I was Big Jake's woman, I'd sure find out why I couldn't be yours."

"Why didn't you look me up when Big Jake left?"

"They were pretty bad days for me, detective. I did come to your police-station, but I see all them white police, and I figures you don't want no black lady asking about you. Then, I find out I be pregnant again . . . ."

"You are something, Pearl," he said, his voice full of respect. He picked up his hat and jacket. "I'll be around to see you and the kids, Pearl. I promise."

"Soon?"

"Oh, I'll be seeing you again about this case. But, I promise I'll come for a social visit real soon." He headed for the door, dreading the closeness and heat of the day. He had to make a couple more visits before he went to pick up Leroy.

CHAPTER 32

The last stop was the house where the boy, Carmine lived. He had rung the bell of the house on the other side of the alley right after leaving Mrs. Furguson's house. He had tried to peer into the house through the side of the curtain on the door and the window, but could see nothing. Satisfied that the house was empty, he had gone to the boy's house, directly across the street. He was met at the door by a dark, fierce-looking man with a long, wild moustache. This guy looks like he just got off the boat, thought Sgt. Petrone. The impression was quickly dispelled when the man spoke in fairly good English.

"What can I do for you?" he asked, making no move to invite him in. By now, the whole neighborhood knew that the detective was going about, asking questions about the burglary.

"Mr. Lannoli, I am Detective Vito Petrone. Can I come in and talk? I just want to ask your boy, Carmine, some questions."

"My son is still in school." The man, small in stature, reminded the detective of a fierce creature guarding his den. He remembered Joey telling him that this man would "kill" his son if he ever stole, and he realized that the boy might already be in for a beating just because he was asking questions about him.

"Well, maybe you can talk to me, Mr. lannoli." The sergeant didn't feel the heat too much since this side of the street was all in shade, making it a bit more comfortable. He was already resigned to speaking to the man in the doorway, when from inside the house, a woman's voice spoke in Italian. "Chiedete di lui(Ask him in)," the voice said.

Without a word, the man stepped aside and allowed Sgt. Petrone to enter. He was met by a large, apple-cheeked woman who must have weighed twice her husband. She was smiling. "Come in, come in," she said, with the peculiar accent of the newly arrived.

Looking about him in the shaded room, the detective saw boxes piled on boxes of clothing, kitchen utensils and bedding. The sight was a familiar one and reminded him of his own childhood days when his parents prepared for a summer on some farm.

"Excuse a me" said the woman. "We getta ready for the country." She motioned toward the boxes.

Sgt. Petrone smiled disarmingly. "I know, Signora," he said. "My family went every summer when I was a boy."

There was a sudden interest from Mr. Lannoli. "You went to pick on a farm?" he asked. In the dimness, he did not look so fierce.

"Sure," Sgt. Petrone took off his hat, put his fingers to his forehead, trying to remember. "Oh yeah . . . we used to go to Gennaro's farm near Williamstown. You know where that is?"

"Gennaro? We go there one year. Then, we find a better place . . . more money . . . ." The ice was broken. "Sit down, please," said the man. Side by side, he and his wife looked like the most mismatched couple the detective had ever seen. If he were to stand behind her, he would not be seen. And he appeared intimidated by her. To make up for his inadequate stature, he spoke forcefully, demanding respect. "What do you wish to speak to Carmine about?" he asked. He has done nothing wrong."

"I'm sure he didn't, Mr. Lannoli, Sgt. Petrone said, trying not to antagonize the man against his son. "As you probably know, one of the houses on Snyder Avenue was robbed last night. Now, the only reason I'd like to speak to your son, is because he went to the house that was robbed and lit the gas for the lady on Saturday."

"Is this a crime?"

"No, of course not," laughed the detective. "But, the only thing I have to go on, is some names that the lady gave me . . . people who were in her house. And then, some people heard somebody walking down the alley across the street last night. So far, that is the only thing I have to go on."

186

Sgt. Petrone looked at the woman who was nodding in an understanding manner. He had found out, long ago, that it was best to be honest with the old Italians,

"Then, you don't need to talk to Carmine because he was home all last night. We pack everything last night, eh, Maria?" He spoke vehemently. "I swear upon my mother's grave that he was here all night." He was not lying.

The detective was mildly surprised at the man's defense of his son. He had figured the man to be a tyrant, ready to beat his son at any provocation. "I take your word, Mr. Lannoli," he said, believing him. He found himself liking him. He was of the old school, much like his own father. Perhaps if more parents were like him, kids would be better off when they grew up. Nothing like a spanking when a kid deserved it. He remembered some beauties his father had handed him, and he was never bitter toward the old man. He still had the old leather razor-strop his father had used.

"Mr. Lannoli," he said as he got up to leave. "I don't want you to punish your boy because I had to question him. Do you understand me?"

"Of course, I understand you. I am not an animal. If my son has done nothing wrong, then there is no need to punish him."

"Good," he said. "And if you ever have a problem, you let me know, capisce(understand)," he added."

By now, both husband and wife were beaming. Mr. Lannoli shook his hand. He no longer looked fierce. "You think it's the colored guy across the street?" he asked.

"What makes you think it's him?" Sgt. Petrone asked. He was willing to bet that every person on the street thought it might be Leroy just because he was black. He was surprised at Mr. Lannoli excellent reasoning.

"Well, you say they hear footsteps down the alley. Then, they don't hear it no more. The colored guy comes down the alley and goes in his back yard. And nobody sees him. Simple."

Sgt. Petrone couldn't hide the grin. Everybody around here was a detective. "Sounds possible, Mr. Lannoli," he agreed. "By the way, when did the people next to the alley move away? I see the house is empty." The detective had only one name left from the three that Mrs. Levine had given him: Eugenio Casadante.

The self-styled jeweler had gone from house to house after Rudolf Valentino's untimely death and had tried to sell rings and broaches with the actor's likeness on them. Mrs. Levine remembered that the handsome man had come to her house, and he was such a nice man that she had offered him coffee. They had sat in the kitchen while he had shown her his jewelry. Like Joey and Carmine, he had become a suspect only because he had recently been in the woman's house.

Mr. Lannoli thought for a moment. "A week . . . maybe two weeks ago?" He directed the question to his wife.

"Two weeks," she agreed.

"You haven't seen them since?"

The man gave a short laugh. "We never see them even when they live there. Sometimes we see the show-off walk up and down the street like a big a shot. But the brother and his wife always work and stay inside the house."

"You never talked to them?" The sergeant looked at Mrs. Lannoli. Surely the women had spoken to each other.

"No, we never talk, she said. "The brother come to sell the Rudolf Valentino rings. But, I say no, and he go away."

"We hear them fight a lot," added Mr. Lannoli. "When the window is open, we hear them argue. The brother always say to the show-off to go to work."

As Sgt. Petrone came out of the house, he glanced across the street. He was positive that Mrs. Furguson's living room curtain had moved. In comparison, the house on the other side of the alley looked lifeless, empty.

He felt many eyes on him as he crossed the street and went into the alley. It was cooler, much like a tunnel. There was even a slight breeze blowing through it. He took a closer look at the hole in the ceiling. He had guessed right when he had suggested that Joey had a hide-out up there. It was probably nice and snug up there . . . better than the one he and his pals had when he was a boy.

Near the end of the short alley were the gates of the two properties, almost abreast of one another. He pushed gently on both of them. They were both locked. Turning into the main alley, he looked up at the second floor of the empty house, his eyes well over the top of the fence. The curtain was all the way down, as was the one in the kitchen window. Apparently, the owner of the house had pulled them all down when the tenants had moved out. As he walked down the alley toward Snyder Avenue, he figured that the fences all along the alley averaged about six feet high. A short person could walk the length of it without being seen from the upstairs windows. He wondered how tall Leroy was. Knowing Pearl, he would be a great big buck.

CHAPTER 33

He wasn't wrong. Leroy Davis was at least as tall as he was, and as wide as a barn-door. He saw him from a distance, and he felt immediate misgivings. Why hadn't he brought along more than just one policeman, the driver of the paddy-wagon? The black man looked awesome, as he easily lifted fifty and seventy-five pound crates and loaded them on a truck. His massive muscles, glistening with sweat, were clearly visible under his drenched shirt.

The driver parked the paddy-wagon near the loading dock, and together they approached the Negro. Leroy had stopped working and wiped the perspiration from his forehead with the sleeve of his shirt. There was a look of fearful anticipation on his face.

"You Leroy Davis?" Sgt. Petrone asked, showing his badge.

"Yes sun."

"I'm Sgt. Petrone, Leroy. We got to take you in for questioning. Now, just come peaceful-like and nobody will get hurt."

"Oh man," the Negro moaned. "I didn't do nothin' to them children. No need to put me in jail."

Sgt. Petrone felt a bit of guilt for what he had to do. "This is not about any children, Leroy. We want to ask you about a burglary," he said.

The Negro turned visibly pale. "I ain't never done no burglary," he cried.

"Well, we'll see about that. You just come with us so we can ask you some questions."

By now, the owner of the company and several other men had gathered around them. The owner, a balding, middle-aged man who looked as though he could lift a crate as well as Leroy, approached the sergeant. "What's up, Sergeant?" he asked.

"We're taking him in for questioning." Sgt. Petrone didn't want to elaborate. The less the owner knew, the better for Leroy when he was let go.

But Leroy began to sob. "Tell him I never steal from you, boss. Tell him I a good worker."

"You must be mistaken. I can vouch for this man." The owner went to Leroy's side and tried to sooth him. "This man's been working for me for twelve years. Never had any trouble with him."

"Well, sir, I'm sure we'll clear it all up at the police-station."

"Go ahead, Leroy. Go along with the officer. We'll get it all straightened out," said the man. Still sobbing, Leroy allowed himself to be hand-cuffed and searched, then led to the police vehicle.

As they rode back to the police-station, Sgt. Petrone found himself in a quandary. When he had first seen Leroy's height, he was sure that the man was innocent. Unless, he had crawled down the alley, anyone looking down from an upstair window would have seen at least his head, he was so tall. And everyone he had questioned had been sure that they had not seen the person who was walking down the alley. They had only heard him. The person could not have been more than five-foot-six. Therefore, it was safe to assume that it could not have been Leroy.

However, while searching the black, he had found a gold pendant on a chain that looked suspiciously like one that Mrs. Levine had described as an old heirloom left to her by her parents. If Mrs. Levine identified that pendant, then Leroy had to be his man.

With the Negro safely in a cell, Sgt. Petrone brought out the piece of jewelry. "Where did you get this, Leroy?" he asked.

Leroy had calmed down, and now looked worried and scared, He had never been in a jail before, and he seemed in awe of the thick, steel bars that held him. He looked at the pendant, as it dangled by the chain from the detective's hand. "Oh, that old thing," he said sullenly. "I found it an' I was gonna give it to my woman. But I ain't no more." He sounded as though he blamed Mrs. Furguson for his problems.

"You say you found it, a real gold necklace. Come on, Leroy. People don't find jewelry like that . . . they steal them,"

"No suh. I didn't steal it. I never steal anything in my whole life."

"All right, Leroy . . . where did you find it?"

The black eyed the detective suspiciously. "Well, suh, I be sleepin' in my woman's back yard las' night cause she done throw me out . . . ."

"Why did she throw you out?" Sgt. Petrone wanted to hear the black admit to molesting the children.

"I be drunk." Leroy smiled sheepishly.

"When we picked you up, you said something about some children. You fooling with your woman's children? Is that why she threw you out."

"Oh, no. I wouldn't hurt them children. They be like my very own. I jus' be drunk . . . ."

Sgt. Petrone sighed. "All right, Leroy, we'll get to that later. Tell me where you found this." He dangled the pendant before Leroy's eyes.

Leroy spoke freely, trusting this cop. He had heard some of his friends tell of beatings at the hand of the police while in jail. They mentioned black-jacks and billy-clubs. This cop was talking to him like a friend. "Well, when I wake up this mornin, I smell real bad cause I be sleepin' in the shit-house. An I be wantin' to wash up and change before I go to work. It still be dark, an I bang on the kitchen door. But my woman don' hear me, so I go out into the alley so I can ring the front door. And jus as I steps out of the yard . . . there it be . . . right on the ground."

Sgt. Petrone frowned. "You expect me to believe that, Leroy. You said it was still dark."

"No suh! It don' be dark in the alley. There be a light there by the big alley. I sees real good."

Sgt. Petrone showed his anger. "Leroy, I don't like it when somebody lies to me. I can make it real tough on you . . . especially when you fool around with young children, too. I can send you to jail for ten years for that. Now, you better tell me the truth about this jewelry."

The black began to tremble with fright at the thought of being locked up behind bars. "Oh, Lord," he cried, "I be tellin' the truth, Mr. Policeman. I swear I find it on the ground."

"Where's the rest of it, Leroy? You throw it down the toilet while you was drunk?" Now, the thought did not seem as amusing as it had when Pearl had suggested it, just to be funny.

"I swear I be tellin' the truth." The huge black was on his knees, his ham-like hands gripping the steel bars for support. "I never steal anything in my life . . . I never steal anything in my life . . . ." He repeated it over and over,

Sgt. Petrone looked down at the pathetic display, and he felt suddenly surprised that Pearl Furguson would have a relationship with someone as childish and immature as this. It was possible that the woman was not as strong-willed as she was eight . . . ten years ago when she had stood up to the likes of Big Jake and the drunks who got fresh with her. She had been tough then . . . a survivor. Whatever the case, she deserved better. He left the Negro, his body slumped against the steel bars, fully convinced that he was not the burglar. The man probably didn't even have the brains to commit the crime. But he would have to make sure, later, when it got dark. In the meantime, he would hold him as a suspect on the strength of the piece of jewelry.

He suddenly felt hungry and realized that he hadn't eaten all day. He would get something to eat, then go to Mrs. Levine's and see if the jewelry was indeed hers. Then, he would go see if he could spot it on the ground from the lamp-light only. It would have to be dark outside.

CHAPTER 34

During recess, Sammy stood against the high, wrought-iron fence with the sharp points on the top which prevented most kids from climbing over when the gates were locked. It was the policy of the school to lock the gates after dark. It helped to prevent vandalism. Sammy stood facing the corner where the trolley stopped. The school was also on Snyder, but at tenth Street. Four trolleys had stopped on the corner during the fifteen-minute recess. And each time he had tried to picture what he had seen the night before.

He was convinced now, that the man he had seen coming out of Eighth Street and crossing Snyder Avenue could have come from the alley behind Mrs. Levine's house. But was it the man who sold the Valentino jewelry? Before going to school that morning, he had gone down the alley, to the empty house where the man had lived. It was still empty, all the shades down tight. It was possible that the person had come down and gone through and out the other end, somebody from another neighborhood. He would have to talk to Joey.

Lunch was a quiet, solemn one, as it usually was. There was nothing said about the burglary, and he felt no need to tell them of his suspicions. His father would probably have told him that it was none of his business anyway. He waited eagerly to see Joey, but he had to help his father get some merchandise from the cellar, so that it wasn't until after school that he finally got to see his friend.

194

He spoke to him through the screen door in the kitchen. It was Sammy's idea to talk back there instead of out front, because he didn't want any of the other kids in on this. "I saw the guy that came up the alley last night," he said. "Did you?"

"No, but I heard him. A lot of people did. I told Sgt. Petrone, too."

"You talked to the sergeant? Honest?"

"Sure," Joey said. "I told him about the colored guy who lives at Sarah's house. He'll probably arrest him."

There was a stunned silence on the part of the Jewish boy. "Joey, it wasn't him," he said in a hushed whisper, "it was a white guy, and he looked like the guy who sells the jewelry . . . you know . . . the guy who used to live next to the alley. He looked like he needed a shave, and he looked real weird."

"It can't be, Sammy. You know that."

"I know those people don't live there anymore. This guy I saw wasn't even dressed smart like him. He was real weird looking. He had something like a cape on. But, what I mean to say is . . . the guy wasn't colored. He was white." They stared at each other through the screen door. "And this guy was short. I couldn't see him anymore, once he went into the alley. I would have been able to see the colored guy."

Joey saw the logic of his friend's words. "Want me to tell the sergeant?" he asked. "I might see him again while you're at school."

Sammy thought quickly. It meant the sergeant would have to come to the house and question him. His parents were sure to be upset. Not a good idea. "Nah," he said. "It probably wouldn't mean anything anyway. Just because somebody came up the alley doesn't mean that he robbed Mrs. Levine's house. The burglar could have gone anywhere after he left there. He could have gone up eighth Street . . . up Snyder. It could even be somebody who lives further down on Mrs. Levine's alley . . . maybe right across the way from them. All they'd have to do, is come out of their back yard, do the job, then go back in. Nobody would even see them."

"You sure it's not anybody else you know?" Joey asked, apprehensively. He was thinking of his father. He was certain that he had not come to the house last night, still, he was relieved when Sammy repeated that he thought it was the man from the empty house. His father didn't look at all like him.

They talked for several more minutes, until Joey realized that Sammy's mind wasn't on the conversation. "What are you thinking, Sammy?" he finally asked.

Sammy grinned. "Nothing," he said.

"Don't lie to me," Joey hissed. "You're going into the empty house. You're going to take those loose bricks out and go in."

"Are you crazy? You know I wouldn't do anything like that."

But Joey knew his friend was lying. "Sammy . . . suppose it is the guy, and he's in there when you go in?"

"C'mon, Joey, you know they moved. The house is empty."

"Promise me you won't go in." Joey was still not convinced. "I'll tell you what, Sammy . . . wait till I can get out. I'll go with you."

Sammy seemed to like the idea. "Okay, Joey. We'll go in together." They sealed the pact by hooking their right pinkies together. A few minutes later, Joey saw the loudmouthed woman poke her head out of the window across the way, and he hurried Sammy out of the yard.

CHAPTER 35

About the same time, Sgt. Petrone was showing Mrs. Levine the gold pendant. She quickly identified it as one of the pieces that had been stolen. "You got the thief, already?" she asked, excited.

"No, Mrs. Levine," the sergeant said. "But if this is yours, then we're on the right track."

"Oh, yes, it's mine all right. My grand-father gave it to my grand-mother when they got married. And when they arrived here in America, they almost had to sell it to get some money. But my grand-mother said no. She wanted to have something to pass on to her daughter. So her daughter, who was my mother, then passed it on to me." She kissed the pendant. "I'm so happy you found this," she said, giving the impression that she was not too concerned about the other pieces. She insisted that the sergeant have coffee and a piece of home-made cake. He accepted the invitation.

Sgt. Petrone liked the friendly woman. On the way to Francesca's restaurant, his favorite dining place, he had decided to stop at her house to show her the pendant and to see how she was faring. She had been in a near state of shock the night before, but now looked relaxed and in good spirits. While he waited for the coffee, he went to check on the kitchen door, saw that the small pane of glass had been replaced. In the daytime, the back-yard fence did not seem very formidable. With the light-post right up close to it, anybody could easily have climbed up the post and over the fence. Afterwards, the burglar, had simply let himself out by unlocking the gate. It had been found unlocked after the robbery. Sgt. Petrone went back to the kitchen table and sat down.

"A funny thing, Sgt. Petrone," Mrs. Levine began, as she poured the coffee. She waited until she had set the coffee pot back on the stove before she continued. "Last night, just before we noticed the broken window, I opened the ice-box to take out the milk and some cheese-cake for me and David before we went to bed. And you know something, it was all gone, except for a little bit of milk. Whoever broke in, ate a whole half of cheese-cake and drank almost a whole pint of milk." The woman laughed cheerfully. "I had to go to the store this morning for milk because my milkman don't come again until tomorrow. And they were all out of cheese-cake. But you shouldn't worry. You'll like my cake. It's my David's favorite chocolate cake."

Sgt. Petrone had to agree with the woman. The cake was delicious and hit the spot. Under the watchful eye of Mrs. Levine, he devoured a large portion in short order, and would have accepted another piece had she offered it. Finally finished, he sighed contentedly. "Simply delicious, Mrs. Levine," he said. "It's no wonder that it's your husband's favorite."

"Oh, thank you, Sgt. Petrone. I just love to see people eat. I would offer you more, but I want to leave some for David," she apologized.

"By the way, Mrs. Levine. Are you sure that you had some cheese-cake left over, that you hadn't eaten and forgot about it? This is more important than you think, so think carefully."

"I'm positive." The answer came without hesitation.

"How can you be sure, Mrs. Levine," The detective looked doubtful. "I couldn't tell you what's in my ice-box, if my life depended on it."

"Sgt. Petrone," sighed the woman. "I agree with you. I forget a lot. But, it so happens that I was thinking about bringing the cheese-cake over to Mrs. Fishbaum's house last night to have with coffee. But when I looked at it, I realized that it wasn't enough for four people, so I told David that we would have it before we went to bed."

The sergeant chuckled. "You should have taken it over to the fishbaums's. Better a little bit of cheese-cake, than none at all."

"You tell me about it." The round face smiled happily. She was totally enjoying the sergeant's company.

"Mrs. Levine, there's something I don't understand." Sgt. Petrone was suddenly frowning. "You say you looked in the ice-box and saw that the cheese-cake and almost all of the milk was gone. Wasn't the empty containers still on the table, where you could have seen them?"

"Would you believe it, Sgt. Petrone?" the woman replied, half amused. This thief has to be the tidiest thief in the world. He took a fork out of the table drawer, and a glass from the cabinet, and when he was done with them, he put them in the sink. He threw the container for the cheesecake in the trash-can and the milk bottle in the ice-box. The table was clear when we came home. Maybe he even wiped it with the dry-rag."

The sergeant's blank expression of disbelief made the woman laugh gaily. He remembered that the table had been clean when he had come to investigate the night before. But the woman had not mentioned the missing food at the time. Was it possible that the woman was putting him on? No, he decided. He was certain that Mr. Levine would have the same story to tell, if asked.

He kept the incident in the back of his mind when he left. Now, the whole three burglaries had something in common. The thief seemed to be a hungry one, and a tidy one. He wondered if Leroy fit that description. He doubted it. He had asked Mrs. Levine if she had smelled anything peculiar when she had first come into her kitchen. She had answered in the negative. He was half hoping that the smell from Leroy sleeping all night in the out-house could have been detected in the kitchen. He had smelled nothing strange,

He was certain that the boy, Carmine, wasn't the culprit either. He would never have cleared off the table. And he doubted that any kid in his right mind would have done anything to bring on the fury of a disgraced parent such as Mr. Lannoli.

Was he climbing up the wrong tree?

What about the gold pendant? How did it get into Leroy's possession?

CHAPTER 36

Something drew him to Carlo Fabrizio's shop. He wasn't quite sure what it was. He knew he wanted to meet Giovanni Nocelli head on . . . to see what he looked like . . . to get his gut opinion of him. Why, he didn't know. He wasn't suspect, although he must have trudged down the alley many times to go to his wife. He had never even considered him as a suspect. Perhaps he wanted to see what type of man had attracted the very beautiful Lucia. Was he a handsome man? He certainly wasn't rich.

Carlo Fabrizio and Giovanni were in the tiny office when Sgt. Petrone walked in. "Amico(Friend)." The balding contractor greeted the detective by coming from behind his desk and shaking hands. "What brings you here?" he asked.

Early in his adulthood, Vito Petrone had worked for the elderly contractor. He had worked for him for a year, the sweat soaking through his clothing in the summer and barely able to keep warm in the winter. He had finally decided that this was not what he wanted to do for the rest of his life. He had explained his feelings to the contractor, and they had parted on good terms now. He kidded the man who had given him his first real job. "I come to get my old job back, Mr. Fabrizio." He still respected the man as a father-figure and addressed him as he did as a young employee.

"No, you don't want your old job back." The contractor grinned. Turning to Giovanni, he said, "This man worked for me a long time ago.

But, he is not happy. He tells me that he wishes to be a police man. Now, look at him. He is a sergeant of the police.

Giovanni froze. Someone had surely reported him for going into his home. He barely heard the introduction. "Giovanni . . . this is Vito Petrone."

The two men shook hands. Not very tall, mused the detective. About five foot six. He could walk down that alley forever and he would never be seen. The contractor's voice interrupted his thoughts. "Giovanni sleeps here because his house is quarantined, Vito. He was sleeping next door to his house, but now, he sleeps here. He's a good man."

"Oh!" The sergeant was not aware of the fact. Somehow, he had figured that Giovanni had been sleeping at Guide's apartment. "I spoke to your family, John . . . a real nice family. And I'm going to see that that damn quarantine comes off."

"You come to see Giovanni?" The contractor was suddenly apprehensive.

"Well, yes and no, Mr. Fabrizio." Sgt. Petrone had gotten a good gut feeling at first sight of Giovanni. The man looked like a good family man. He had beamed with satisfaction when he had praised his family. "John," he said, "I want to ask you just one question." Looking Giovanni straight in the eyes, the detective said, "I know that men like yourself who are forced out of the house because of these damn quarantines, usually sneak in to be with their families. I don't care about that. I think every man should be with his family. All I want to know is, did you go near your house last night. I'm only interested in last night, John?"

Giovanni and the contractor exchanged glances. "No, I did not," Giovanni said. "We played cards . . . briscula . . . right here in this room. We played all night."

"That's right, Vito. I played a little bit, too," the contractor agreed.

"What time did you break up?"

"About half past ten," the contractor answered. "I tell them it's getting late . . . we gotta go to work tomorrow."

"You checked the time?" The detective looked about for a clock, found none.

"Sure, I look at my watch." The contractor took a large, gold watch from his vest pocket and held it in the palm of his hand. "Hey, Vito . . . don't you believe me? What's wrong?"

"Mr. Fabrizio . . . I'm sorry. I just had to make sure." Sgt. Petrone gave the contractor a genial hug. "I'm really sorry. What happened is, somebody robbed one of the brown-stone houses on Snyder Avenue, and a lot of people heard somebody walking down the alley in back of John's house. I just wanted to make sure it wasn't John sneaking down the alley to his house."

"You're satisfied . . . right, Vito?" The contractor demanded an answer.

"Sure, Mr. Fabrizio."

Giovanni's voice suddenly registered concern. "Dio . . . it could have been my house," he cried. "Who would protect my family if I am not there?" He grabbed the sergeant's arm. "Sgt. Petrone . . . please," he begged, "please get that damn paper off my door. I wish to be with my family. If this person knows that I am not home . . . he will surely try to break into my house."

"That's right, Vito. This poor man has to live like an animal. He should be home with his family," the contractor added.

"I agree with you, Mr. Fabrizio. I'll get that paper off, even if I have to bang some heads in City Hall." Turning to Giovanni, he said, "I'm glad you were here last night, John. I'm really glad." Shaking hands, he added, "You have a really nice family . . . a smart boy, too." Turning to the contractor, he shook hands with him. "Mr. Fabrizio, it was good to see you again," he said. "You look good . . . God bless you."

"Don't be no stranger, eh, Vito. Come around again," Carlo Fabrizio said, his face beaming. Many boys from the neighborhood had started their working years with him, most quitting school as soon as they reached working age. Vito Petrone was one such lad. He had changed all that, however. After a year with the Fabrizio Construction Company, he had quit and gone back to school. The old contractor was proud of him.

"Maybe I will. Maybe I'll come and play some cards. You still play for drinks?"

"Sure, Vito. You know how we play . . . boss and under-boss," the detective said. "You think I forgot?"

"Good boy, Vito. I'm glad you don't forget."

"I'll never forget Mr. Fabrizio. I gotta go now." He waved to Giovanni and left, satisfied that the beautiful Mrs. Nocelli had made a wise choice for a husband.

CHAPTER 37

Sgt. Petrone parked the police-car outside of Mrs. Levine's house, walked up the brown-stone steps of the porch. He wondered what had possessed the builder to build this one row of big houses with the somber, brown-stone fronts. Even the porches had a short wall and rail of the stone. It gave the houses an appearance of strength, like a fortress or a prison, and it looked out of place in this community of red-brick row houses owned mostly by new immigrants. These were the houses of the "rich people" and were the envy of the neighbors on the other side of Snyder avenue . . . the other side of the track, so to speak.

He was greeted at the door by Mr. Levine, just home from his store where he sold children's clothing. He looked tired, but broke into a smile when he saw the detective. "Libby tells me that you recovered her pendant," he said. "Have you caught the thief?"

"We found the pendant, all right. But we haven't caught the thief yet, Mr. Levine. It won't be long now."

* "Good. Come in, come in."

"I'll only be a minute, Mr. Levine. I want to ask Mrs. Levine one question." From inside the house came the smell of Jewish cooking, of chopped chicken liver. He was glad he had eaten. He didn't like chicken liver, and he knew he would be invited to dinner by the genial, out-going housewife.

He followed the tall, spare Mr. Levine into the kitchen. The length of the house seemed almost twice that of the houses on Fremont Street, where Pearl Furguson and the Nocellis lived. In the dimness, he could see that the furniture was much more expensive and in extremely good taste.

"Hello, Sgt. Petrone," chirped Mrs. Levine, as though she had not seen him in ages. "You got, maybe, some good news?"

"No, Mrs. Levine . . . just a question for you." In the kitchen, the smell was overwhelming.

"Sure. You'll stay for supper?"

"I would really like to, Mrs. Levine, but I just ate. Thanks, anyway."

"You're welcome." She was already opening the ice-box. She drew out a pitcher of lemonade and poured a glassful. "So ask your question," she said.

The sergeant accepted the lemonade. He knew Mrs. Levine would insist. Besides, it looked refreshing. "Mrs. Levine, when that man came to sell you the jewelry, did he act funny?" he asked. "I mean; did he ask any questions or anything?"

The woman looked thoughtful, shaking her head just a little bit. "He was such a nice man, and he couldn't speak very good English. But he was very well dressed. I asked him to have coffee and some cake."

"Libby . . . you mishuga(crazy)?" Mr. Levine exploded. "Somebody you don't even know . . . you bring him in and have coffee with?"

"Don't get excited, David. I know this man. I see him every day, almost. He comes to the corner across the street, and he looks over here like he wants he should buy one of these houses." Mrs. Levine turned to the detective. "Did I do something wrong?" she asked.

Sgt. Petrone smiled gently. "I'm afraid so, Mrs. Levine. You should never invite somebody that you don't know."

"Oh, my." The woman smiled sheepishly. "But he was such a nice man. He even put his cup and saucer into the s . . . ." She stopped. "Oh, my God . . . just like the thief did." She remained with her mouth open.

"You're sure?"

"I'm positive. He needed some room to lay his jewelry out on the table, so I started to pick up the cup and saucer. But, he stopped me. Then, he cleared the table and put them in the sink himself." She looked at her husband, then back at the detective. "Do you think it's him?" she asked, in a subdued tone.

"It's possible." But the sergeant wasn't too sure. Put in the man's place, he probably would have done the same thing in order to make a sale. But he wouldn't have been so tidy after robbing somebody. Besides, the man and his family had moved. What he had been looking for, when he had asked his question, was whether the man had been inquisitive, had looked at some of the nice things that the Levines had. He, himself, had noticed several vases that looked expensive. And the large china-closet with the fancy-glass doors were full with expensive knick-knacks. "Mrs. Levine . . . did this man show any interest in anything at all in your house?" he asked.

"I don't think so. He walked behind me when we came into the kitchen. Maybe he looked around," she answered.

"Oh," moaned Mr. Levine. "Libby . . . he could have grabbed you from behind . . . ."

"Oh, David . . . you're such a worry-wart."

"Are you going to arrest this person?" Mr. Levine asked.

"I would certainly like to question him Mr. Levine. Unfortunately, the man doesn't live around here anymore. He and his family moved away two weeks ago, and I don't where to find him." Sgt. Petrone saw the look of concern on Mr. Levine's face. "But you can bet that he won't be back Mr. Levine," he added quickly. "I hope so," Mr. Levine sighed. "I hope you have learned, a lesson, Libby."

"Your right, David. I'll never let in a stranger, ever again." Mrs. Levine said meekly.

Sgt. Petrone left, after finishing the cold drink, but once again refused dinner.

CHAPTER 38

He decided to leave the police car in front of Mrs. Levine's house, hoping it would give her a sense of security. The sky was just beginning to lose the light from the sun. There would not be much moonlight either, not as much as last night. It was just like he wanted it to be. In the meanwhile, it was still light enough for people to see him go to Pearl's house. He did not want it to look as though he was sneaking around after dark.

He recognized Sarah immediately. There was not much of a change in her face, the hazel eyes, skin as smooth and a little lighter than Pearl's. Her hair was as dark as her mother's, but straighter . . . like Big Jake's. Of course, she had grown taller. This was no longer the small, shy, seven-year-old he had known. This was almost a woman, her breasts already poking out against the material of the thin, cotton dress. He felt an instant revulsion for the huge black who had wanted to defile this lovely child. He wished that somehow, it was Leroy who had committed the burglary.

"Hello, Sarah," he said. "Do you remember me?"

"Yes, Officer Petrone. I remember you. You look different without your uniform."

"But you haven't changed . . . except gotten taller. You're still the pretty little girl who used to sit on my lap and wear my policeman's hat."

The girl smiled at the memory. Turning her head, she called into the house. "Momma . . . it's Sgt. Petrone."

"Well, let him in, child," came the reply from the kitchen.

Little Hebert came running from the kitchen. There was no doubt who his father was. Sgt. Petrone had never seen the boy, since Pearl had disappeared completely after Big Jake sold out to the mob. And by her own admission, she had not even known she was pregnant until after Big Jake disappeared. "Are you really a cop?" he asked, his eyes on the sergeant. "You not dressed like no cop."

"He's a detective, Hebert. Detectives don't need to be dressed like a policeman." Pearl had come in from the kitchen. She had changed, and Sgt. Petrone suspected that she had known that he would be back and had dressed up solely to impress him. And he was impressed. The years had rounded out her figure, made her more seductive than the slim, beautiful girl who used to tease him in Big Jake's saloon.

"Hello, Pearl," he said, admiring her openly.

"Hello, Sergeant."

"You're doing a great job with your children, Pearl."

"Thanks. I'm tryin with the help of the Lord."

Sgt. Petrone was mildly amused. Knowing Pearl Ferguson, he was sure she needed no help from anyone. And she had never been religious. "You getting religious, Pearl?" he asked.

"Momma goes to prayer meetings," said little Hebert.

"That's good. Do you go with her?"

"No, I'm too little."

"This is Hebert, Sergeant. You never met him. You remember Sarah."

"Sure, I remember Sarah. She still is my best little girl. And pretty as ever. She's gonna be a fine looking young woman. You should be proud, Pearl.

"Thanks." Pearl Furguson beamed. "You got homework to do, Sarah?" It was more an order than a question. "Go help her, Hebert."

The children left without a word. When they had settled down at the kitchen table, the woman took Sgt. Petrone's hand and led him to the chair by the window. She sat across from him, on the sofa, her knees demurely covered.

"So you're getting religious," the sergeant said, faintly amused.

"That's right. I'm just getting ready to go," she answered.

Sgt. Petrone showed his disappointment. She had not dressed up for him after all.

"We done with the meetin' about ten," she added. "Just in case you got some other business with me." she added.

Sgt. Petrone could not mistake the invitation. "Well, I have a couple things I want to check out now, if you have the time. But I would like to come later."

"You can come, Vito," she said quietly.

"Thanks, Pearl."

"Did you see Leroy?" she asked, keeping her voice low.

Sgt. Petrone nodded. "We found this on him," he said, taking the pendant out of his pocket. "And it belongs to the lady who was robbed."

"Oh, no," Pearl moaned.

"He claims he found it."

"Well, I believe him. Leroy is no thief."

"I'd like to believe him, Pearl. But you just don't find things like this." Sgt. Petrone pulled the curtain of the window to the side. It was completely dark. He stood up. "I want to see something out in your alley," he said.

She didn't question him. She led him through the kitchen into the yard. "Wait here," he said. She waited by the kitchen door without a word to Sarah and the boy, who looked on with questioning eyes.

The detective opened the fence gate. Several feet down, across the alley, was the gate of the empty house. Without thinking, he looked up at the empty window. He saw nothing unusual. He took the pendant and laid it carefully on the ground. It was clearly visible by the illumination from the gas-light where the two alleys intersected.

"Sgt. Petrone." It was the woman, her voice low but penetrating in the darkness.

"Come out here, Pearl," he called. Then, he moved several steps down the alley to the gate of the empty house. He could hear her footsteps on the bricks of the yard. Then, she stepped through the gate, looking down to avoid the wooden bottom-plate that ran the full length of the fence.

"Oh," she cried. She had seen the pendant and chain instantly. She remained still until Sgt. Petrone came back to her and picked it up.

"This is where he said he found it," the detective said. "I wanted to make sure it could be seen under these conditions."

"Then, you believe him?"

208

"I'm gonna hold him for a few days," the detective said, evading her question.

"That means the thief came through here." There was just the slightest hint of fear in her voice.

"Yeah." Sgt. Petrone did not want to frighten her any further with what he was thinking. It was all he could do to keep from looking up at the empty window again. It was possible the thief was looking down at them at this very instant. Should he break in? The question had occurred to him from the moment he had last talked to Mrs. Levine, He would have to call for more policemen. The house was dark and the man could probably hide in a dozen different places until he got a chance to get away. He could have done it while it was still light, but he had wanted to make sure that Leroy had told the truth about finding the jewelry. By now, he was almost positive that Leroy was innocent.

He made up his mind quickly. He would go to the real estate company who handled the house. It was possible that they might know where the people had moved to . . . or where they worked. It was possible that the suspect still lived with them, although from all the people he had talked to, the reason the couple had moved was to get away from him. Some character, he thought. He just might have enough balls to remain in the house after they left, hiding like an animal, stealing food to survive. This could very well be a portrait of his suspect. If all checked out, he would get his search warrant, surround the house after the kids from the street had gone to school in the morning. With a little luck, the man, if there was one, would still be groggy from sleep.

In the meanwhile, he might consider spending the night right here in Pearl's house. For their protection, of course. He smiled at the thought.

"C'mon, let's go inside," the woman said softly. They brushed against each other in the dimness of the yard. Inside the kitchen, the children were still at the table, the boy eating cookies and drinking milk. The girl was getting together her books, apparently done with her homework. "Stay with me tonight, Vito," the woman whispered. She pressed against him, and Sgt. Petrone felt her lips searching for his mouth. They met and the kiss was long, searching.

She had called him Vito again. A long time ago, when as a patrol-man he had stopped by Big Jake's saloon on a New Year's Eve while on duty.

He had refused a drink in front of the revelers, but Pearl Furguson, barely twenty at the time, came from behind the bar and walked him to the small vestibule that protected the tap-room from the harsh, wintery blasts. She had a pint of whiskey in a paper bag. "Here, Vito, take this. It's cold out there." She waited for a moment, expectantly. "You gonna give me a New Year's kiss?" she asked.

Reaching down, he avoided her lips and kissed her on the cheek. "Happy New Year, Pearl," he said.

"Happy New Year, Vito," she said. Then, she was gone, back to the bar. He had left to continue on his rounds, sheltered from the cold by the bottle and his thoughts of Pearl Furguson.

When they pulled apart, the woman whispered, "Will you stay, Vito?" She too, had remembered that night long ago, for it had been the only time she had addressed him by his Christian name.

"Not now, Pearl. You go on to your prayer meeting."

"I don't need to go." The woman's vibrant body was once more pressed to him.

Had it not been for the children in the kitchen, he would have taken her willing body right there in the tiny yard. Instead, he took a deep breath, taking in the musky odor of her, and drew away. "I can't stay," he said. "I have to report back to the precinct with the police car. I can't leave it parked out all night. But I'll be back later. Is that all right with you, Pearl?"

For answer, she kissed him again. When they parted, she whispered, "I'll be waiting, Sergeant. Taking his arm, she led him into the kitchen where he tousled the boy's hair. "So long, Hebert. You be a good boy," he said.

"Okay, Sergeant," the boy retorted, imitating his mother.

"Good-bye, Sarah."

"Good-bye," the girl answered. She was disappointed to see him leave. She had expected him to stay all night, now that Leroy was gone. She hoped he would.

At the door, they were extremely formal, for the benefit of the neighbors, many still sitting on their front steps, enjoying the cooling air. "I will let you know as soon as we get more word, Mrs. Furguson," he said.

"Thank you, Sergeant," she replied. She closed the door and went inside immediately.

Sgt. Petrone nodded to the people on the steps. Some of the men were dozing off. He stopped at Joey's house. He was in his window, and two boys were sitting on his steps. They were listening to a radio program that was easily heard outside. It was a comedy show, and occasionally the boys burst into a fit of laughter at the jokes. The detective stopped for a moment, burst out laughing at the humor, then left, telling Joey and the boys to be good.

As he crossed Snyder Avenue, he noted that the Levines were sitting on their porch. They wouldn't be going next door for a while, he thought, with some amusement. But the Fishbaum radio could be heard quite clearly, so all was not lost. He waved to them and left in the police-car.

CHAPTER 39

S ammy looked out of his bedroom window and saw Sgt. Petrone wave to the Levines then leave in the police car. He relaxed then, waiting another hour to make sure his parents were asleep. It was several minutes after ten by the alarm clock on the bureau. He quickly dressed and made his way silently out of the house, leaving the kitchen door and the yard gate unlocked.

Making his way silently up the alley, he passed Joey's house, then reached the empty house. He tried the latch to the gate. It was locked. If anyone was hiding in the building, he was still in there. Perhaps when he got up into the hide-out he could hear something through the wall.

Sammy had never been in the hide-out this late at night, and now the darkness became a sinister enemy that frightened him. It was no longer the cozy, friendly place where he had dreamed and planned the future along with Joey. For the first time since planning the adventure, he thought of calling the whole thing off. It's the damn dark, he thought as he crawled toward the loose bricks in the wall. The darkness even seemed to distort his sense of distance, so that he had to touch the wall every so often. Finally, he reached the spot. One of the bricks actually moved in his hand. He relaxed, making himself comfortable. Now, he did not feel so nervous. Instead, he felt a tingling feeling of exhilaration coursing through his body. And his eyes were getting accustomed to the darkness. He pulled out the loose brick. It came out easily, like a tiny drawer. He listened, putting his ear to the hole. Silence.

The half hour that passed seemed like an eternity. And he had heard nothing. When the family lived there, he had been able to hear even the footsteps from different parts of the house.

Through the opposite wall, on the Furguson side, he had already heard Mrs. Furguson wishing Sarah and the boy a good night, sleep tight. "Good night, Momma," they had answered, almost in unison. Then, he had heard footsteps, as the woman went back down stairs. He was glad that Leroy had been arrested. He would not be fooling with Sarah any more. But he also felt bad for him because he was sure that he was not the burglar.

It was impossible to believe that the man could be so quiet, if he was still in the house. Perhaps he was asleep.

But that didn't seem at all logical. This was the time for the man to go about his business. The daytime was for sleeping, in his case. He waited a few more minutes, trying to make up his mind. Suddenly, he was not so sure he should go in. Perhaps he should go in in the daytime, and with Joey. They would surely be able to see better. There would be some light filtering through the drawn curtains. On the other hand, maybe the man had left while he was getting settled in the hide-out. Maybe he was even now gone about his business.

He made up his mind. Taking a small screw-driver from his pocket, he began to loosen more bricks by prying in the joints. It wasn't difficult because the mortar had long ago dried out and had been cleaned out by some mischievous boy or boys, and the prying merely loosened the bricks from the plaster on the inside of the house. Soon, he had over a dozen bricks out and lined carefully along the wall. The hole was big enough for him to crawl through, except for the plaster. There was nothing but a thin coating of it between him and the inside of the house.

Now came another short period of waiting, of indecision. He reviewed his arguments, and once more he decided to go in tonight. He put his ear close to the bare plaster, but still there was no sound. Was the man playing cat and mouse with him? There was the possibility, of course, that the man was not in the house at all . . . had not been for the past two weeks. Then, there was nothing to fear.

He began turning the screw-driver into the plaster, using it as he would an awl. And in a surprising short time, he was through. The plaster was thinner and softer than he had anticipated. He put his eye to the hole, and saw that the room was brighter than the hide-out. At least some of the lamp-light in the alley was seeping around the edges of the curtain. At least he would be able to see.

He grew bolder. He began to gouge out the plaster all around the hole, not worrying about the small amount of noise he was making. If the man was in the house, and he came to investigate, he, Sammy, would have plenty of time to scamper out of the hole and run for dear life. He had even planned to run down the alley in the opposite direction from his house so that the man would not know who he was.

With the hole large enough to crawl through, he poked his head half way through, listening for any sound. He was certain now, that the house was empty, else the man would surely have shown himself by now. He put his arms through and began to squirm through. The jagged edges of the plaster caught at his clothing, but easily broke off. The room seemed empty, except for a shapeless form against the far wall-a box or a suit-case.

The trunk of his body was in the room, his knees and legs still on the other side of the wall, when he saw the apparition . . . a flowing, shapeless thing that let out a horrifying, blood-curdling laugh. "Uccidere il infidelei (Kill the infidel)," it growled. It rushed at him from the doorway as Sammy tried desperately to back out.

The first blow on his head stunned him. The second caused bright flashes in his brain, and he collapsed to the floor, blood running down the side of his head. As he passed into unconsciousness, he heard the shrill, insane laughter, felt hands on his face, turning it. He heard a match being struck.

The nightmare ended in God-sent blackness.

CHAPTER 40

Lucia hummed noiselessly to herself. At last the children were asleep, and the hour was getting near. She had on only a thin robe that she had worn only once before: the last time he had come to her. Giovanni had been deeply excited, but had made love to her almost reverently, as though he knew her deep secret. They had made love silently for most of the night. They had slept, finally, then he had left before dawn broke. But she had not told him her monumental secret. She was pregnant. She had not told him because she had only guessed then. But tonight, she would tell him. Tonight she was sure, for only this morning, she had gotten the morning sickness.

She sat in the darkness of the kitchen, waiting for his signal. The kitchen door was wide open, and a steady breeze wafted through the screen door. She listened intently, wondering why he did not come. It was at least a half hour since she had sat down to wait for him, a half hour past the time that he usually came.

Then she heard it . . . the wiggling of the gate, making the slide bolt rattle, metal against metal. She opened the screen door carefully and closed it soundlessly behind her. She walked silently, barefooted, on the bricks of the yard. She whispered into the darkness as she reached the gate. "Giovanni, is it you?" She remembered the burglary of the night before.

"Yes," came the muffled reply.

She slid open the well-oiled slide-bolt and opened the gate.

Before she could scream, a figure in a burnoose-like cape and hood rushed in and grabbed her. Putting a long, slim kitchen knife to her throat, he whispered, "Silenzio." Then, with one hand holding the knife to her throat, he locked the gate with the other. He motioned her to the kitchen.

The short walk to the kitchen was the most horrifying moment of Lucia's life. Her legs felt as though they would crumble beneath her at any moment and when the man ordered her to sit at the kitchen table, she did so gratefully. He had not tried to harm her, she reflected, after the first shock. He had walked behind her without touching her, as though afraid of doing so. But now, he threatened her, speaking in the eloquent Italian that she quickly recognized. "Do as I say, or I shall cut off your pretty head," he said.

He stuck the knife into his belt and lit the electric light-bulb hanging over the kitchen table. He stood in front of her, arms folded across his chest. "At last we are alone, my love . . . my slave," he said. "Don't you know who I am?"

In spite of the unkempt two-week old beard and the odd cape of deep maroon, Lucia had recognized him immediately, mostly because of his beautiful and flawless enunciation of the Italian language. It was the man who sold the Valentino jewelry. Diomio (My God)," she thought, keeping her wits about her. The man actually thinks that he is the great Valentino. She now recognized the costume, the posturing. It was from a scene she had seen twice in the theatre. It was from a scene from "The Sheik."

Now, totally in command of her wits, she answered him. "Of course I recognize you, my master," she said, in Italian. "You are my sheik." Her voice trembled. "But you frightened me."

The man seemed to relax. "Ah, no, my darling. You need not fear, for I would not harm a hair of your beautiful head." The man brought himself to his full height, and for a moment, Lucia thought she saw a slight resemblance to the great actor. His wild eyes glared at her. "I have searched for you all of my life. And now that I have found you, I will make you my virgin bride." he said.

"Yes master, Lucia knew that she had to keep the man occupied. She no longer feared for herself. She was sure that he would not harm her. But she feared for her children . . . if Joey should awaken and come down abruptly . . . . And what if her Giovanni came now? Seeing the light on

216

in the kitchen, he was certain to know that there was something wrong if she did not open the gate for him. He might come bursting in and get hurt. Perhaps, if she could somehow get rid of the knife. She was sure that Giovanni could overcome the man. "Madonna mia, give me strength," she prayed, as she decided to help the man play out his wild fantasy. "You look famished, my master," she said. "I will feed you. I have food and wine." A thought came to her. Perhaps she could get him drunk and he might fall asleep.

"Yes, you must feed me," said the man, suddenly showing signs of fatigue. "I have not eaten well, I will eat, then I will take you to my tent,[11]

"As you wish, master. Lucia got up and went to the side-board. She came back with a glass and a bottle of wine and set them on the table. "Sit down, master, and I will get food," she said. She hoped that the man would not be inflamed by the sight of her fear-thickened nipples that probed against the thin cloth of her robe.

He sat down quickly his hunger now foremost on his mind.

Lucia got a large piece of cheese out of the ice-box and a loaf of round, crusty bread out of the bread box and brought them to the table. Guido had brought them yesterday morning and still had the aroma of freshness about them. She set them before the man. He had already emptied the glass of wine. She refilled it and stood before him in a position of servitude. And just as she had hoped for, the man took his own knife from his belt and proceeded to cut large chunks of cheese and bread. He ate as one who was famished, washing down each mouthful with wine. Lucia kept filling his glass. "You must eat hearty, for it is a long journey to your tent," she said.

"It is no great distance." There was a cunning smile on the man's face as he stopped eating for a moment. "We cannot go there immediately, however, for it is under siege."

"They have attacked your tent?" Lucia's heart suddenly began to pound furiously. Standing before the man, she could see through the doorway into the living room. There, at the foot of the stairs, stood Joey, looking on, his eyes reflecting the questioning uncertainty of what he was witnessing. She needed to warn him not to try anything foolishly heroic. "How did you manage to escape them?" she continued, thankful that the man sat with his back to her son.

"I killed one of them . . . a mere boy," he snorted. "The fools have sent children to fight a man's battle. But I struck him down as he tried to tunnel into my tent." The man's cunning eyes were on Lucia, 'absorbing her beauty. "But it matters not that they have invaded my camp. I have conquered this magnificent castle." He looked about him, admiring his conquest. "And of course, I have you, my beautiful virgin. Come, sit with me, for soon I will make you my wife."

"Very well, my master. But first I must go for more wine." She poured the remainder of the bottle into his glass, "May I not eat and drink with you?"

"Of course." He began to cut another slice of bread.

"It is down in the wine-cellar, my master."

"Go, then." There was a noticeable slurring of his words and Lucia noticed it. Her plan was working. As she passed momentarily behind the man, she motioned for Joey to go for help with a wave of her hand, pointing it toward next door where Angelina lived. Then, she went down into the cellar.

CHAPTER
41

Joey saw his mother's hand-motion. It was clearly a signal to go next door for help. But, should he leave his mother and his brother at the mercy of this man? He hesitated momentarily, trying to make up his mind. He had seen the knife in the man's hand and knew he was no match for him. Also, he had heard the man bragging about striking down a child . . . killing him. Sammy? Had he tried to get into the empty house through the loose bricks? The man had mentioned that the boy had tried to tunnel into his tent. Was he dead?

Suddenly, Joey hated this man more than anyone in the world . . . even Leroy, for what he had done to Sarah. He knew what he must do. Making his way slowly up the stairs, he went into his parent's bedroom, opened the top drawer of the bureau. Digging down under a pile of socks and underwear, he felt about until he found it. Now, he needed the shells. He felt around some more, but couldn't find the small box that contained them. He knew that the revolver was not loaded. His father had told him so, once when he had to work at night for a week. He had shown him where it was and how to load it and fire it. "Do not ever use it except if your mother and Jimmy are threatened," he had instructed Joey. And Joey had felt elated when he felt the thirty-two caliber revolver in his hand. None of his friends had ever held a gun in their hand. Of this, he was positive.

But the gun was not loaded his father had shown him where the shells were. He kept them separated, he told him, in case a thief finds the gun. He would still have to search for the shells.

But where were they? He racked his brain, picturing that day when his father had entrusted him with the protection of his family. Then, he remembered. The high bureau across the room. "So little Jimmy can't reach them," his father had said.

Joey found them easily in the top drawer. Then, standing by the window, where he could see better, he loaded the revolver, the tension in his body mounting. He was about to shoot a man. Would he be able to do it? They did it so easily in the movies. He could hear his mother's laughter downstairs, but he recognized the fear, the false hilarity. He knew what she was up to. She was trying to get the man drunk. His father usually fell asleep after drinking too much wine. Hopefully the man would. If he didn't, he would be ready.

He crawled down the steps, stepping gingerly where he knew the stairs would creak. He heard the man's voice, thick with emotion. "Enough wine, woman. Come here to me." There was the sound of struggling.

"Finish your wine before it spills. Lucia's voice was now shrill with fear.

With one arm about Lucia's waist, the man emptied his glass just as Joey reached the bottom of the stairs. He was now able to see into the kitchen. The man was trying to kiss his mother as she twisted her head back and forth, trying to avoid his lips. Her robe had opened and one of her breasts was perilously close to becoming bare. And the man was reaching for it with his free hand. His mother had become a wild woman, struggling furiously. She fought him silently, praying that little Jimmy wouldn't wake up, praying that Giovanni would come . . . that Joey would come with help . . . . Suddenly, freeing one hand, she raked the man's face, trying to gouge his eyes out, in her fury.

The man screamed as blood quickly surfaced on his face . . . his beautiful, handsome face. He let go of Lucia and his hands flew to his face, touching his torn skin, coming away with his own blood. He looked with horror at his bloodstained hands, Lucia forgotten. "Oh, my God," he screamed. "Whore . . . what have you done?"

Lucia had twisted away from him, picked up the knife and held it, blade pointing at him. She glared at him defiantly, eyes blazing as his body tensed for a rush at her.

At that moment, Joey stepped into the kitchen. The revolver was leveled at the man's head. "Don't move or I'11 kill you," he screamed.

The man stood on unsteady legs. The wine had finally taken its toll. "So they send more children to do battle," he growled. With a flourish, he flung his chair aside. "We will see if you dare to kill Valentino, the Sheik." He started toward Joey. **fc.**

CHAPTER
42

Sgt. Petrone stopped in at Carlo Fabrizio's shop. With several hours to spare before visiting Pearl Furguson, he had decided to spend some time with the men, perhaps get into one of the friendly games and have a couple of glasses of wine to fortify himself. The reason . . . he was not certain that he was about to do the right thing. It certainly would not help his career. It might even hinder it. It was well known how the powers that be in the police hierarchy felt about mixed racial relationships, especially now, since there had been several racial incidents nationwide that had resulted in several deaths. But the sight of Pearl, that afternoon, had sent the blood coursing through his veins, and had rekindled a flame that had been dormant since the days, long ago, in Jake's saloon. She had been unattainable then. Now, she was not. Even now, as he played with the men, he could think of nothing other than the ivory-hued body of the woman. Several times, his partner had chided him for not keeping his mind on the game, thereby losing it. He took the criticism and the good-natured kidding and laughed and joked with the men. And he got his share of drinks. For in the game "Padrone e sote . . . boss and underboss," one could lose and pay for the bottle of wine, but then, a boss and underboss was chosen by a one hand deal of the cards. And it was these two who dispensed the glasses of wine to whoever they pleased. So it was that Sgt. Petrone had a drink in all the games that he played in, the men all wishing to stay in the good graces of the detective.

In the back of his mind, lurked another consideration. It had been over two years since his divorce, and except for several disastrous meetings with known prostitutes, he had been as chaste as a new born babe. And now, it left him questioning his manhood. Here was a ripe, vital woman who had been bedding with a big, vigorous buck, and he was trying to replace him. He had heard of the capabilities of black men, and he was certain that he could never compare with Leroy. So where did that leave him? Would he make a total jack-ass of himself? This bothered him. He could picture Pearl laughing at him, like one whore he had slept with. Or her pleading for something that he might not be able to give her. So he made his mistakes in the card games and took the kidding and drank the wine that the under-boss offered him and the boss permitted.

It was getting close to eleven, and he could see that Giovanni was getting fidgety. They no longer played cards, and most of the men had gone home. Carlo Fabrizio had stopped in and watched the play for a while. He had been pleasantly surprised that the detective had visited his shop again. He had left at ten, giving his customary suggestion that they break it up and get some sleep. They had played another game after he left. Now, there was only the detective, Giovanni and another man. It was not necessary to be a detective, to guess that Giovanni was going to visit his wife this night. He was only waiting for Sgt. Petrone to leave before he made his way home. The other man lived near him, and he was going to walk the several blocks with him.

"If you are going to visit your wife, 1 will be glad to give you a ride in my car," Sgt. Petrone said, in the best Italian that he had learned from his parents.

It caught Giovanni off guard. Was this a trap? "You know that I cannot go to my house, Sgt. Petrone," he said. "You know that my house is quarantined." He had learned the word well and detested it.

"I understand, my friend. And you will not have to worry about it, ever again. For tonight, I will take the damned thing down. Of course, I will not do this if you do not want me to." The sergeant winked at the other man.

It was the wine speaking, thought Giovanni. "Please do not play with me, Sgt. Petrone," begged Giovanni. "If you would do this for me, I would be forever in your debt."

"I was thinking of a bottle of your best wine."

"You shall have that too." Giovanni was elated. There was no more reason for pretense. "Vincenzo, here, was going to walk with me. We live near one another."

"Come along, Vincenzo." Sgt. Petrone was happy, the wine making him do preposterous things. "Tonight, Giovanni, you will walk into your home through the front door."

"Grazia Dio (Grace God)," said Giovanni.

Soon, they had left the man off at his house and parked in front of Giovanni's house. He would go in for his bottle of wine, then he would be off to visit Pearl, mused the detective. He felt marvelous. Tonight, he could do no wrong,

"Lucia will be waiting for me in the kitchen. She must be worried because I have not come sooner, Giovanni said. "I will surprise her."

On the top step, Sgt. Petrone motioned to the quarantine on the inside of the door. "Would you like the honor, my friend?"

"No," said Giovanni, searching for his key. "It is best that you do it. It will be such a surprise for her."

Then they heard Joey's scream. "Don't move or I'll kill you." It was faint, coming from inside the house, but quite clear.

Sgt. Petrone was the first to enter, silently, motioning for Giovanni to stay back in the vestibule. He had his revolver drawn. He saw the boy's back first, defiant, just inside the kitchen door. He could not see anyone else yet. Then, he heard the man's voice, thick with wine. "So they send more children to do battle." Then he heard a chair being thrown aside, "We will see if you dare to kill Valentino, the Sheik," the man continued.

Oh, Lord, Sgt. Petrone thought. A nut! He made his way toward the kitchen, slowly, carefully, fearful that any sound on his part would cause the boy to turn on him with whatever weapon he might have.

"You better stop or I'll shoot, Mr. Casadante.

"Don't you take another step." The boy's voice was firm, with no sign of fear.

Sgt. Petrone stopped in his tracks. It was worse than he thought. The damned kid had a gun. God only knew what his reaction would be to a voice behind him. If the kid began firing, should he return the fire. He was still too far away to rush him. Not tonight, Vito, he thought. Let's not get shot by a kid. Then, he heard the booming voice of Giovanni.

"Don't shoot Joey. Me and Sgt. Petrone are here."

Joey's body seemed to go limp, and he half turned, a look of relief on his face. At once, the sergeant reached the boy. "Nice going, kid," he said, soothingly. He took the revolver from the boy, whose hands had suddenly begun to tremble. He turned to face the man in the bizarre costume, prepared for the worst. But the man had suddenly slumped into a chair, confused, brought back to reality when Joey had called him by his true name.

By now, Giovanni was holding his wife and son, and all were in tears. Sgt. Petrone handcuffed the man, now completely subdued. He submitted without a word as he watched the tearful scene with dull, emotionless eyes, his mind hovering between his tiny world of grandeur and reality.

Suddenly, Joey broke away from his parents and faced the man. "Did you hurt my friend?" he shouted.

"The Jewish boy?" The man shrugged. "He crawled into my home, and I struck him down . . . as you have the right to strike me down for breaking into your home." He looked at Giovanni and Lucia for signs of affirmation.

Without a word, Joey ran out of the room and up the stairs. Lucia followed him because little Jimmy had begun to cry. In an instant, Joey was down again, fully clothed. He ran out of the house. A moment later, Lucia came down,

"He has gone to the house." She pointed to the man. "He fears that his friend is in trouble."

Sgt. Petrone stifled an oath. These damned kids trying to play detectives could be a pain in the ass, he thought. He grabbed the man, still slumped in the chair. "Come on, you," he snarled, dragging him out of the house.

"Go," said Lucia to her husband. We will be fine."

Without a word, Giovanni followed the two in front of him. By now, lights were lighting up in the houses and heads were poking out of the windows. "Who's got a phone?" thundered the detective.

"Mr. Gleason . . . the ward-leader, he's gotta the phone," a voice shouted back.

"John, go tell Mr. Gleason to call the police. Break his door down if you have to," the sergeant told Giovanni. "Tell him I sent you, and to call an ambulance, too."

"My son . . . ?"

"Don't worry about him. That boy can take care of himself. I'm worried about the other boy."

Giovanni ran ahead to the house of Harry Gleason and banged on the door. And just as Sgt. Petrone and his hapless felon reached the alley, the front door of the empty house opened and Joey stood in the doorway. Behind him stood Sammy, a sickly grin on his face. He had taken off his shirt and was pressing it against the back of his head. There were signs of blood where he had wiped his face.

"Are you all right?" asked Sgt. Petrone, his voice grim, angry.

"He's okay, said Joey, happily.

The two boys came down. The detective told his prisoner to sit down on the steps. "Watch him," he told two men who had appeared from the nearby houses. Others were coming, some with just their trousers on. "If he moves, break his legs," he said.

He took Sammy to a nearby gas-lamp and looked carefully at his head. The blood had begun to coagulate, no longer flowing. His hair was matted with dried, crusty blood. Satisfied that the skin cuts looked worse than they were, he asked him, "Do you feel dizzy or faint?"

"I'm okay," laughed the boy, as though it had been a minor accident.

But Sgt. Petrone wasn't laughing, or even smiling. He turned the boy so that he faced him. "What in God's name were you doing in that house?" he asked in a low tone.

"He's the guy that broke into Mrs. Levine's house. I found her jewelry in . . . ." Sammy stopped, the look in, the detective's eyes scaring him.

"I didn't ask you that, son. "I asked you what you were doing in that house, I've been looking for a burglar. How do I know you're not it? How do I know that-this isn't where you've been hiding your loot . . . that you didn't put Mrs. Levine's jewelry there?" Sgt. Petrone's voice was rapier sharp. This was a smart-ass kid. He would make him squirm a little.

Sammy was dumb-struck. He had expected only praise for what he had done. "I didn't do it . . . I swear. I was with my mother and father last night. We were watching you and your men from across the street, where we live," he said, lamely. "But before that, I saw that guy come out of Eighth Street, and go in the alley. He was dressed just like he is now." Honest, it wasn't me."

"I know," sighed the detective. "But how can I get it through your thick skulls that what you did was wrong . . . I mean going into that house. I could arrest you for breaking and entering." He looked over at his prisoner. He wouldn't go anywhere, as more men had gathered about him. He turned back to Sammy. "Do you realize that what you did was wrong, boy?" he asked him. Not only was it wrong, but you could have been hurt. You were lucky he didn't hit you with something heavier. You might have been killed."

The boy did not respond, his head hanging low.

"What's your mother and father gonna say about all this?"

This alarmed Sammy more than anything else the detective had said. "Please don't let them know," he said, the fright apparent in his eyes. His mother would be devastated, and his father would probably disown him. "Please/' he begged/ "don't let them know. Please let me go home. You don't know my father. He would never forgive me."

Joey had never heard Sammy whining like this. It was strangely out of character for his friend. But he knew how Mr. and Mrs. Cohen would react. He could visualize the Cohens moving in the middle of the night in disgrace. It could be even worse. "Please, Sgt. Petrone," he said, "Sammy's right. His mother and father would probably kill themselves from shame."

"That bad, huh? The detective was amused, although he had heard and witnessed such things happening. One man had killed his whole family because his unwed daughter had become pregnant. "All right, go on home . . . but make sure you go see the druggist tomorrow, and have him look at your head."

"Thanks, Sgt. Petrone." Sammy almost kissed the detective's hand. "Thanks a lot."

*

Sgt. Petrone^ caught him by the arm, just as he began running for the safety of his house. "If I ever run into you again, you'd better be wearing a halo," he said. He hoped the boy had truly learned his lesson. He would have to leave him out of his report. Perhaps the prisoner would also have another lapse of memory. There was no doubt that he would also be questioned by a psychiatrist, when they saw the way he was dressed. Who would believe him? Sgt. Petrone was sure he was doing the right thing. The boy would be safe from involvement.

"Thanks, Sgt. Petrone." Joey was still at his side.

"And that goes for you too, son. Don't you ever touch your father's gun again. If that man had come at you and you had struggled . . . who knows what would have happened. Your mother might have been hit." The sergeant chuckled. "And don't you think I wasn't worried about my hide. I was never shot at by a boy, but I sure was worried then, when I was creeping up on you." Suddenly serious, he continued. "1 might have had to kill you to protect myself. Do you understand, son?"

"I understand."

They walked back to the group of men, the sergeant's arm over Joey's shoulder. The men were heaping ridicule upon the man and his ridiculous costume. He remained silent, his head bowed. Giovanni had returned with word that the police-wagon was on the way. Along with him was Mr. Gleason the ward-leader, wearing a robe over his pants.

"Hello, Harry," the detective greeted him.

"Vito . . . nice going." He greeted the detective with a firm hand-grasp. He looked over at the men and gave them a big wave of his beefy hands. "Nice going, men," he called over to them. Harry Gleason knew how to please a crowd. His political career depended on it. He approached them so that he could see the prisoner. When he recognized him as the man who used to walk up and down the street dressed like a movie actor, he could not help but quip, "Now, I know where he got all that jewelry he was selling." It got a big laugh from the men and perhaps some votes for his candidate in the coming election.

"That was quick work, Vito. I'll have to let them know down at City Hall," said the politician, pulling Sgt. Petrone aside.

"Well, I had some help from the Nocelli family," replied the detective. He pointed to the prisoner. He broke into their house while only that poor woman and her kids were there."

"The people with the quarantine?"

"That's right, Harry. And if me and her husband hadn't come in time, there might have been a real tragedy there." The detective did not want to give the politician too much information. "Me and Mr. Nocelli had to go in, in spite Of that thing on the door even though the doctor said it could come off. It's not fair, Harry. That family has got to be separated because those ass-holes can't get off their butts and come down to take it off."

"I'll see what I can do." The ward-leader sounded sincere. But then, he always sounded sincere.

\\ *n*

"What happens to me and Mr. Nocelli and Valentino, over there. We've all been in that house. Do we all go back in until somebody takes it off?" said the detective, bitterly.

"Take it off," said the ward-leader. I'll take care of it down at the hall. Probably, nobody will ever know the difference."

"Thanks, Harry. You're gonna make some people real e> happy."

"Yeah . . . well, make sure they know I did it for them," said the politician.

"You can tell Mr. Nocelli yourself. He's right there." "Nah. You can do it better. You talk their language." Soon, the police-wagon came, and the prisoner was locked safely in the back. Telling the two policemen who had come with it to wait for him, he walked with Giovanni and Joey back to their house. "Listen, you two," he said. "I want both of you to forget about that gun. I think it's better if I don't mention it in my report. It could only hurt you both . . . go on Joey's record."

"But what of the man. He will tell," said Giovanni.

"Nobody would ever believe him. There's nothing to worry about from him. But you, Joey, you have to promise me that you won't tell anybody . . . not even your friend, Sammy. Do you understand, don't tell anybody."

"I promise," said Joey, dejectedly. He had already been planning it in his mind. He would tell Sammy, then the guys, and maybe little Carmela. They would surely think he was quite a big-shot. It might even get around at school.

"I know you'd rather tell your friends and show off a bit." The detective said. "But it would only cause trouble. You and your father would have to go to court as witnesses. Maybe, even your mother. But, if you keep your mouth shut, I will take care of the rest, and all this will be forgotten. Understand?"

"He will not say anything," Giovanni said.

And Sgt. Petrone believed him. "And it might be a good idea to find a better hiding place for that gun," he said.

"I will get rid of it, if you wish."

"Do what you want. I don't want to ever see or hear of it again. The important thing is that this young fellow doesn't ever touch it again." He gave Joey a good-natured nudge. He was betting that if Mrs. Nocelli had anything to say about it, that gun would be gone before long.

They had stopped in front of the house, the quarantine staring them in the face. Without a word, the sergeant opened the door and tore it off, leaving a ragged edge where the glue held.

Lucia had opened the vestibule door. She took the scrap of paper from him. "God bless you, Sgt. Petrone. I will pray that you will never be harmed." With that, she kisses his cheek, and for an instant, the detective felt her full breasts hard against him.

"Thank you, Mrs. Nocelli. I can use a prayer like that," he said. He stood aside and motioned for Giovanni to enter. "It is legal to come into your house tonight, John," he said with a grin.

As Giovanni and Joey came in, some of the neighbors, including Angelina from next door, had gathered outside. "Can I come in, too?" she asked. "I'm her best friend."

"You'll have to wait until I leave, Signora," he said. "There's still some official business I have to take care of." Closing the door behind him, he warned Giovanni to explain to his wife that she should not mention the gun . . . not even to her best friend from next door.

Giuseppi nodded. "I will get your wine," he said.

"Not tonight, John. I have to go back to look inside the house. Then, I have to go back to headquarters to make my report. Maybe, tomorrow night."

"Do you want me to go with you? I can show you where the stuff is," Joey said, eagerly.

"No, thanks son. You've done enough." With three separate good-byes ringing in his ears, he went back to the empty house. Mrs. Nocelli's kiss and breasts pressing against him had reminded him of Pearl Furguson. She had felt like that. A pity he would not be able to go to her tonight. Perhaps tomorrow night. He had Sunday off, and he surmised that she did too. He could stay the night and not worry about work next day. He was glad she had wisely not shown herself. Maybe he would knock and see if all was well when he was through in the empty house and the rest of the crowd had dispersed. "Give me one of those lanterns, and you come with me, Davis," he told one of the policemen. Together, they went into the dark, empty house.

CHAPTER 43

A week later, Joey and Sammy, regaining some courage and dying with curiosity, crawled up into the hide-out. The hole in the brick wall had been sealed up. The bricks were no longer loose. No sound came from the house. It was now truly empty.

On the Furguson side, they could hear Sarah and her brother speaking quite clearly, evidently, from her bedroom. And it was apparent, from the conversation, that Mrs. Furguson was not at home.

"You like the white man, Sarah?" Hebert asked.

"Yes, Hebert. He's nice."

"He won't be trying to fool with you . . . like Leroy?"

"Of course not."

"Why, cause he a cop?"

"Maybe."

"You think he be movin' in like Leroy?"

"No I don't think so."

"Why, cause he white? He been comin here a lot."

"That don't mean nothin". Our daddy was white. How you think we so light-colored?" the girl said, matter-of-factly.

"You remember our daddy? I don't."

"Course, you don't. You never seen him. He had to go far away before you was born. But, you'd a liked him, Hebert. He was big . . . almost as big as Leroy, and he had blue eyes and blond hair. And he always gave me nice things."

"Gee he as nice as the cop?" asked the boy. "Why can't he move in with us?"

"Hebert, I don't know why," said the girl, suddenly grown tired of talking. "Now, git! I want to put on that nice dress that Sgt. Petrone gave me. Momma said I could, cause he comin' to visit tonight."

"Let me watch you, Sarah?"

"I swear. You're gonna be just like Leroy when you get big."

"Will I be big like him?"

"Will you get out of here." There was the sound of scuffling, then childish laughter that grew faint as the boy ran down the stairs.

"I'm gonna make Sgt. Petrone throw you in jail for doing that," the girl shouted. Her voice was quite clear and didn't sound at all serious.

Joey nudged Sammy. He began to crawl toward the opening. Down in the alley, they looked at one another. It was as though by mutual consent. They would never reveal what they had heard.

"You glad Sgt. Petrone is going with Mrs. Furguson," Joey asked Sammy.

"Yeah. I'll bet she's part white, too. How do you feel about it?"

"It's okay with me."

They never brought the subject up again.

CHAPTER 44

Every year, the Feast of Our Lady of Mt. Carmel was celebrated by the parishioners of St. Nicholas of Tolentine Church. The festivities began on Friday after supper and lasted until Sunday evening. A band-stand was built every year for the occasion, and a band played Souza marches, semi-classical and Italian music. The small street next to the church was lined with games of chance, and all the receipts went to the church. So did all the profits from the various food-stands that were also there. Hot-dogs, soft pretzels, as well as Italian sausage sandwiches, meat-ball sandwiches and fried chicken were all sold by volunteers from the church members. It was impossible to venture into the street without partaking of the succulent foods, or gamble a few dollars for the good of the church. There were others who were content to sit on the steps across the street from the church or mill about and listen to the band.

On Sunday, after the last mass, the procession would begin. The statue of Our Lady was hoisted on a pedestal and carried through the main streets of the parish. The band preceded it and many of the congregation would follow on foot to honor a pledge that they had made for a favor granted them by Our Lady of Mt. Carmel.

Lucia, Joey and little Jimmy were among the throng that followed the statue, for Lucia had vowed to do so if her Joey would recuperate from the dreaded diphtheria. They walked slowly in the blazing July sun. And already, little Jimmy was tiring and getting cranky. Giovanni, wearing a brightly colored sash diagonally across his chest, was leading the procession, for he had been made honorary Marshall because he had built the new platform for the statue of Our Lady. She was now being carried, in all her glory, by four strong men. Bright colored streamers were attached to her, and one, two and five dollar bills were pinned to them. A straw plate at the Lady's feet was almost filled with coins from the people who watched from the side-walks.

They had entered the street, unlike any of the others they had gone through. Instead of the red-bricked row houses that seemed to be everywhere, this street had a row of neat twins with porches and tiny plots of ground, lush with roses and many-colored flowers. Some even had trees. Lucia saw these houses, and instantly, her mind was back to the village of her birth, the houses with the tiny yards and the mountains in the distance.

They had neared the middle of the block, and she was suddenly aware that Giovanni was by her side, handsome in his bright colored sash of honor. His eyes were shining as he picked up little Jimmy. "Cara," he said, "look there."

Lucia followed his eyes. He was looking at one of the houses with the porches. This one had a fig tree in the yard that almost reached the roof. It was lush with fruit, hanging heavy with ripeness, ready to be picked. And wonder of wonders, there was a "Sale" sign showing above the heavy, wrought-iron fence. An elderly man was reaching out from his porch, picking one of the succulent fruits.

"Do you like it, Cara?" Giovanni asked.

"Oh, yes," Lucia answered.

"Then, we shall go and buy it as soon as the procession is over."

"Oh, Giovanni . . . can we?"

"Yes, Cara. Just think, all of our friends from the old country are close. And the Italian market is only three blocks away . . . and the church is so close."

"Yes . . . yes," cooed Lucia, as she watched a young woman, her own age, in the other of the twin houses. She was sitting on her porch and was smiling pleasantly as she watched the procession. She said something that made the old gentleman laugh, and he offered her a fig. She seemed like a nice person and would make a good friend like Angelina was. She would miss Angelina, of course, but they were not that far that they could not visit each other.

An alley separated the twins, with many windows along the side to give the house plenty of sunlight during the day. An elderly couple stood inside the wrought-iron fence of the next twin. The woman reminded her of her dead mother, she had her hand on her husband's shoulder, moving it ever so slightly and affectionately. What a nice person she must be, Lucia thought . . . a mother figure.

Reluctantly, they passed the house, and the rest of the day became as a dream for Lucia, the house always in the back of her mind. She dreamed of little Jimmy and the new baby she carried in her belly, going to the school on the corner. She would walk with them every day Joey, of course, would be going to higher-grade school, but he was big enough to go alone. And she and the women on either side of her house would go to the Italian market at least once a week. And they could go to church of their choosing, only a block away. Her prayers were being answered twofold.

Joey had overheard his parents, and to his delight, he had also noticed the school on the corner, the imposing stone building, much like the school where he now went. The school-yard was smaller, but it was full of boys about his age. They had evidently jumped over the wrought-iron gates, since they were padlocked. Surely, he would find someone among them who would be his friend like Sammy was. Of course, he would miss Sammy, but he could easily walk back to the old neighborhood. And in a couple of years, he would probably be going to school with him at Southern High.

He thought of Sarah and Carmela. He could see them, as well, when he went back to visit. He hoped that Sarah would be able to go to Southern as well. He would see her somehow, even though she would be in a lower grade and separated from the boys, since the school was not co-ed. The school, which took up a whole city block, was separated in two, half for the girls and half for the boys. There were no classes with boys and girls together.

He would miss Carmela, the impish, carrot-top that had given him his first glimpse of the female anatomy, albeit a very immature one, Carmela who was wise beyond her years. In a few years, when he was twenty, she would be sixteen, and they could go out together. She would probably know everything there was to know about "doing it' by then.

He dwelt upon these thoughts until the procession ended and the Lady of Mt. Carmel was safely back on her pedestal by the alter.

When it was ended, they had gone to the home of Nicolina Flaviano's parents. There had been shrieks of laughter and happiness when Giovanni told their childhood friends that they had seen a house only a little more than a block away, and that they were going to look at it. And when Giovanni described the house, Yolanda Flaviano said that they knew the man, that his wife had recently died, and he was anxious to sell the house and move in with his daughter. She and her husband agreed to go with Giovanni and Lucia in hopes of making the man lower his price. Joey and Nicolina were left at the house with little Jimmy, who had fallen asleep as soon as they had arrived.

"I hope they buy the house, don't you?" the girl said, as soon as they were alone.

Joey agreed, not saying much more. He felt awkward in the girl's presence, perhaps because they had never been this alone before. He remembered the kiss on his birthday quite vividly . . . the teasing, warm wetness of her lips. Not quite a year had passed, but the girl had lost most of her baby softness, and was now reaching for womanhood. There was no mistaking the tiny bumps that would become breasts, large and soft like his mother's. This made him nervous, and it didn't use to when they would lie down on the floor together and read the Sunday comics and laugh together.

"Maybe we'll go to the same school . . . maybe in the same class," Nicolina added, trying to keep up the conversation.

"That would be swell." Joey was sitting at the kitchen table, drinking a glass of home-made root-beer, while the girl moved about the kitchen, finding things to set on the table to pick on.

"We could do our homework together." She was behind him now, her hands on his shoulders, caressing him. Her tiny breasts pressed against the back of his head for just a tantalizing moment, then it was gone. Now, her soft, moist mouth was nibbling at his ear, sometimes taking the tip of his ear-lobe and sucking it into her mouth. "Maybe, they'll leave us alone, like now. And suddenly she was gone from behind him and now faced him, dark, brown eyes laughing at him.

Joey felt his face burning, and he knew that he was blushing. Hidden by the table, he touched his crotch, not understanding the transformation. His penis had stiffened and pressed painfully against his underwear. It felt like when he awakened with the urge to urinate. "I have to go to the toilet," he said, in a panic. He got up, but there was no hiding the small bulge in his knickers.

The girl stared, eyes bright. "Oh, Joey," she giggled, "did I cause that?"

Joey hated her at that moment. She was poking fun at him, teasing him. Without a word, he ran upstairs, to the toilet and stared in awe at what she had caused. It felt oddly and painfully delicious, even better than how he felt after thoroughly emptying his bladder. It was strange, but the same thing had happened at his birthday party when they had kissed. But it had been nothing like this. And now it wouldn't go down. What would happen if they kissed now?

He heard the girl call from downstairs. "Are you all right, Joey?"

The thought came to mind, not to answer. Then, she would run up, and he would show her what she had caused. "I'll be down in a minute," he called, instead.

Soon it was limp, and he was able to urinate. He went downstairs after washing his hands and face. The girl was looking at his crotch from the moment he went back into the kitchen. "Did you play with it?" she asked, giggling.

Joey was speechless. What had happened to the nice girl he had known only months before.

"Jerry Peretti says he goes to the boy's room and plays with himself whenever that happens to him." The girl was enjoying herself.

"Who's Jerry Peretti?" Joey felt a tiny twinge of jealousy. He was back in his chair, and the girl sat opposite him.

"He's in my geography class, and every time, I go into the cloak-room, he comes in and tries to kiss me. Sometimes, he tries to make me put my hand on his thing." The girl no longer seemed to be teasing him. She had suddenly grown serious.

"Do you let him . . . do you do it?"

"No, of course not." She was frowning. "But when I try to fight him off, he manages to touch my . . . ." She touched her breast, daintily. She

238

had suddenly become the perfect little lady. "And that's when he runs to the boy's toilet." She shrugged her shoulders, indicating that it was not her fault.

Joey suddenly felt the need to protect the girl, much like the feeling he had for Sarah. He somehow felt that he had helped solve her problem with Leroy. Now, he must solve Nicolina's. "Why don't you tell your teacher?" he blurted.

The girl lowered her eyes. "Oh, he's such a silly boy. I don't want to get him in trouble."

"Do you like him?"

"No, of course not . . . not like I like you."

"Do you really like me, Nicolina?"

"Of course I do."

"Well, if I ever come to your school, he won't do it anymore. I'll see to that." Joey wanted to go on and tell the girl about how he had almost shot a man, but he wisely did not.

"Oh, Joey," the girl cried, her eyes bright, "would you fight him because of me?"

"Well, if he bothered you, I would."

Without a word, the girl came to his side, turned his head and kissed him full on the lips, her tiny tongue probing the inside of his mouth, her mouth making tiny sucking sounds. She did not laugh at him when he again ran upstairs, holding his crotch and hoping that the grown-ups did not return before his penis returned to normal.

Joey and the girl were sitting at the table, reading the Sunday comics when their parents returned, all in a joyous mood. Lucia carried a brown bag full of large, sun-ripened figs, all bursting with sugary syrup. The man who owned the house had picked them earlier in the day, and when Giovanni had inquired about how much fruit the tree yielded, the man brought the bag out of his ice-box. "Here is what is left after the neighbors help themselves. Every Sunday, they come from early morning. I tell them to take one bag-full apiece, but I know some of them cheat," the man chuckled. "I will pick figs until the middle of August," he added. Then, he had offered them the fruit.

"But what about yourself?" asked Lucia.

The man laughed. "Tomorrow morning, I will go out on the roof of the porch, and I will pick another bag-full that that they could not reach from the ground."

The man had been as anxious to sell as they were to buy, since he intended to move in with his daughter. "My daughter married "uno Americano" and they have a little farm in New Jersey. In my old age, I will go back to the farm," he said, happily.

The price, forty-two hundred dollars, had been happily agreed upon by both sides, and the deal had been struck. The man, Francisco Quatrone, would see the real estate man in the morning.

The figs were placed in a large bowl and set on the table. The wine and a crusty loaf of bread were brought out and the grown-ups ate to their heart's content. It was a bit of Italia in the new country. Joey and Nicolina tasted one each and decided that gum-drops and chewing-gum tasted better.

CHAPTER 45

The reality of what they were about to do hit home the next morning. Lucia awoke, and instead of the luxurious awakening that followed a night of love-making, she awoke with anxiety spasms that finally erupted in a fit of morning sickness such as she had not experienced in either of her other pregnancies. She blamed it on her condition, of course, and she did not mention her moving to Angelina, next door, until a week later for she could not bear to see how her friend would react.

Finally, one morning, as Lucia was hanging some clothing she had just washed in the big, galvanized wash-tub, Angelina came out into her own back yard. They spoke for a few minutes as a radio from one of the back yards played some Italian tunes on the all-Italian program. They spoke of the weather and the usual joking and chatter that drew so much laughter whenever they were together was strangely missing. "Is something wrong, Lucia?" the older woman finally asked.

"I have not been feeling well because of the baby," Lucia said, patting her belly.

"No, there is something else," countered Angelina. "Several times, you have tried to tell me, but always you held back. Is it something that happened that night with our friend, Valentino?"

"No, Angelina, it is nothing like that." Lucia was quick to ease her friend's suspicions, for Joey and the revolver had quickly come to mind.

She was sure that Joey had not told anyone. It must forever be a family secret. Not even Guido knew about it.

"What is it then? I know that something is bothering you."

And Lucia finally blurted it out. "I think that we are going to move. Oh, Angelina, I am so worried that we are doing the wrong thing. Where would I find another friend like you?"

Had it not been for the fence, the two friends would have been in each other's arms, shedding tears. Angelina would have been trying to console the younger woman, almost like a younger sister to her. "You are moving . . . when?" Angelina could not hide the disappointment and sadness she felt.

"I don't know. As soon as . . . how you say . . . the settlement is made. But we are not moving far. We will see each other often."

"Of course we will."

"We are near the Italian Market. You can come to my house and we will go to the market together."

It was then that Angelina told Lucia about her husband's desire to move. Up till now, she had not mentioned it for the very same reason that Lucia had kept her secret to herself. She had not wanted to hurt her friend. But now, it didn't matter. He had mentioned it after the burglary at Mrs. Levine's and again after the man from up the street had broken into Lucia's house. "This neighborhood is getting worse and worse," he had said. "That crazy character from up the street could have killed everybody in that house . . . and us right next door." He had eaten a few mouthfuls, then spoke again. "What do you say we move out of here, Angie?" he had asked.

And Angelina had kept it to herself until now.

Lucia's face brightened happily, a huge load now off her back. "Oh, Angelina, move near us. I will look every day until I find one for you."

When Angelina went back inside, she heard Lucia's sweet voice singing in accompaniment with a song that was being played on the radio across the way. The song, "Ritorno a Sorriento," was a song that every Italian knew. It told of a wish that every Italian immigrant held in his heart: the wish to return for one last visit to the country of their birth before they died. Angelina was happy that Lucia no longer felt the guilt of leaving her behind. But she knew that once she moved, it would never be the same for them. First of all, it was highly improbable that they would ever live in close proximity to one another. Tony, her husband, had even suggested New Jersey, where most of his family now lived . . . so far away. And even if they moved fairly close to one another, Lucia would now be among her childhood friends from her village in Italy. And she was bound to make new friends . . . . Angelina sat down and had a good cry over a cup of coffee.

Giovanni was ecstatic. He had already found a buyer for his house. One of the men who worked with him, who had arrived in America two years before with only his wife, had suddenly discovered that the one-bedroom apartment they lived in had become too crowded with the addition of two babies, one year apart. He and his wife had visited one night and had been awe-struck by the new bathroom and the electricity in the house. They had quickly agreed on a price.

Giovanni could not believe how smoothly everything was falling into place. If everything continued as it was, soon his family would be living in their new house, perhaps in time to pick some of the late figs. The house was only a block or so from the St. Nicholas church, and he would become a legitimate member of its congregation. Another thought. Hopefully, he could be settled in so that he could make his new wine in the autumn. In his mind, he had already designed one end of the cellar for this purpose. He would have to build a wall and insulate his wine-cellar from the heater. Perhaps he would buy more barrels and make more wine. It could become a lucrative business, as long as Prohibition lasted. He knew he had a market for all the extra wine he could make. He still could not believe that he had earned enough money to pay for his new home if he wished to. At this rate, he could buy many fine things for Lucia and the children. He could buy things that could make life easier for his wife. There was such a thing as a refrigerator that ran on electricity, which the new house had. There would be no more ice, with Lucia having to wipe up after the iceman. And there were such things as washing machines and electric sewing machines, all run by electricity. Perhaps he could afford an automobile send his sons to college to become lawyers or doctors. It was the dream of all immigrants. Giovanni sang a lot these days.

CHAPTER 46

S ammy was not surprised when Joey told him that they might soon be moving. "I always said you would be moving to a bigger house. But I thought it would be one of them," he laughed, pointing to the big, brown-stone houses on Snyder Avenue. "I wish we could move," he said, no longer laughing.

"We're only moving five blocks away," said Joey. He saw the look of sadness that Sammy had failed to hide. "I can come and hang out with you and the guys. And in a couple of years we'll both be going to Southern High, and I'll get to see you plenty."

"I hope so. Anyway, you'll be here for the rest of the summer. Carmine and the guys will be back from the farms by then. I'll be all right." But Sammy knew that it would not be the same. He had never been as close with the other boys as he was with Joey. There would be no more trips to Shibe Park with Mr. Guido. "The Yankees are coming to town next week. They'll be here for three days," he said, trying to change the subject.

"Oh, by the way, Sammy, Uncle Guide's got tickets for Thursday." Joey had wanted to surprise his friend, but he decided to spring the news now, knowing that it would bolster his friend's spirits. "He wants to know how many home runs you think Babe Ruth is gonna hit this season."

"He'll probably break his old record. He hit fifty-nine in 1921, you know," Sammy said, smugly.

"Go on. Uncle Guido will think you're nuts."

"Well, he ought to bet on it if he wants to make some money. He'll probably get great odds."

"You can tell him Thursday . . . if you think you can come with us," Joey said, slyly.

"You're sure I can go with you?" Sammy's spirits were quickly revived "I have to ask my father if it's okay."

"I'm positive, Sammy."

Sammy got up from the store-steps, where they had been sitting, and ran into the store. He came out after a few minutes, grinning, two glasses of soda-pop in his hands. A short time later, Mrs. Cohen came out to get the empty glasses. "I want you should thank your uncle for me," she told Joey. "He's a nice man." She was smiling, but there was something in her eyes that told Joey that Sammy had told her of his parent's plans to move.

They had almost decided to walk down to the school-yard when Sammy suggested they go down to the alley where their hide-out was. A new family had moved into the empty house two days before. Maybe there were some kids their age.

They went down the main alley. They heard the radio from one of the back yards, an announcer advertising the R.C.A. Victor radio in Italian. It sounded musical to Sammy's ears. They heard Joey's mother humming in the back yard, and little Jimmy calling for her from the kitchen. The two exchanged glances, Joey putting his finger on his lips in a "keep quiet" sign. They slowed down, walking on tip-toes. But no sooner had they reached Joey's house, then they heard Lucia's voice. "Is that you, Joey?" she called.

"Yeah, Mom." Joey opened the gate and poked his head in. "We're going to see if the new family has any kids," he said.

"Very well. Do not cause any trouble." Lucia understood a boy's need for friends.

They reached the house with the new family and heard childish voices, laughing and chattering. They peeked through a large crack between the fence-boards. The two children, a boy and a girl, were perhaps three and four years old, and they were chattering in pure Italian. A woman was wiping down the glass on the kitchen door. She turned her head, a proud look on her pretty, dark face as she scolded her children. She did it playfully, her voice caressing them. Petite in body and hair in a bun, she appeared to be almost a child herself, younger than Joey's mother. "Silenzio" she called.

Joey understood the woman quite clearly. She wanted her children to be quiet so that the neighbors would not complain and perhaps chase them back where they had come from. It was the concern of most immigrants in those days: to be liked and to be approved of. This was of the most importance.

Next door, across the alley, Sarah could be heard talking to her brother. "No, you can't go play with them," she said, trying to keep her voice down. "Momma don't want you to leave the house."

"Can they come to play over here?"

"No not till Momma says so."

Joey and Sammy moved silently until they could look into the Furguson's yard. The early afternoon sun was no longer directly overhead, and the house cast a shadow in the yard. Sarah was washing some clothing in a galvanized tub that was close to the house in order to take advantage of the shade. She rubbed and ground the clothing against a ribbed wash-board, every once in a while dipping it in the sudsy water. Hebert sat watching her, his feet in several inches of water in a small pail.

"I like it when your dress gets wet," said the precocious child. "I can see right through it."

"Oh, hush, Hebert." Sarah looked at herself. The boy was right. The cotton print was almost transparent where she had been leaning against the tub. She tried to pull the dress away from her skin, but it clung to her body, making every contour of her belly and legs evident. There was the hint of pubic hair. Her breasts seemed to have gotten larger in the several weeks since Joey had seen her in school.

Joey felt Sammy tugging at him in his excitement. He turned and saw him grinning broadly, making his nose even more prominent on his thin face. His eyes were glued to the crack in the fence. He pulled at Sammy's arm and the boy came away reluctantly. He had wanted to speak to Sarah, to tell her of his moving, but under the circumstances, he decided not to. There would be time.

They went down the narrow alley and stopped under the hole to their hide-out. Joey pointed upward, indicating his desire to go up. When

246

Sammy nodded agreement, Joey went to the street to see if all was clear. They could spend the rest of the afternoon up there.

But it was not to be. Joey was met by Mr. Petrosano an old man with a ragged moustache who did odd jobs about the neighborhood. He was tugging at a small wagon that he had made himself, using the wheels from a discarded baby coach. On it he had some sand, a partially empty bag of cement, some wood lath and some tools and a ladder. "Hello, Mr. Petrosano," Joey greeted him, a sinking feeling coursing through him. "You got a job for me?" he asked, as he always did.

"No, Joey, you don't want this job. You go to school . . . you be a doctor or a lawyer."

"What are you gonna fix, Mr. Petrosano?" asked Sammy, knowing full well what the old man was about.

The old man looked up at the ceiling, ran his eye down to where the boy was standing under the hole. He walked slowly, dragging the wagon behind him. He surveyed the hole,

"It's about time they closed that hole up," Sammy said with a straight face. "Every time I pass under here, I feel like some animal is gonna jump on me."

"Yeah, or maybe a boy or two," the old man responded, with the wisdom of age. He smiled knowingly as the boys grinned. "But don't you worry no more, because Mr. Petrosano will now close it up." Without another word, he set up the ladder, climbed up on tired legs until his head was through the opening. He lit a match and peered into the darkness. He eyed the boys below. "It's a shame. Two boys like you could have a lot of fun up here." He shook his head sadly as he prepared to close up the hole in the ceiling.

Joey and Sammy watched for a time, then move on out of the alley. When they returned the next day, the hole was done, neatly patched up. They left sadly.

That night as Joey listened to the muffled noises from behind the closed door of his parent's bedroom, he thought no more of what they were doing. He knew that his mother was carrying another baby, and that what they were doing right now had made her pregnant. And had it not been for him, Sarah might have been made pregnant. And had it not been for him, God knows what might have happened to his mother that night, had he not confronted the crazy man with his father's revolver. All this whirled through his mind, worse than any of the nightmares he had had during the worst time of his illness. And somehow, it all related to the hole in the ceiling. It was closed now, gone forever. And gone with it, in a sense, was his childhood innocence.

The End